A Slaying in Savannah

A *Murder, She Wrote* MYSTERY

OTHER BOOKS IN THE *MURDER, SHE WROTE* SERIES

Obsidian
Published by New American Library, a division of
Penguin Group (USA) Inc., 375 Hudson Street,
New York, New York 10014, USA
Penguin Group (Canada), 90 Eglinton Avenue East, Suite 700, Toronto,
Ontario M4P 2Y3, Canada (a division of Pearson Penguin Canada Inc.)
Penguin Books Ltd., 80 Strand, London WC2R 0RL, England
Penguin Ireland, 25 St. Stephen's Green, Dublin 2,
Ireland (a division of Penguin Books Ltd.)
Penguin Group (Australia), 250 Camberwell Road, Camberwell, Victoria 3124,
Australia (a division of Pearson Australia Group Pty. Ltd.)
Penguin Books India Pvt. Ltd., 11 Community Centre, Panchsheel Park,
New Delhi–110 017, India
Penguin Group (NZ), 67 Apollo Drive, Rosedale, North Shore 0632,
New Zealand (a division of Pearson New Zealand Ltd.)
Penguin Books (South Africa) (Pty.) Ltd., 24 Sturdee Avenue,
Rosebank, Johannesburg 2196, South Africa

Penguin Books Ltd., Registered Offices:
80 Strand, London WC2R 0RL, England

First published by Obsidian, an imprint of New American Library,
a division of Penguin Group (USA) Inc.

First Printing, October 2008
3   5   7   9   10   8   6   4   2

Copyright © 2008 NBC Universal Inc.
Murder, She Wrote is a trademark and copyright of Universal Studios. All rights reserved.

OBSIDIAN and logo are trademarks of Penguin Group (USA) Inc.

LIBRARY OF CONGRESS CATALOGING-IN-PUBLICATION DATA:
Bain, Donald, 1935–
A slaying in Savannah : a Murder, she wrote mystery / by Jessica Fletcher and Donald Bain.
p. cm.
"Based on the Universal television series created by Peter S. Fischer, Richard Levinson & William Link"
ISBN: 978-0-451-22505-4
1. Fletcher, Jessica (Fictitious character)—Fiction. 2. Women novelists—Fiction. 3. Savannah (Ga.)—Fiction. I.
Murder, she wrote (Television program) II. Title.

PS3552.A376S63 2008
813'.54—dc22   2008012339

Set in Minion Regular
Designed by Alissa Amell

Printed in the United States of America

A Slaying in Savannah

A *Murder, She Wrote* MYSTERY

A NOVEL BY
JESSICA FLETCHER & DONALD BAIN

Based on the Universal television series created by
Peter S. Fischer, Richard Levinson & William Link

AN OBSIDIAN MYSTERY

For Zachary, Jacob, Lucas, Alexander, Abigail,
Eleanor, Sylvan, and Gray

Acknowledgments

Erica Backus, Katie Foster, and the other wonderfully helpful folks at the Savannah Area Convention and Visitors Bureau who sent us in the right direction while researching this book. It must be a joy to promote a place as lovely as Savannah, Georgia.

Captain Robert Merriman of the Savannah-Chatham Metropolitan Police Department. This personable, savvy thirty-year veteran of the Savannah police force graciously shared his time and knowledge with us of policing procedures utilized in Savannah not only today but historically as well. And thanks to **Mike Wilson,** who put us in touch with him.

Wally Campbell, laboratory manager of the Georgia Bureau of Investigation's Coastal Regional Crime Lab. His love of the science practiced there is contagious and undoubtedly contributes to the lab's place in the top tier of crime labs. Thanks for giving us a solid education in forensic science and for introducing us to **Brian Leppard** and **Rachel B. Duke**, both of the Division of Forensic Sciences.

Jacqueline L. Allen, real estate consultant extraordinaire for Re/Max, whose love of her adopted city shines through and who helped us navigate the neighborhoods.

Robert Edwards, general manager of the venerable Forest City Gun Club. We wish you well with your book, too.

Last but not least:

Shane Sullivan, whose wife, **Deborah Sullivan**, is the proprietor of "The Book" Gift Shop, nerve center for everything *Midnight in the Garden of Good and Evil*, the John Berendt blockbuster set in Savannah, and the shop's **Trese Newman**, who graciously gave us permission to borrow their ghost story.

Chapter One

"Ah'm hoping to make contact with a Mrs. Jessica Fletcher."

"Well, you have," I said. "May I ask who's calling?"

"My apologies. Ah seem to have forgotten my manners. My mother would be horrified. This is Roland Richardson the Third, attorney-at-law in Savannah, Georgia."

"Savannah! I haven't been there in a long time, although I've always enjoyed my visits."

"Yes, it is a lovely place to call home. My family goes back many generations. You might call me a true native son."

Judging from his pronounced Southern accent, I didn't doubt him for a minute.

"What can I do for you, Mr. Richardson?"

"It's what Ah can do for *you*, Mrs. Fletcher."

My antennae went up. Was he about to try to sell me something, a parcel of land in a swamp, or a hot stock that couldn't lose? I waited for him to elaborate, my hand poised to hit the OFF button.

"Allow me to explain. You see, I have been the attorney for one of our leading, and I might say loveliest, citizens for many years. I believe you were acquainted with her— Miss Tillie Mortelaine."

"Tillie? My goodness, it's been ages since we've spoken. I hope she's all right."

"It is my sad duty, Mrs. Fletcher, to inform you that Miss Tillie has passed from this earth to a heavenly place of rest and repose."

In other words, she's dead.

"Oh! I'm so sorry to hear that. She was a charming lady."

"I would certainly agree with you. And a long-lived one. Ninety-one years on this earth, and every one of them active and productive."

"I appreciate your calling me with this news," I said, wondering why he had. The explanation was not long in coming.

"You must be curious why I've made this call," he said. "Let me be direct, Mrs. Fletcher. Miss Tillie—that was how she preferred to be addressed—left a v-e-r-y long and detailed last will and testament, in which you are prominently mentioned."

"I am?"

"Yes, ma'am, you certainly are."

"It's been so many years since we've seen each other. May I ask why she remembered me in her will?"

"Of course you may, and it is my pleasure to enlighten you. According to Miss Tillie's document, she worked many years ago on a literacy program with which you were very much involved."

"That's true. We met in Washington, D.C., at the founding meeting of the National Coalition for Literacy. I'm still involved with literacy programs."

"A truly worthwhile undertaking. Miss Tillie cites in her will the work you and she did together to establish such a program here in Savannah."

A flood of memories warmed me. "I loved working with her, Mr. Richardson. It was an extremely satisfying undertaking, and I was delighted to see it spread throughout Georgia and to other states in the South. She was the spark plug that got the program off the ground. And, of course, her generosity was crucial to its success."

"Exactly so. Well, Mrs. Fletcher, Miss Tillie obviously wanted the program you and she created here in our fair city to continue on long after her passing. It is for that reason that she has left you the sum of one million dollars."

"Left *me*?"

"Yes, ma'am."

"Why would she leave *me* a million dollars?"

"I must admit it isn't quite as simple as I may have led you to believe."

"I'm listening."

"You see, Miss Tillie was known in Savannah as a woman who did not easily part with her money. I suppose you could say she was parsimonious in the extreme. Although she did support many charities, her gifts more often than not included conditions."

"Conditions!"

"Yes, ma'am, conditions."

"And what conditions are attached to this bequest?"

He chuckled. "Excuse me while I clean my glasses," he said. "The eyes are not what they used to be. Actually, I am in quite good health, aside from my vision and a weakness in the toes."

"Pardon?"

"Weakness in my toes. My physician says it's a form of peripheral neuropathy. But that's of no concern to you."

Although we'd never met, I pictured an elderly man in a three-piece suit and bow tie, sitting barefoot at his desk and wiggling his toes.

"Ah, yes, that is better, much better. Now, let me see what it says here. Miss Tillie has left the million dollars to you with the understanding that you will use it to further the literacy program with which the two of you were involved."

"That's hardly a difficult condition, although I wonder why she didn't leave it directly to the foundation."

"Obviously, Mrs. Fletcher, because she trusted you implicitly to do the right thing."

"Which I certainly will do."

"But there's more."

"Oh?"

"Are you aware of a gentleman named Wanamaker Jones?"

"Yes. I mean, I certainly didn't know him. He was long dead before I first met Tillie. What about him?"

"Are you aware that Mr. Jones died under mysterious circumstances?"

I rewound my memory. "Yes," I said. "Tillie told me that he'd been shot by an intruder right there in her home."

"Exactly! And are you also aware that Mr. Wanamaker Jones's killer has never been apprehended?"

Another pause for me to recollect what Tillie had told me. "I believe I did know that, Mr. Richardson. If I recall correctly, his murder was very big news in Savannah. It's still an unsolved crime?"

"Very much so, Mrs. Fletcher, notwithstanding the professional efforts of the local constabulary. Very much so, which brings me to the condition of the bequest Miss Tillie has made to you. She is leaving you this money on the condition that you solve Mr. Jones's murder."

My laugh burst out of me. "That's—that's—that's a most unusual condition, isn't it?"

His laugh was gentle and wise. "Miss Tillie was an unusual woman, Mrs. Fletcher. There is a limit to the time you have to honor her request, however—exactly one month from the day you arrive here in Savannah and have the specifics of the will read to you by yours truly."

I'd been standing during the call. Now I sat and tried to make sense of it all. Mr. Richardson continued.

"I should mention that the million dollars bequeathed to you, Mrs. Fletcher, is but a portion of the wealth Miss Tillie has left behind. Having no direct descendants, she has directed that sizable amounts of her estate go to various social and charitable organizations here in Savannah. But she seemed to take particular pleasure in incorporating you into her final wishes."

"You must know I'm not a detective, Mr. Richardson."

"Oh, Miss Tillie makes that plain in her will. She says—excuse me while I find that precise section—it's the longest will I've ever seen, more than fifty pages—aha, here it is. I can read it to you word for word when you arrive in Savannah. For now, allow me to paraphrase. She says that while you are a writer of murder mysteries and not someone who sets out to solve murders, you have had the good fortune to have ended up doing precisely that. She goes on to say that her experience with law enforcement officials has left her skeptical as to their ability to solve particularly difficult crimes, especially murder. I must add, however, that I myself have always found them most efficient. Nevertheless, Miss Tillie was hard to convince otherwise once she'd taken to a notion. Therefore, you, Mrs. Fletcher, are the one in whom she is placing her trust."

I shook my head, then realized he couldn't see the gesture. "This is too bizarre for me to contemplate at the moment."

"I can certainly understand that, Mrs. Fletcher. But let me reiterate that there is the question of time. You have one month once you've arrived here in Savannah. But you must also plan to be here within a month of my phone call to you. Miss Tillie was e-x-t-r-e-m-e-l-y specific about such things. It would be a tragedy if the million dollars were lost to your literacy foundation. Tragic indeed."

"Who will receive the money if I decline to do this, Mr. Richardson?"

"That remains to be seen, I'm afraid. If you decline to come to Savannah, Mrs. Fletcher, or if you do come and fail to solve the crime, we are to open a sealed envelope that contains further instructions, including the disposition of the house and the million-dollar bequest. But until then, no one is privy to its contents—not I nor any of my colleagues. To my knowledge, everyone else is already provided for. Of course, there are Miss Tillie's niece and nephew." Mr. Richardson's voice rose, and his speech became clipped. "They are expecting to inherit the property in town, which is worth more than a million dollars. In any case, they are—and this is entirely off the record—not in the least deserving of any additional money. But, of course, that is purely my personal judgment."

"The house is historic, as I remember," I said, thinking to divert him from giving negative opinions of people I had yet to meet. "And the garden is lovely."

"They have no interest in history, that pair. There is some talk already that they plan to sell the house—should it become theirs, of course. Would be a shame to sell it out of the family, but young people have no respect for tradition. The house is quite old. The historical society might be interested in acquiring it if they could raise the funds.

And it is reputed to be haunted. Haunted houses in Savannah sell quite well."

His comment was intriguing, of course, but I declined to follow up on it. I was still thinking about Tillie. Could she really have intended to disinherit the literacy program if I chose not to go to Savannah? I wish I knew what was in that sealed envelope. Or had she deliberately made that provision in her will as an added inducement to me, knowing that I was an easy mark where literacy programs are concerned?

"Mrs. Fletcher?"

"What? Oh, yes, sorry. My mind wandered."

"There is a fairly new hotel next door. However, Miss Tillie directed that you were to stay in the main house. No point in wasting money where it isn't necessary. A room has been freshly made up and awaits you. The housekeeper, Mrs. Goodall, is still on staff and will tend to your every need. There are others living in the guesthouse on the property. Temporarily, of course, but—"

"Others? Family? Her niece and nephew?"

"No, I'm afraid not. As Miss Tillie advanced in age, she developed a greater need to have people around her. She began taking in guests at the house—against my best advice, I assure you."

I'd stayed in the guesthouse the last time I'd visited her, which was quite a number of years ago. It had been recently renovated at the time and was lovely, spacious and beautifully decorated, dripping with Southern charm. The main house was a bit of a mausoleum, with heavy, dark drapery and stiff, uncomfortable chairs. I remember wondering when I'd visited which decor best reflected its owner, the guesthouse she'd had refurbished or the family home that she occupied. I knew which one I favored, but Tillie chose to live in the main house. I'd never asked her if she'd left its furnishings as they were out of a sense of maintaining tradition or if she truly enjoyed surrounding herself with the possessions and interior style inherited from her ancestors.

Mr. Richardson interrupted my thoughts. "You should know that the reading of Miss Tillie's will takes place on Wednesday next. If you decide to come, that would be a propitious time to meet people."

Wednesday was five days away. I glanced down at my desk calendar. I was relatively free for the next three weeks. I'd finished a book just a week ago and had proudly sent it off to my publisher, Vaughan Buckley. I then did what I always do upon finishing a novel: attacked the piles of paper that I hadn't gotten around to filing, started to catch up on correspondence, including answering dozens of e-mails that had accumulated, and spent a day entering new phone numbers and addresses into my address book from small slips of paper on which I'd hastily noted them. My schedule called for me to begin the research for my next book in two months. The timing for a trip to Savannah was good. Not only that, but I found myself enamored of the possibility of visiting that lovely Southern city again, although I had to admit that the circumstances for such a trip were off-putting.

Wanamaker Jones had been murdered forty years ago. Certainly, many of the people who might have something to offer to an investigation into his death would be gone now, either deceased or having relocated. But it also occurred to me that Tillie's death, and the impending reading of her will, might draw a few of them back to the scene of the crime, especially if they knew Jones's murder file was about to be reopened. Word was bound to get around.

"Mr. Richardson," I said.

"Yes?"

"Give me a day to think about this."

"Of course. I'm aware all this must come as quite a shock. But I urge you to consider her request favorably. It would be such a shame to see that million dollars go—shall we say—'astray,' rather their being used to advance the cause of literacy."

He gave me his phone number, and we ended the call.

"What kind of lawyer lets a client put conditions like that on her bequests? Didn't he realize she was not in her right mind? Probably suffering from dementia. Absolutely preposterous."

My dear friend Seth Hazlitt, Cabot Cove's favorite physician, was in high dudgeon. He picked up the black knight and moved it forward on the chessboard. "You should tell them what they can do with their million dollars," he said, setting the piece down with a sharp rap.

"You know I can't disappoint the literacy program."

"I don't know, Mrs. F. I don't think I'd go if I were you," Sheriff Mort Metzger offered as he moved behind Seth to get a better look at the chessboard. He had dropped in to keep us company while his wife was at her cooking class.

"For once I agree with the sheriff," Seth said. "There's a chance they'll be disappointed anyway if you can't solve the murder—not that I don't have complete confidence that you can—but they would certainly understand if you declined such a ridiculous assignment. You're a writer, Jessica, not a private detective."

"Crackpots like that lady are a dime a dozen in New York City," Mort said. "Did I ever tell you about the guy who left a fortune to his cat? Park Avenue apartment, limo, the whole works."

"Is 'crackpot' a technical term they use in New York?" Seth asked. "And stand somewhere else, please. You're blocking my light."

Mort moved to the side.

"She was a little eccentric, I'll admit," I said, contemplating the chessmen. " 'Pixilated' is the word Charmelle used."

"Who's Charmelle, Mrs. F?" Mort asked.

"Charmelle O'Neill, an old friend of Tillie's. They knew each other as girls. She worked with us when we set up the literacy program. Her family is nearly as venerable as Tillie's. The O'Neills were in Savannah before the Civil War. The Mortelaines, I believe, arrived even earlier than that, sometime in the late eighteenth or early nineteenth century."

"A lot of oddballs in those old families," Mort said. "When I was on the force in New York, some of the craziest crazies came from society families. I remember a guy, filthy rich, who used to walk around in a cape singing opera on the street corners. Wasn't looking for a handout, just attention."

"Comes from too much money and not enough responsibility," Seth said flatly.

"Maureen bought me a book about people and their crazy wills," Mort said. "There was this guy who drank a lot. His wife was always on his back about it, so when he died, his will said she'd only get his money if she had a drink every night at the local saloon with his buddies."

"Idiot!" Seth snarled.

"And there was this crazy rich old German lady who left something like eighty million bucks to her dog. Oh, and there's that Leona Helmsley down in New York, who left *her* dog twelve mil. People do weird things with their money when they die."

"I prefer the term 'insane' rather than 'weird,'" Seth pronounced.

"Charmelle told me that Tillie was always 'a bit off'— her words—even before she started drinking," I said. "Tillie was a young woman when Prohibition was repealed, and afterward her odd behavior was attributed to overindulgence with a bottle. But I have to say that in the time we worked together I never saw her inebriated. At least as far as I knew. Check!"

"With some people you can't tell that they're drunk

without looking in their—Wait a minute! Did you say 'check'?"

"Ha! She got you good, Doc."

"See your king?" I said. "I have him boxed in."

"How did you do that?"

"I did very little. You moved your knight into a vulnerable position. I just took advantage."

"Well, I must have been distracted by your tales of a peculiar old lady and the outlandish provisions of her will," Seth said, frowning down at the board. "And, Sheriff, your peering over my shoulder did not help my concentration."

Mort raised his hands in surrender. "I'm just an innocent bystander."

"I find the provisions of Tillie's will just as distracting," I said, marking my win on a pad we used to keep track of our games. "But I didn't let that divert my attention from the board."

Seth harrumphed. "What does that make it?" he asked, reaching for a homemade butter cookie.

"Two games to one, my favor." I held up the cookie plate for Mort to take one.

"You owe me another game, then," Seth said. "Have to let me catch up."

"I'll be delighted to accommodate you, but not tonight. This lady has to pack in the morning." I gathered up the chess pieces and started putting them away.

"I'd better get home," Mort said, looking at his watch. "Maureen will be back soon from her class."

Maureen, a big-hearted redhead, was an enthusiastic cook who embraced each food trend as it came along. Fortunately for her future guests, she was dedicated to improving her skills. She'd come into Mort's life at a particularly low period for him, after his first wife, Adele, decided the bright lights of the big city were preferable to country life and took off. Maureen adored her husband, and took on community activities in Cabot Cove with the same energy that she devoted to her culinary endeavors.

"Let me give you some cookies for her," I said.

"Don't bother, Mrs. F. She's on another diet. Has me on it, too. Not that I don't cheat every now and then." He held up half a cookie. "These are delicious."

"Thank you."

Seth cleared his throat. I offered him another cookie, and asked, "You were just saying you can't always tell if someone is drunk without looking into something. What is that?"

"Their eyes," he replied. "It's called alcohol gaze nystagmus."

"AGN for short," Mort added.

"And what exactly is that?"

"Alcohol depresses the central nervous system and affects fine-motor coordination, including the movement of the eyes," Seth said. "If you have someone look forward and then gaze to the side, you can see a kind of jerky movement of the eye if they're intoxicated, rather than the smooth control they'd have without alcohol in their system. The change is like the difference between a ball rolling over smooth paper versus sandpaper. You can see the lack of control."

"It's been used as a field sobriety test for the police to check drivers," Mort said, "but the courts don't always accept it as evidence. That's why additional tests are usually required."

"Like the Breathalyzer or walking a straight line?" I asked.

"Exactly."

"And standing on one foot," Seth added, "although I don't think I could do that anymore anyway. My balance is not what it used to be." He patted his stomach. "And your cookies are no help."

"I put out a bowl of apples," I reminded him. "It was you who requested the cookies."

"Can't resist your butter cookies. They're every bit as good as the ones at Sassi's Bakery."

"A high compliment indeed," I said. "Would you like me to wrap up a few for you to take home?"

"Seeing as you're going to be away, and not baking anytime soon, I wouldn't be averse to having a stash to put in the cookie jar."

Mort grabbed a cookie from the plate. "Saving you a few calories, Doc," he said, smiling at Seth's scowl. "I'm outta here. Have a good trip, Mrs. F. Good night, Doc."

"And good riddance," Seth said, but he winked at me.

I wrapped the remaining cookies in aluminum foil. "Just parcel them out slowly so you don't go into withdrawal until I can bake a new batch."

"I'll make them last, but if you stay away too long, I may have to break down and buy some at the bakery."

When he'd gone, I straightened up in the kitchen, made myself a cup of herbal tea, and settled in my favorite chair in the living room. I've never been one to shy away from a challenge, but this trip to Savannah had me at sixes and sevens. Seth was right; I'm a writer, not a private eye. I'd never before been officially asked to solve a murder, although I'd ended up doing just that on too many occasions. Those were flukes, examples of my being in the wrong place at the wrong time, and with the wrong people in many instances.

Was this a foolish errand to satisfy the whim of a woman who wasn't even around to see the final result? Was I being used to punish her relatives? They certainly would not want to cooperate with someone who could cost them a potential inheritance. Why did Tillie jeopardize an important social program that she had worked so hard to establish? I would be a very unhappy person if I ended up depriving the literacy program of its donation.

I sighed, and hoped I was up to the task. I would soon find out.

I was leaving for Georgia in the morning.

Chapter Two

The shops in the Savannah airport were decorated for Saint Patrick's Day. Cardboard shamrocks hung on strings from the ceiling in the newsstand. A table in the front of a bookstore was piled with works by Irish authors. A young woman serving coffee had dyed her hair green. (I assumed it was in honor of the occasion.) And everywhere I looked, windows were festooned with green ribbons. Of course! I'd forgotten that Savannah has the second-largest Saint Patrick's Day celebration in the country, trailing only New York, a tribute to the thousands of Irish who'd helped found and develop the city. Good timing for this lady with Irish roots.

I pulled my rolling suitcase across the floor of the glass-roofed atrium that linked the gates to the rest of the terminal, and stepped onto the escalator leading to baggage claim and ground transportation. I always try to pack lightly whenever I travel, and since Tillie's attorney had informed me I was to stay in her house, I assumed I would have access to a laundry during my visit.

At the base of the escalator, a group of people, some in chauffeur uniforms, held up hand-lettered signs with the names of arriving passengers. I searched the little forest of white cardboards and smiled at the young woman who waved my name on a sheet of lined paper. She was in her late teens or early twenties, dressed in blue jeans with high heels and a bomber jacket edged in lace; she looked as if she could have stepped out of the pages of *Cosmopolitan* magazine. She jumped forward and grabbed the handle of my suitcase.

"Welcome to Savannah, Mrs. Fletcher," she said. "I told my mama I'd have no trouble finding you. You look just like the picture on your books."

"Well, that's nice to hear," I said, laughing, "considering that's a picture of me."

She giggled. "I guess that didn't make much sense, did it?"

"It made all the sense in the world."

"Is this all the luggage you have, Mrs. Fletcher?"

"That's it."

"Great! Then just follow me. I had to put the car in the parking garage. You get a ticket if you leave it outside, even for just a few minutes. I can't afford another ticket and I only have a few dollars in my pocket." Her final words were barely audible as she strode off in front of me toward the door.

"You have an advantage over me," I said, hurrying to catch up with her. "You know my name, but I don't know yours."

"Oh, sorry about that, ma'am," she said, twisting around to face me without breaking her stride. "I'm Melanie Goodall. My mama is Miss Tillie's housekeeper—or rather *was*, seeing as Miss Tillie has passed on. Mr. Richardson sent me to carry you home. Know him?"

"Only over the telephone," I replied. "He had said he would be picking me up himself if he had the time."

"He did? Mr. Richardson drive? Then this is your lucky day, Mrs. Fletcher. That man must be a hundred and two—and half blind to boot. I wouldn't trust him behind the wheel of a baby carriage. He drives so slow, the turtles pass him. You're much better off with me."

Once outside, Melanie held up her hand to stop the traffic and jogged across the roadway toward the garage with me in hot pursuit. I was glad I try to keep myself in relatively good shape, or I could easily have lost her in the crowd. Given her single-minded goal of reaching the car in record time, I had visions of being left behind at the airport while my luggage made the trip into town. Mr. Richardson's reportedly slower pace was looking favorable to me.

"Here we are," Melanie said as she reached a blue Honda that had been parked halfway into an adjacent spot. "I'm not usually so greedy with parking spaces," she said as she lifted the trunk and deposited my bag inside, "but I was afraid I'd miss you. Front seat or back?"

"I'd prefer to sit next to you," I said, "if you don't mind."

"Fine with me. I usually drive with the window cracked. Let me know if it's too airish."

As we exited the airport, I was relieved to see that Melanie's highway driving did not mimic her sprint to the parking garage. We chatted easily on the way into town. She was the only daughter of Emanuela Love and Andrew Goodall, who had married late in life. While Mrs. Goodall had been Tillie's housekeeper for forty years, and had a room of her own off the kitchen for the times it was needed, she had also maintained her own home farther uptown, which she'd shared with her husband until his death and, until recently, with Melanie, who was a student at the Savannah College of Art and Design, known locally as SCAD.

"Mama nearly took a fit when I told her I was moving into a place near the school with my girlfriend, LaTisha," Melanie said, "but we were workin' all hours and it was just too far to go uptown after."

"What are you studying?" I asked.

"Historic preservation."

"You're certainly in the right place for it," I said.

"Yes, ma'am. You don't find too many colleges with that major, but Savannah has a really big historic district. And our college has renovated a mess of buildings downtown. We get hands-on experience, which is good. I think I'd get bored pretty fast if everything I learn came only from books."

"That's wonderful," I said. "You've worked on some of the renovations?"

"Not really. Not yet, anyways. But Miss Tillie was lettin' me research the history of Mortelaine House. That made Mama happy, cooled her down a tad about my living elsewhere. When I was snooping around Miss Tillie's house looking for some history, it meant Mama could keep an eye on me while she was doing her job. Mama is pretty protective of me. Don't get me wrong. I know she's that way 'cause she loves me."

"A doting, loving mother," I offered.

"She sure is." She abruptly shifted verbal gears. "It's a great old house, even has a couple of ghosts." Melanie glanced over to see my reaction. " 'Course, I've never seen one, and believe me, I've tried. Tish and I stayed up till three in the morning one night, goin' from room to room trying to raise a soul. Nothing. Not even a cold breeze. Thank goodness for that. I would have been scared to death if I'd actually seen one."

"So how do you know the house has ghosts?"

"Has to have, an old house like that where somebody—Mr. Jones—was murdered, especially since no one has ever found his killer. I expect Mama has seen the ghosts, but she won't talk about it—leastwise to me—but Miss Tillie, she swore up and down she saw them. She once said to me, 'There's Mr. Jones over to the fireplace.' He was her *betrothed*—that's what she called him—till he got shot. Died in the upstairs hall. I looked real hard, but I didn't see anything. I like that word, 'betrothed.' Sounds like something from Shakespeare, doesn't it? What does it mean exactly? D'you know?"

"It means she was engaged to marry him," I said.

"That's what I thought." She was quiet for a rare moment. Anyone who believes in the stereotype that Southerners move and speak slowly hasn't met Melanie Goodall. "It's really sad that she never got to marry him," she continued, "but it's pretty awful if he's haunting her. That's just plain scary."

"Well, maybe now that she's gone, too, he'll stop haunting the house," I said to her, not adding, *if he was ever really there.*

Melanie sighed. " 'Course, you always had to take everything Miss Tillie said with a very large grain of salt. She was a mite loopy. Not all there, if you take my point. Meaning no disrespect. Don't get me wrong. I loved her to death. Oops! That doesn't sound right either."

"I knew what you meant," I said, trying not to laugh.

"She was always very good to me. But she was like a dotty old grandmama, talking to herself and seeing things. Even Miss O'Neill said so. And she was her best friend."

"That would be Charmelle O'Neill?"

"Yes, ma'am. You know her?"

"It's been many years since I've been to Savannah," I said, "but I did meet her when I was here."

My first encounter with Charmelle O'Neill had been brief but memorable.

It was the afternoon before the opening of the new literacy center, which was actually just a room in a multipurpose building, but its official designation had been long in coming. The U.S. Department of Health had extended a grant for screening hospital patients to determine if they were able to read and follow the doctors' directions. Those deemed to need extra help were to be directed to our center, where evening classes would be given by volunteers trained in elementary education. Plans were to move people into special computer programs once they'd mastered the basics, so our clients would become proficient in two areas at the same time—reading and using a computer. It was an ambitious program, one of which we were very proud.

Tillie and I were setting up refreshments in the classroom. While the hospital would provide our first customers, we hoped to draw from a wider population and had invited the press to see our new quarters in the hope they would get the word out across the city. Over my objections, Tillie had insisted that I be her "celebrity spokesperson."

"Would you put the teapot over there, Jessica?" Tillie said, pointing to a scarred wooden table we'd pushed against the wall. "The cups and saucers are in the box on the floor. I don't want anyone spilling tea on my nice tablecloth." She arranged a dozen small plates of tea cakes, and lined up forks and linen napkins on the embroidered blue tablecloth, smoothing its surface with hands gnarled by arthritis. "This was such a good idea of yours, Jessica."

"It's always been my experience that if you feed the press, they're in a better frame of mind to hear and disseminate your message," I said, lifting the saucers from the box. "Of course, I think they probably would have been just as happy with cookies served on paper plates."

"Maybe so, but I wouldn't be," she said, grinning at me. "I have my reputation as a hostess to maintain." She looked at her watch. "The mayor and the reporters will be here in ten minutes. I told Charmelle to come at three to help us set up. That woman is always late."

"I think we're in good shape," I said, looking over the computer stations lined against one wall. My publisher, Vaughan Buckley, had twisted a few arms at a big computer company, and five brand-new machines, complete with the appropriate software, had been donated to our center. Computers were not as common back then as they are today, but their growing popularity in businesses promised to spread to homes across America. We were excited to be using the latest technology to give our students their training.

"You could have waited for me," came a wail from the door.

Charmelle O'Neill must have been a beauty in her youth. She was tall and spare, and posed in the doorway as if waiting to be admired. Even as age had begun to claim her, she fought to maintain her looks with careful application of bright pink lipstick and rouge to her powdered face. She was dressed meticulously in a soft green suit, a pink cashmere sweater, and a silk scarf pinned to her shoulder with a gold brooch. I smiled in greeting as she smoothed down a stray hair and tucked it into her chignon with perfectly manicured fingers.

"If we waited for you, Charmelle," Tillie said, "we'd be setting the table while the mayor gives his speech."

"The Ladies Auxiliary meeting ran dreadfully late," she said. She took one of Tillie's napkins from the table, and with flicking motions dusted off a chair before allowing herself to perch on it.

"Charmelle, you know Jessica, don't you?" Tillie said, grabbing the napkin back and folding it next to the others.

"I don't believe we've had the pleasure," I said, extending my hand. "I'm Jessica Fletcher. I've heard so much about you."

Charmelle gave me the tips of her fingers to shake and managed a small smile. "You're the writer. Tillie mentioned you." Her gaze took in my shirtwaist dress and sensible shoes, and I felt as if my attire was being scrutinized and found wanting.

My eyebrows rose at this less than cordial greeting and I returned to the table, where I busied myself putting teacups on the saucers.

"Charmelle, get off your derriere and give me a hand over here," Tillie said, trying to hold up the blue cloth and simultaneously wrestle a box under the table.

"Really, Tillie. Don't you have people to do this?"

"You're people. Now move. We don't have all day. They'll be here any minute." She looked up at her friend. "I see you're dressed to the nines. Hoping to snag one of them newspapermen? I swear, Charmelle, is no man safe from your clutches?" Tillie winked at me and tried to cover a smile.

"Hush your mouth," Charmelle said as she grabbed the edge of the tablecloth and held it up while Tillie shoved the box under the table with her toe. "I always dress this way."

"You do not. And don't be snotty to my friend Jessica. I know all your secrets, and I'm not above blabbing them. Remember that."

A short time later, the room filled with lots of officials and a sprinkling of press. The mayor, the superintendent of schools, the hospital administrator, and several others accompanying them stood around admiring the shiny computers, while a photographer recorded the moment for posterity. Tillie introduced me, and I made brief comments on the importance of ensuring that every adult and child have the opportunity to learn to read. "You are so fortunate to have dedicated teachers volunteering their time and expertise to this center," I said. "We hope they'll be aided by these computers and the revolutionary program written especially for the Savannah Literacy Center. If it's successful here—and we're sure it will be—the program will be rolled out all over Georgia and to other states in America. Savannah is leading the way in this important educational initiative."

As I spoke, I noticed Charmelle examining the table where I'd set the cups and saucers. Using one pink fingertip, she pushed the cup handles to the right so they all lined up in exactly the same direction.

"Why did you get involved, Mrs. Fletcher?" a reporter called out, drawing my attention back to the matter at hand.

"I'm a former English teacher," I said, "so education and literacy have always been particular interests of mine. Besides, a writer always needs more readers."

There was polite laughter and I was invited to pose with Tillie, the mayor, and the school superintendent for a picture to appear in the *Savannah Morning News*.

"How have you been, Miss Tillie?" asked the mayor, a short, compact man with ruddy cheeks and a patch of reddish hair on the top of his head.

"I couldn't be better, Harold," she replied.

"You look a bit tired," he said.

"What would you expect from a woman my age?"

The mayor laughed. "How many years is it now, Miss Tillie?" he asked, mirth in his voice.

"That is none of your business, Harold, and if you insist upon asking women their age, you'll never win a second term. Thanks for coming today. You've always had a nose for being where the press will be."

"She knows me only too well," he said to me. "It's a real pleasure meeting you, Mrs. Fletcher. You come back to Savannah soon, y'heah?"

"I certainly hope to, Mr. Mayor."

"Where's Charmelle?" Tillie asked after the dignitaries had gone and we were packing up her china.

"I didn't see her leave," I said.

"She can't stand it if she's not the center of attention," Tillie said, shaking her head. "But I'll fix her good later."

Tillie wouldn't tell me how she "fixed her good," but Charmelle's attitude had changed dramatically the next time we met. She was unfailingly pleasant on that second meeting, and continued to be from that point forward. Though we never became good friends, we did keep in touch for a few years, mostly through holiday greetings, until the cards stopped. I never knew if it was her health, or disposition, but I didn't hear from her again after that.

"How is Miss O'Neill?" I asked Melanie. *She must be about eighty-five or eighty-six now,* I thought. I was looking forward to seeing her again. She could be the key to my deciphering Tillie's true intentions. Would she remember me? And could she explain the reasons behind Tillie's strange bequest?

Melanie concentrated on making a left turn off the highway onto a crowded street, her bottom lip caught between her teeth. I thought for a moment she hadn't heard me. Then she sighed. "Not too good," she said. "When Miss O'Neill got the news that Miss Tillie had died, she collapsed and hit her head on the corner of a table. She has nurses taking care of her all day and all night. My mama doesn't think she'll pull through."

Chapter Three

Savannah was the first planned city to have been
built in North America. General James Edward Oglethorpe, for whom dozens of entities are named—
schools, streets, parks, hotels, clubs, a university, even a
mall—sailed up the Savannah River in 1733 and gained
permission from the Yamacraw tribe to establish a settle-
ment. Together with his colleague and co-planner, William Bull, he set up a city designed in the London manner
around a series of twenty-four green squares with public
buildings to occupy the east and west sides of the quad-
rangle and settlers' homes to be situated on the north and
south. Later, as wealthy merchants, planters, and states-
men vied to outdo each other by erecting lavish homes
in a variety of architectural styles, no side of a square was
exempt from construction.

The distinctive architecture of Savannah is without doubt part of the city's charm, a fact that the local historical foundation fully appreciates. Its members, a cross section of the community, have campaigned over the years to save many beautiful homes from the wrecker's ball. Some have been accused of being overzealous in their mission; critics and cynics snidely term them members of the "hysterical preservation review board," but these detractors have never succeeded in dampening the board's missionary spirit.

Tillie's house was located in the historically protected landmark district and was a monument to the wealth accumulated by her great-great-grandfather, a banker and investor who cannily put his money into the manufacture of arms in businesses located both above and below the Mason-Dixon Line. Built of Savannah Grey brick, which is really more mauve than gray, it was designed in the Italianate style that was popular in the 1860s and later augmented by flourishes in the Queen Anne and Romanesque Revival styles. It seemed to have passed through the twentieth century without ever having put its foot down. The only nod to modern times was the addition of electricity and indoor plumbing. And in the twenty-first century, a ramp at the back door to accommodate Tillie's mobility-challenged friends.

Melanie steered carefully around the cars that were double-parked in front of the hotel next door, and pulled into a driveway at the right side of Tillie's house, which fronted on one of the city's beautiful squares. Ahead was a high wrought-iron fence that surrounded the garden. To the right was the guesthouse in which I'd stayed on my last visit. It had been the servants' quarters when the house was originally built. Melanie collected my luggage and escorted me up the front steps. "Be prepared. My mama's going to want to feed you," she said as she pressed down on the brass latch and pushed open the tall, paneled door.

"That's all right," I said. "The only food I've had since breakfast were the pretzels they gave out on the plane. I'll be happy for a snack."

"Mrs. Fletcher! So kind of you to come."

Mrs. Goodall, in a black and white flowered dress beneath her starched white apron, greeted me as I walked in. She was a tall, sturdy woman with slightly bowed legs that gave her a rocking gait when she walked. Her face was unlined, and only her steel gray hair in tight curls cut close to her head gave away her age.

"It's good to see you again, Mrs. Goodall," I said, "but I'm sorry that it's under these circumstances." I pressed her hand. "You have my condolences."

"Forty years I worked for Miss Tillie, Mrs. Fletcher." Her eyes filled with sadness. She gave her head a sharp shake. "I was just a girl when I come here, no older than Melanie." She waved her daughter in, took my jacket, and hung it on the coat tree in the front hall. "I can't believe she's gone. I thought she'd live forever."

"She had a good long life," I said. "A lot of people would be grateful for ninety-one years."

"That they would," she said. "That they would. May the good Lord keep her." She turned to lead me inside and I

31

heard her mutter to herself, "And may she not come back like that other one."

While Melanie took my suitcase upstairs, Mrs. Goodall led me across the marble foyer to a sitting room. "Please make yourself to home," she said. "I'll bring you up some refreshment. I know they don't give you no food on those airplanes anymore. I already have a tray ready for you."

"That's very kind."

"No bother at all. When Miss Tillie was alive, I was serving food all day. She did like to entertain, that one. Now, it's just the general and that pair from the institute."

"I beg your pardon?"

"Her tenants. Stayin' in the guesthouse. You'll meet them at supper. I told her she should be charging them rent, they been here that long. Taking advantage of her hospitality, that's for sure. But she wouldn't pay me no mind. Said they were her guests. Guests, my foot. Hangers-on. That's what they are."

"How long have these guests been here?" I asked.

"Too long. Don't see as how Mr. Richardson lets them stay now," she said. "But the house is going to go to the niece and nephew, so they tell me. They'll kick 'em out soon enough. Me, too, I 'spect. Lucky I got my own place. You just relax now. I'll be right back."

I paced the room while waiting for Mrs. Goodall. It was hard to relax in the formal atmosphere of Tillie's parlor. The sun that might have come through the tall windows and reflected off the high ceilings was effectively muffled by heavy velvet drapes, in a deep red, trimmed with gold fringe, behind which were closed wooden plantation shutters. The walls were covered in a paper so old it was difficult to discern what the pattern was supposed to be. Light had never been given a chance to fade it; instead, the years had left their mark in dark patches and streaks that no amount of cleaning would ever erase. The atmosphere could only be described as decidedly gloomy.

The mahogany furniture was familiar from my last visit, and I chose a stiff upholstered settee, which crackled when I sat on it. While it wasn't what I would call comfortable, at least it had the benefit of not capturing the sitter in a soft trap, as so many old sofas can do.

Across from where I sat was an ebony fireplace with intricately carved columns supporting a marble mantel. It had been fitted with an elaborate overmantel and a central mirror framed in tiny reflective squares, and four outer mirrors with shelves to reflect the back of finely carved figurines that had been placed on them. I wondered if Mrs. Goodall needed to tote a ladder around when she was doing the housework—dusting the recesses within and above the overmantel must have made for an athletic workout.

My eyes wandered the room, conjuring up the days when Tillie entertained me by telling tales about the figurines and other memorabilia she had collected or had inherited from her ancestors. She knew the history of every piece, and many times would snicker about the wool she'd pulled over an antique dealer's eyes when she'd tricked him into giving her a bargain.

*　　*　　*

"You're thinking that dealer is no fool, I bet," Tillie told me the last time I was with her.

"I didn't say any such thing."

"But you were thinking it, Jessica. You'd make a bad poker player the way your thoughts are written all over your face. I was a damn good poker player. Yes, I was. I could bluff anybody and everybody at the table, take all their money. You think that shifty dealer probably knows all my wiles."

"He wouldn't stay in business for long, Tillie, if he lost money on every piece," I replied.

"I let him make money on some of the pieces. That oil painting *Judith Holding the Head of Holofernes*, for instance." She pointed to a gruesome picture of the Old Testament story. "He told me it's eighteenth century, but I know for a fact it's a twentieth-century copy."

"How did you know?"

"My mama didn't raise me to be a lackwit," she said, her Southern accent deepening. "I hired an art historian from the college to check it out before I made an offer. I can see you don't like it, but I do."

I studied the painting. It was a murder scene, the knife still in Judith's right hand, her left holding her victim's head. "What appeals to you about it?"

"The story. It's been painted by many artists over the centuries. Do you know it?"

"I do," I said. "Judith seduced Holofernes and killed him

while he slept. By beheading the general who had come to conquer her people, she saved them."

"She was a widow, but she was strong. She did what she had to do. I admire that. Too many women are timid, afraid of offending. They never stand up for themselves. I tell that to Charmelle all the time. Don't let people walk all over you. I tell it like it is. People think I'm crazy, but they watch their step around me."

The wall held a different painting now, and I wondered if Tillie had finally tired of the violent scene, or if someone had talked her into hanging it elsewhere.

Mrs. Goodall entered with a tray of sandwiches, two cookies, and a glass of iced tea. She followed my gaze. "I took it away," she said, setting the tray on a small table in front of me. "Never could stand that awful picture. I asked Mr. Richardson. He said it was okay to move it. I put it in Miss Tillie's room, seein' as how she liked it so much. The lady had some mighty strange tastes in pictures. I like pretty pictures, nature scenes, blue sky with clouds, not ones to give me nightmares."

"I didn't care for that particular painting either," I said, smiling. "This sandwich looks wonderful. Thank you so much."

She straightened her shoulders. "It's crab salad and arugula. It's a kind of lettuce. Grow it myself in the garden in summer, but this one's store-bought. Should hold you to supper. I serve at six; we're finished by seven thirty. Don't usually rush you, but I got a meetin' at the church tonight and I got to clean up before I go."

"Of course," I said. "If you need to leave early, I'll be happy to clean up."

"Now don't go taking away my job, Mrs. Fletcher," she said with a frown, but there was a twinkle in her eye. "Don't know how much longer I'll have it."

"I wouldn't think of it, Mrs. Goodall."

"You can call me when you're finished and I'll take the tray back down."

"Can't you sit with me a while?'"

"Well, I—"

"If you have work to do, I understand. It's just that I was hoping to talk to you about Tillie. It's been so many years. How did she die? Mr. Richardson never said. And how is Charmelle O'Neill? Your daughter told me she's not well."

"I guess I can set a spell," Mrs. Goodall said, lowering herself into a side chair. She picked up a silver bowl, pulled a cloth from the pocket of her apron, and began wiping the bowl's side. "Supper's already made. Just needs heating."

I picked up a half of the sandwich. "I understand Tillie was ninety-one. Was she in failing health?"

"Never say so. She was strong as an ox, that one." Mrs. Goodall smiled at the memory. "Never sick a day. And her brain was sharp as a knife, too. No one could put anything by her. She rush around from here to there. She'd get swimmy-headed from time to time. The doc said it's not unusual at her age. But Miss Tillie, she didn't want to act her age. Maybe that's the problem. I come in one morning and find her at the bottom of the stairs, all curled up."

"That must have been awful for you."

"I left at seven thirty the night before. Them people in the guesthouse told the police that they went back to their rooms right after supper. Miss Tillie shooed them outta the house. Said she had a headache and was goin' right upstairs. She should've stayed up there. She tripped on the rug at the top of the stairs."

"Oh, my."

She nodded. "Found her slipper up there. Blue with gold embroidery. Brand-new, too. A gift from Miss O'Neill. When the box come, Miss Tillie run upstairs to open it. First time she ever wore them, and look what happens. I kept warning her that rug was dangerous. Too worn, it was, with the threads showing and all. It needed to be replaced, but she wouldn't let me."

"If the rug was dangerous, why wouldn't she let you have it fixed?"

"Oh, it was passed down from her great-grandfather, who brought it back from some country he visited on his honeymoon. She'd say, 'You mind that rug with the vacuum, Emanuela. We don't want to tear a piece of history.' And I clean it by hand. Don't let no machine pass over it." She shook her head. "I hate to think what she was feelin', falling down all them stairs. But there was no breath in her when I find her. And she was cold. I feel so bad. Maybe if I didn't go to church that night, she'd still be here."

"You must not blame yourself," I said. "The rug was

worn. She was wearing new slippers. You know how the soles of new shoes can be slippery. It was probably dark and she didn't see clearly. These kinds of accidents can happen, especially with elderly people who might be unsteady on their feet."

"She was careful, though. Kept a light on at the top all night long. 'Wasting power,' I said, but she insisted. Now I'm glad she did. She probably would have fallen sooner."

"Why do you suppose she wanted to come back downstairs that night?" I asked.

Mrs. Goodall sighed. "Sometimes, she have trouble sleeping. When I'm here, I bring her up a glass of warm milk."

"So you think perhaps she wanted to heat some milk for herself? Would she do that?"

"Couldn't say." She replaced the silver bowl on the table and took a long time to fold her polishing cloth into a tiny square, her brow similarly creased.

"Have I made you uncomfortable, Mrs. Goodall? If so, I apologize. I only meant to ask if there was something else that might have prompted Tillie to come downstairs."

"This is an old house, Mrs. Fletcher," she said, her eyes still on the polishing cloth, "with a lot of memories and a lot of noises. Creaking boards and such. Miss Tillie, she was convinced we have ghosts, said she saw them, heard them wandering in the night. They always bothered her. I used to see her all the time talking to herself. Come to find out she was talking to them."

"So she may have heard a noise and gone to investigate?"

"Wouldn't be the first time. That pair in the guesthouse churn her up. They been testing the air, bringing in Geiger counters or some such. Tell her when the needle moves, that means a spirit is here. Had her believin' Mr. Jones is haunting the house. Could be others, too, they say."

"That would be Wanamaker Jones, the man who was killed here?"

"Yes, ma'am."

"I take it you don't believe in ghosts, Mrs. Goodall."

"I'm not saying yes and I'm not saying no," she replied. "I seen some strangeness from time to time. I don't pay it no mind."

Melanie poked her head in the door. "I have to leave for school, Mama," she said.

Mrs. Goodall's frown eased into a smile. She pressed her palms on her knees, rocked forward, and rose from the chair. "I put some cookies in a sack for you."

"Don't get up. I got 'em," Melanie said, waving the paper bag. "'Bye, Mrs. Fletcher. Nice to meet you."

"Nice to meet you too," I called after her.

"I got work to do anyway," Mrs. Goodall said, brushing off the chair in which she'd been sitting.

Melanie's interruption clearly had been a relief for her mother. The topic of ghosts and haunting didn't seem to be one she was happy to discuss and I didn't want to press her. She'd already been generous with her time. I would ask about Charmelle later.

"Thank you so much for your company, Mrs. Goodall, and for this wonderful snack. It was delicious."

"No bother at all, Mrs. Fletcher. You just leave the tray when you're finished. I'll come collect it. Your room is the first door on the right, top of the stairs, across from Miss Tillie's room. I made it up fresh this morning."

"I think I'll go up now and unpack."

"Supper's at six."

"Yes, I remember."

"And, Mrs. Fletcher?"

"Yes, Mrs. Goodall?"

"Please mind the rug."

Chapter Four

Mrs. Goodall was nowhere in sight when I came downstairs at a quarter to six, but some of her guests were already in the parlor, helping themselves to Tillie's brandy from a glass-topped cart next to the fireplace. A tall, stooped gentleman holding a half-filled snifter turned as I entered the room.

"Ah, the guest of honor," he said, holding out the glass. "May I offer you some Armagnac, Mrs. Fletcher? General James J. Pettigrew, Fourth Infantry Division, Retired, at your service. These are the Grogans." As he gestured with the hand holding the snifter toward a couple sitting on the settee, he sloshed liquor over the rim of the glass.

I captured the drink from him before he could spill any more on the carpet, thanked him, grabbed a napkin from the cart, and went to shake hands with the Grogans, who wore matching blue jackets. "How do you do?" I said.

Mr. Grogan handed his drink to his wife and stood. "Professor Arthur G. Grogan of the Institute for Paranormal Relations," he said, pumping my hand. "It's a pleasure, Mrs. Fletcher."

"Please, it's Jessica," I said.

"Then call me Artie. This is my wife and business associate, Sammy Grogan."

"Samantha," she said, shooting her husband an annoyed look.

Artie Grogan was an egg-shaped man of medium height. He wore a bright green silk neckerchief in the open collar of his white button-down shirt. His wife was a taller version of her husband. She'd dressed for the evening in a brown and blue paisley dress. I took note that they both had some sort of insignia on the breast pockets of their jackets.

"Sorry, I can't shake your hand," Samantha said, holding up the two glasses—hers and her husband's. "We heard you were coming."

"Oh? Did Mr. Richardson tell you?"

"Oh, no. We have better sources than that," she said brightly.

"Please sit down," I said. I waved Artie back to his seat and took the chair Mrs. Goodall had occupied that afternoon. There was no coaster on the table next to me, so I held on to the drink, not wanting to rest a damp glass on the housekeeper's highly polished wooden tabletop.

Artie resumed his place on the settee, which creaked under his weight, and took his drink back from his wife, while Mr. Pettigrew busied himself pouring another Armagnac.

"Will Mr. Richardson be joining us for dinner tonight?" I asked.

"I believe so," Samantha said, wrinkling her nose. "He doesn't tell us when he's coming, but the general"—she nodded toward Pettigrew—"was talking to Mrs. Goodall this afternoon and she let the pig out of the poke, so to speak."

"Don't you mean 'the cat out of the bag,' my dear?" her husband said.

"No, I don't."

I gathered that Mr. Richardson was not a favorite of Tillie's tenants. And he had already indicated to me his displeasure that they were in residence.

"Ah, yes," said Mr. Pettigrew, sinking into the chair opposite mine. "This evening, we are to be honored with the presence of Roland the Third, Rollie to his buddies." He took a big gulp of his drink, and hummed his satisfaction. "Between the two of you, I imagine we shall learn our fate."

"I beg your pardon," I said. "I'm afraid I don't understand."

"Mr. Richardson has been threatening to evict us," Artie said, looking to his wife for confirmation. "Miss Tillie had told us we could stay as long as we needed to conduct our research. We've been making great progress, but her untimely demise has put us all in jeopardy."

"That's right," Samantha added. "Now that the poor soul is no longer here to defend us, her lawyer wants to kick us out." She sighed and slowly shook her head. "And after all we've done for Miss Tillie. It's so unfair. She would be so upset. I'm sure she's rolling in her grave this very minute."

The image that came to mind was disconcerting.

"I don't mean to sound rude," I said, "but what exactly have you been doing for Tillie?"

"We're cataloging her spirit complement," Artie said.

"Researching the paranormal phenomena in Mortelaine House," Samantha clarified.

"Houses of this generation often show evidence of supernatural presence," Artie continued. "It's important to know who you're dealing with and why they haven't passed into the next world. We research their history, communicate with them, and discover the reasons why their spirits are so unsettled. It's essential to know why they're still here in order to help them gain their heavenly reward and rest in peace. Right now, the spectral beings in Mortelaine House are not resting."

"Nor are they at peace," his wife added.

"How many beings are we talking about?" I asked.

"At least two," Artie said.

"Maybe more," Samantha put in.

"We believe—and Miss Tillie agreed, I might add—that her great-great-grandfather is still here in the house that his son built. Miss Tillie thinks—or rather *thought*, I suppose is more appropriate at this juncture—that the renovations made to the building when the plumbing was brought indoors may have disturbed his spirit. Our equipment has registered quite a number of psychic manifestations around the bathrooms."

"I see," I said. I did not see at all, and wanted to know more. "What would these manifestations consist of?" I asked.

"Cold spots, orbs of light, disturbances of the physical plane, things of that sort."

"I have felt a hand on my cheek," Samantha said, smiling at the memory. "Great-great-grandfather Mortelaine was apparently quite the ladies' man."

"And the others?" I asked.

"One would be Mr. Wanamaker Jones, who was killed in the hall above this very room," Artie said, lowering his voice. He looked around as if to see where Jones was. "His killer has never been caught. The police never even found the murder weapon. Miss Tillie thinks that's why he's still here. His spirit is very disruptive."

"In what way?"

"Oh, the usual, locking and unlocking doors, stomping in the halls, banging on the pipes, flinging the occasional item across the room. Miss Tillie wanted us to help the soul of Mr. Jones attain his rightful heavenly rest."

"I can see why," I said.

"We heard that you're being brought in to do the same thing," Samantha said, "although I don't see how you can be successful with no prior experience with the spirit world."

"Nor do I," I said, "although that wasn't exactly my understanding of why I was asked to come." I turned to the man Samantha had called "the general." "And you, General Pettigrew, are you part of this research as well?"

"Oh no, no, no. I leave that to my esteemed colleagues over there. No, I have no talent in ferreting out leftover souls who haven't figured out how to make it into heaven. While I'm a firm believer that the present is informed by the past, if you will, Miss Tillie and I had a different relationship."

"And what relationship was that?" I nodded at Pettigrew, encouraging him to continue, and took a sip of the drink I'd been holding all this time.

"I believe we were fulfilling our destiny. I had asked Miss Tillie to be my wife and she had consented."

That took me by surprise. Plus, the drink was very strong. I gasped and started coughing. Samantha jumped up and pounded on my back. I put my hand up. "I'm all right," I managed to get out.

She took the snifter and put it on the glass-topped cart. "That stuff is too powerful," she said, as she returned with a glass of water. "Really, General, why did you give it to her?"

"Wanted to see what stuff she was made of," he said. He raised his glass. "Welcome, Mrs. Fletcher." He consumed the drink in a single swallow.

The water soothed my burning throat, but I was afraid to speak in case the effort would set off another paroxysm of coughing. I drank it slowly, eyeing Pettigrew and wondering what I had done to gain his animosity so quickly. Mr. Richardson owed me a lot of explanations and I intended to get them from him.

As if I had conjured him by thinking of his name, a small man, easily in his eighties, limped into the doorway, leaning on a cane. He wore a three-piece suit and a bow tie, just as I had pictured him in our telephone conversation.

"Ah, the cavalry has arrived just in time," Pettigrew said. "Mrs. Fletcher, have you met your sergeant at arms? Say hello to the esteemed Roland Richardson the Third."

Chapter Five

The dining room table had been set for six. Two tall chairs upholstered in a floral tapestry were drawn up to either side of the oval table, with matching armchairs at the head and foot. Extra chairs had been pulled back out of the way and lined one wall. For some reason they reminded me of the row of chairs outside the principal's office when I taught high school English, except these were much prettier.

The room had a sparkle that the parlor lacked. Mrs. Goodall had placed silver candlesticks on the mahogany sideboard with a matching pair flanking an ormolu clock on the mantel. A gilded Cupid rested on the clock, his head cocked at a little bird perched on his hand. Light from a crystal chandelier above the table was reflected by Tillie's good china and glassware, lending the room a warm glow.

Mr. Richardson, the attorney whose phone call had lured me to Savannah, indicated the chair at the head of the table—it must have been Tillie's—and nodded at me. He rested his hand on the top until I took my seat; then limped around to the other end and claimed his spot. The tenants of the guesthouse sat in what I presume were their usual chairs, with the one between the general and me left empty.

Once we were seated, Mrs. Goodall arrived with a tray containing the first course. The kitchen was downstairs on the basement level, which was not uncommon in many of the houses in the landmark district.

"We're missing one," Richardson observed.

"The doc says y'all go on ahead and eat without him," Mrs. Goodall said. "He's still at the hospital, but he say he join you when he can."

"What do you have for us tonight, Mrs. Goodall?" Artie Grogan rubbed his hands together in anticipation.

"Shrimp and grits," she replied, pointedly circling the table away from Grogan and his wife even though Samantha's seat was closest to the butler's pantry and the back stairs.

Samantha stretched her neck to see what was on the tray. "Isn't that traditionally a breakfast dish?" she asked.

"Up north, mebbe. But not this 'un," Mrs. Goodall said.

Richardson smiled. "By 'up north,' she means South Carolina. Don't you, ma'am?"

Mrs. Goodall chuckled, and came to my side.

I took a small plate from the tray. On it were three large shrimp, sprinkled with lemon and bits of bacon and onion. Accompanying the shrimp was a triangle of deep-fried grits.

"I made this special for you. I remember you liked it last time."

"I'm sure I did," I said, marveling that she could remember what dish I had liked so long ago.

She brought the tray to Attorney Richardson next and announced, "I'll serve the appetizer; then y'all jus' help yourselves to the rest I be putting on the sideboard: baked buttermilk chicken, green beans, hush puppies."

"And biscuits?" Artie Grogan asked.

"And biscuits," she growled. "I know what y'all like."

The housekeeper took the tray back downstairs to the kitchen and emerged a minute later with a silver basket piled with biscuits. She surveyed the table in search of some space and decided to leave the basket next to me. There wasn't a lot of room. Mrs. Goodall had draped cream-colored lace over a white damask tablecloth. A trio of Delft bowls filled with pale pink roses was complemented by blue and white ceramic figures of a shepherd and shepherdess. At opposite ends of the table, crystal swans, their silver wings drawn back, held the salt and tiny spoons for serving it. Each place setting included multiple plates, and glasses for water and wine, as well as a silver napkin ring in which squares of linen had been arranged to resemble an open flower. Tillie may have liked to entertain and had been known as a gracious hostess, but she'd unquestionably been aided by Mrs. Goodall, who clearly enjoyed setting a beautiful table, even when she wasn't pleased with all the guests.

Mr. Richardson concentrated on his food, and all conversation halted. The clinks of forks and knives on china sounded especially loud in the lingering silence. I looked around at my dinner companions. All eyes were narrowly focused on their plates.

I used this moment of quiet to process the circumstances of my being seated at this table with these people whom I'd just met. No one seemed aware of the reason for my being in Savannah, which led me to believe that Mr. Richardson hadn't shared it with them. I hadn't volunteered information, and although Samantha had guessed I was there to help the resident ghosts find their eternal peace, they hadn't pursued the subject. Did they assume that because Tillie and I had worked on launching the literacy center years earlier, I'd traveled to Savannah to memorialize her life and contribution to society? I somehow doubted that. Of course, they may have known my mission and considered it impolite to inquire further. Or it was possible that they were reluctant to bring up the subject of Wanamaker Jones's murder so close on the heels of Tillie's demise. They may have feared that my investigation would get in the way of their own self-interest. That was more likely. Whatever the reason, my motivation for having arrived in Savannah would become public knowledge the following morning when Richardson gathered all interested parties in his office and read Tillie's last will and testament.

I looked at the general and contemplated what Tillie might have seen in him. He had nice features and could have been a handsome man were it not for the disagreeable expression on his face. Would Tillie really have gotten married at ninety-one? And to a man easily twenty years her junior? I hated to think it, but it was possible of course that by now Tillie had been more than pixilated. Was her mind starting to go? The provisions of her will could have been the work of someone off balance or perhaps with undiagnosed dementia. Would Mr. Richardson have recognized the symptoms?

I put that unpleasant thought aside and took a biscuit, passing the basket to Artie Grogan. "Tell me about your institute, Artie. Is it here in Georgia?"

A strange look came over his face. He held his napkin to his lips as though buying time before answering. Finally, he lowered the napkin and said, "Actually, we're kind of in between permanent locations at this moment." He shot a look at Richardson, who ignored him, before going on. "We traveled around quite a bit until founding the institute, doing research, of course. We did have an office in Durham at one point, but not during the heyday of paranormal research at Duke University. But still, those were the days, huh, Sammy?"

His wife gave him a small smile.

"Um. Then we moved to New Jersey, to Princeton. Unfortunately, that program closed, too, but we met Miss Tillie at one of the sponsored lectures. The rest is history, as they say, and so here we are." He smiled broadly, seemingly pleased at his response to my question.

"Not a very lengthy history, is it?" General Pettigrew said. It was more of a dismissive grunt than a clear statement. He'd been silent during the early stages of the dinner.

"I beg your pardon," Grogan said.

"Just stating the obvious," the general said.

"I don't attack your credits, Pettigrew," Artie said, and "I'll thank you to keep away from mine. General, indeed!"

"Come now, Grogan, don't be so touchy," Pettigrew said. He had a remarkably large, prominent Adam's apple that sprang into action each time he spoke. "Your so-called institute is not exactly at the forefront of paranormal research, now, is it?"

"How dare you, sir. I'll have you know that . . ."

Although Richardson appeared to be entertained by this budding confrontation, I rarely find dinner-table arguments beneficial to anyone's digestion. I interrupted Grogan before he could finish. "Artie," I said, "how did you become interested in paranormal research to begin with? Did you see a ghost as a child?"

"Huh?" His eyes swiveled back to me. "No, not exactly."

"Tell me how your interest developed. This is a whole new area for me."

"No one's ever asked me that before," he said. "I imagine I always had an interest in the spirit world, and in parapsychology, too. My grandmother always knew who was calling before the phone rang."

"And she was forever talking to her dead ancestors," Samantha added. "Before she died, of course."

"Did she *see* those ancestors as well?" I asked.

"I never asked her," Artie said, sounding surprised that it hadn't occurred to him. "But it's entirely possible. If you go back in history, there has never been a society without a mention of spirits, or ghosts of some kind." He was warming to his subject. "Although there is a great deal of skepticism these days, spirits were an established part of civilizations going far back in time. Today, people want 'proof,' but not everything falls neatly into a scientific category. You can't produce a ghost on demand. They exist in a different dimension."

"Yet don't you use all kinds of scientific instruments?" I asked. "Those things exist in this dimension."

"Yes, of course. We have your basic recording equipment in place—audio and video—extraordinarily sensitive cameras. We have several EMF meters to measure electromagnetic fields."

"What does that tell you?"

"It's more a rule-out than a rule-in device," he said. "Sometimes your strong electromagnetic fields set up false sensations that people interpret as spirits, when actually it's the charge in the air that makes them think something is there. I had a lady who was sure she was being watched every time she went down to her basement. Come to find out she had a strong electromagnetic field set up around her fuse panel, which was hung exactly where she was feeling those 'eyes' on her coming from."

Artie's explanation of his view of the supernatural and the paranormal was interrupted by Mrs. Goodall, who placed the platters of chicken, green beans, and hush puppies on the sideboard. The Grogans sprang from their seats to fill their plates, followed by General Pettigrew, Attorney Richardson, and me. The food was, of course, superb; Mrs. Goodall had the same deft culinary hand as I remembered from previous visits.

As we ate, there was little conversation, only innocuous chitchat about myriad subjects that did not include the supernatural. Pettigrew and Artie Grogan avoided each other during the discussions, but Samantha exchanged pleasantries with the general. Curling a lock of hair around one finger, she was almost flirtatious, which seemed to feed into Pettigrew's ego.

Richardson, so soft-spoken that it was difficult at times to hear what he was saying, offered a number of observations about Savannah and the upcoming Saint Patrick's Day celebration. "They come from all over the United States for our Saint Paddy's weekend," he said, "bringing their tourist dollars and enriching our merchants. You are welcome to watch the parade from my office, if you like, Mrs. Fletcher. It's quite a good view."

"That's very kind of you to offer," I said, a bit embarrassed that he hadn't extended his invitation to the others at the table.

"Personally, I tend to avoid all the festivities," he said, scraping up gravy with a hush puppy. "They can become raucous at times. The criminal attorneys in our fair city pick up many cases over the weekend, and the police are out in droves. A good weekend to lock the doors and engage a good book." He turned to me. "I must admit, Mrs. Fletcher, that I had not had the pleasure of reading one of your works prior to your coming here, but I have rectified that grievous omission in my literary life. You write quite well, although I must admit that I identified the killer in the first few pages, undoubtedly because of my legal training and experience."

I smiled but didn't respond. The particular book of mine he'd read was devoid of any information in the first three or four chapters that would allow any reader to pinpoint the murderer. But I didn't challenge him. During my writing career, I've experienced others making similar claims, undoubtedly to bolster their self-esteem in my eyes. Who am I to rain on their parade?

Mrs. Goodall had quietly come to take away the dinner plates. She put a crystal bowl of banana pudding on the sideboard together with smaller bowls of blueberries and whipped cream. Mr. Richardson was first up for the dessert, which he seemed to know was going to be on the menu. The rest of us followed, and again conversation lagged while the next round of food was consumed.

"Mrs. Fletcher—er, Jessica—you were asking earlier," Artie said through a mouthful of pudding and cream, "about the times when Samantha and I are able to point to natural physical reasons for the presumed presence of supernatural fields."

"Yes, I found that interesting," I said. "If you find that an electromagnetic field is causing people to think they're experiencing a ghost when they're not, then your research is debunking the very thing your institute is based upon, the existence of unexplained phenomena."

He took another spoonful before answering. "It may seem that way, at times," he replied, "because we need to show we recognize a false alarm in order to be taken seriously when we discover a true spirit haunting."

"Not that you often are—taken seriously," said the general. He was obviously fond of baiting Artie, but his target ignored him this time.

"You take your stories of ghosts rattling chains," Artie said. "In a lot of houses that can be easily explained away. Not all, mind you, but some. Vibrations can come from underground streams or tunnels—Savannah is loaded with underground tunnels."

"It is?"

"Many," Mr. Richardson chimed in, deciding to join the conversation. "They were used by privateers to shanghai sailors for their ships."

"I've heard that the hospital had an underground morgue in one of the tunnels," Pettigrew added, suddenly interested.

"Quite right," said Richardson. "There had been a major yellow fever epidemic in the nineteenth century, killing hundreds of people. The medical community didn't want the citizens to know how many had died and used the tunnels to keep the death toll from becoming public. The bodies were buried after most citizens had gone to bed."

"Store them underground in the day, huh, and then bury them at night? Sounds reasonable," said Pettigrew.

Artie saw the spotlight slipping away and wrested it back. "Anyway, getting back to the chains, noises from a tunnel or an abandoned mine nearby or even loose water pipes in the house—those can sound like chains. And if that's the case, we always say so. We pride ourselves on our honesty."

"Which is why our institute *is* taken so seriously," Samantha said, her eyes darting between the general and Richardson. "But as many times as not, there is no other explanation for the noise, and we have to consider that it may be a signal from another world."

Her husband nodded sagely. "We try to develop concrete proof, but we recognize that it's not always possible. You take your Loch Ness Monster, for instance," he said, looking at me. "Have you ever been to Scotland, Mrs. Fletcher?"

"As a matter of fact, I have," I said, thinking fondly of my trip to Wick and the ancestral home of my good friend George Sutherland, an inspector at Scotland Yard in London.

"Well, there are folks who've seen the monster for centuries, drawn pictures of it, even photographed it, but it's never enough. Until someone pulls a dead one from the murky waters, the skeptics will rule. Skeptics doubted the giant squid until some Japanese fishermen killed one."

"The first mountain gorilla wasn't discovered until 1902," Samantha put in. "It was certainly in existence before that. Just because you haven't seen something doesn't mean it doesn't exist."

"We're still battling prejudice and cynicism. But that's why it's so important for us to finish our research here," her husband said. "With the reports we write up on Mortelaine House—on its spirit life, so to speak—when we publish our research, we expect the institute will garner quite a bit of attention, and we can further our goals in this area." His eyes turned to Attorney Richardson. "Of course, our findings will considerably add to Savannah's ghostly reputation and increase the value of this property."

"What do you say to all this, Mr. Richardson?" I asked. "Do you believe in ghosts?"

"I cannot say with conviction that ghosts exist or not," he said, never looking up from his second helping of banana pudding. "I have never encountered any in my experience, but I do have friends and colleagues who are, shall we say, sensitive to their existence." He scraped his spoon along the edge of the bowl until every last bit of yellow pudding had been secured and swallowed, licked his lips, and smiled up at me.

"You must know Savannah is one of the most haunted cities in the country."

"So I understand," I said. "Why do you suppose that is?"

"There are many theories, not the least of which is the existence of the large Irish population here. The Irish have a strong tradition of communing with supernatural beings—leprechauns, for example—as well as a rich history of storytelling."

"I'm Irish," Artie Grogan said. "Are you suggesting that

we make these things up?" His voice had risen in volume and his face was reddening.

"You completely misinterpret me," Mr. Richardson said, every word clipped. "Mrs. Fletcher asked why Savannah has such a haunted history, and I'm attempting to explain some of the *theories*. And that is one of them. May I continue?"

"Be my guest."

His gaze moved from Artie to me. "Another *theory* is that the slaves brought their belief in spirits with them from Africa. Yet a third attributes the strong spirit presence to Native American tribes that occupied this land." He looked at Artie again. "I have also heard that cities on waterfronts have more spirit stories than those that are landlocked, something to do with the ebb and flow of tides preserving spiritual energy. I don't cotton to that last one at all."

"I don't believe in the water theory either," Artie said, waving his hand as if batting the theory away like an annoying fly, "but without doubt energy from a different dimension can be attached to a place. You take your typical haunted house, like this one, say, and if you do your research, you'll find that there were times of extreme stress or emotion, tragedy or disaster, and those kinds of experiences can bind a spirit's energy to the place where it occurred."

"Such as the Wanamaker Jones murder?" I suggested.

"Exactly." Samantha smiled at me in approval.

"Have you ever seen him?" I asked.

"I haven't, no," she said, "but Miss Tillie said she did. And I'm betting Mrs. Goodall did, too, although she denies it whenever I ask her."

"Why would she lie to you?"

"She's not happy that we're here and she hasn't made any bones about it. I'm not sure why, although I'll bet Mr. Richardson here has put ideas in her mind."

"I did no such thing," Richardson said, mustering as much indignation as his soft voice and frail body could manage.

"She's been against us since the first day. Maybe *she'll* tell you why."

"She doesn't care for me either," General Pettigrew noted. "Not that it's important."

I made a mental note to ask Mrs. Goodall if Tillie had told her about the general's proposal. Would the housekeeper have made her dislike of him so plain if her employer were about to marry the man?

The woman in question opened the door from the butler's pantry. "Y'all finished?" she asked. "I got to clean up before I leave."

"Yes, of course, Mrs. Goodall," said Richardson. "We'll go into the parlor and leave you to your duties. The banana pudding was superb, as always."

"The whole meal was wonderful," I added. "Thank you so much."

"Yes, of course," Mr. Richardson amended. "The whole meal."

Mrs. Goodall picked up a silver snuffer and extinguished

the candles on the mantel and the sideboard, a clear signal that the meal was at an end. "You're welcome, sir, ma'am," she said, nodding at Tillie's attorney and me.

I noticed that the Grogans and Pettigrew hadn't bothered to thank her. Perhaps that was one source of her irritation with them. If so, I didn't blame her. Simple courtesy would have required thanks for any meal, and this one had been special. Given her culinary skills, Mrs. Goodall would have no difficulty finding another position—should she want it—when Mortelaine House passed into other hands.

Who *would* get the house? That answer would be revealed soon, presumably in the morning after the reading of Tillie's will. But I edited that thought. According to Richardson, there was a sealed envelope that was to be opened in the event I'd declined to come to Savannah, or failed to solve the murder of Wanamaker Jones. The answer to the question could remain a mystery for a bit longer.

"Time for some post-dinner spirits of the liquid variety," Pettigrew announced, pushing himself back from the table and preparing to lead us to the parlor. But as he got to his feet, the room suddenly, harshly descended into blackness. Samantha Grogan let out a frightened squeak.

"Another power failure," the general intoned.

"They've been occurring with greater regularity lately," Richardson noted. He asked Mrs. Goodall to fetch some candles for the parlor, and I heard her leave the room.

"Nothing to worry about," Artie Grogan said to me. "They'll get it back on in short order. Usually do."

The blackout hadn't concerned me in the least, although I appreciated his expression of concern. But then my eyes saw something that drew me from the table, across the room, and toward the spacious foyer into which visitors entered through the front door. I reached the hall and confirmed what I thought I'd seen from the dining room. A small antique table lamp with a lovely Tiffany shade, whose single bulb was of very low wattage—was on! I reached out my hand, touched the shade, and all the lights in the house came to life again.

"Hooray!" someone proclaimed from the dining room.

I looked down at the table lamp. It was off now. *Was it a special emergency light? Or was it battery-powered?* The frayed cord from the lamp's base to a wall socket disabused me of that explanation. And the lamp was clearly very old. Why would that one lamp have remained on while the rest of the house's electricity failed?

I was still staring at the lamp when the sound of the front door opening caused me to stiffen and turn. A large older gentleman with a shock of gray hair sticking straight up stepped into the foyer. He was wearing a suit and carried a black raincoat over one arm.

"Goodness, you startled me," I said, my hand over my thumping heart.

"That wouldn't do for a physician, now would it?" he said, closing the door behind him. "Can't have a doctor scaring people to death, can we? I'm Dr. Warner Payne. Hardly a proper name for a physician, but you'll have to blame my parents for that. I take it I'm late for dinner. My apologies."

With that, and without asking who I was, he hung his coat on the clothes tree, strode past me, and joined the others in the dining room.

"I got your plate warming on the stove," Mrs. Goodall called back to him as she passed through the foyer carrying two candlesticks to the parlor. "There's always some sorry thing when I'm studyin' to get gone," she muttered.

"Mrs. Goodall," I said, standing at the entrance to the formal room as she placed the candlesticks on two tables. "About that lamp in the hall."

"The little one on the table?"

"Yes," I said. "It's off now, but it was on during the blackout. How can that be?"

"Cain't," she said, hurrying out of the parlor back toward the dining room. "Been outta kilter for years."

"You mean it doesn't work?"

"Not since nineteen and sixty-seven."

I looked down at the lamp again.

It wasn't cold in Montelaine House, but I was suddenly chilled to the bone.

Chapter Six

"So, Mrs. Fletcher, what brings you to Savannah and specifically to Mortelaine House? Miss Tillie's funeral was back some."

Dr. Payne leaned his sizable frame against the tapestry back of the dining room chair, his unbuttoned suit jacket revealing a pair of flowered suspenders that framed a small paunch. He held a cup of tea, the large fingers of his hands surprisingly gentle with the delicate china.

The other dinner guests had departed not long after his arrival, the general taking with him a glassful of the harsh Armagnac that he favored. He and the Grogans had used the back stairs, going through the kitchen and crossing the garden courtyard to reach the guesthouse.

Mrs. Goodall locked up after them but wasn't about to

wait around for the doctor to finish his plate. She didn't want to be late for her church meeting.

Mr. Richardson had made his excuses—citing a need for at least nine hours of sleep before the arduous task of reading Tillie's will the following morning. As I closed the front door behind him, I was at a loss as to whether I was expected to play host to our belated dinner guest, Dr. Payne. Reluctant to interrupt his meal, but not wishing to be rude, I poked my head in the dining room and inquired if he would like a cup of tea.

He was bent over his plate, rapidly forking food into his mouth. He looked up, an expression of confusion on his face, and nodded. A little later, he entered the kitchen carrying his plate. "Did I just meet you in the hall?" he asked, running his fingers through his gray hair in an attempt to smooth it down.

"Yes." I introduced myself. "You came in right after we had a short blackout."

"Thought it looked a little dark when I came up the front steps." He went to the sink, washed his plate and utensils, and left them in the drainer.

I'd already filled the kettle with water and had set it on the stove. I looked about trying to guess where Mrs. Goodall might store tea bags.

"Allow me," Dr. Payne said, going to a cupboard to take down a tin of loose tea and a strainer, and to another to remove a brown and white porcelain teapot and two matching cups and saucers. "I can find my way around this kitchen as well as Mrs. Goodall," he commented. "She likes to hide things, but I know how she thinks. If you'll get the cream from the refrigerator over there, I'll set us up for tea. While you're at it, see if she left me a dish of her pudding. I'll be a sad soul if she didn't."

Now, back in the dining room, the teapot between us on the table, a dish of banana pudding consumed, the doctor had relaxed considerably. "I thought I'd met all of Miss Tillie's friends," he said. "Was her doctor for—let me see now—must be at least fifty years. I knew about you, of course, through all the media stories about the literacy program you and she created. Quite admirable. But I never had the pleasure, Mrs. Fletcher, of shaking your hand. Miss Tillie liked to keep some of her friendships secret from me." He chuckled and took a noisy sip of his tea. "Of course, you know that the lady had quite a few secrets. It was part of her considerable charm."

Was the general's proposal to Tillie one of those secrets? I asked myself.

The conversation turned to the reason for my having come to Savannah, and I expressed my surprise about Mr. Richardson's having called to inform me that I was mentioned in Tillie's will. I opted to leave out the specifics of what she expected me to do. The doctor, along with others, would learn them soon enough.

"Well, she was certainly a generous woman," he said. "There should be quite a crowd there tomorrow: charity officials, no doubt, Richardson, of course, myself, and the judge, those idiots in the guesthouse—although I can't believe she would leave them anything." He speared his fingers through his hair. "Then there's her niece and nephew," he continued. "Have you met them?"

"I haven't."

"I think they're her only living relatives."

"I didn't know she had any brothers or sisters."

"She didn't." He watched my face, waiting for me to ask the next question.

"Courtesy titles?"

"Nope." He smiled, waiting.

"I never realized she'd been married," I said. "Was she not a Mortelaine by birth?"

"You're a sharp one," he said, thumping his hand on the table, making my cup rattle in its saucer. "Oh, yes, Miss Tillie was a Mortelaine through and through. She married young, lost him in the war. Battle of Midway. No children. Not sure if that was good or bad for her. She took back the family name when some of her husband's relations tried to make a claim against her property, arguing what was hers was his and, by extension, theirs. The niece and nephew are children of her husband's brother."

"And were they party to that claim?"

"No. No. Not even born at the time."

"The claim was unsuccessful, I take it."

He nodded slowly. "Frank O'Neill was her attorney. I thought he was a little young and inexperienced. 'Course, I was pretty young and inexperienced myself at the time. But Tillie liked him, and he proved me wrong. He's gone on to prominence here in Savannah, now the Honorable Frank O'Neill, a retired judge. He's grand marshal of this year's Saint Patrick's Day parade. Frank set those interlopers straight. But it gave Miss Tillie a bad feeling, sharing the name of those would-be thieves, so she went back to Mortelaine and stayed that way."

"And she never married again?"

"Not to my knowledge, although there's been many a man would've had her. Always had her beaus, even up to the day she died." He chuckled.

Tillie obviously had her admirers. I'd heard Mr. Richardson speak fondly of her, and given his expression when discussing Tillie, perhaps Dr. Payne had had a crush on her, too.

"Was Mr. Pettigrew one of her beaus?" I asked.

"You don't miss much."

"The general told me that he'd asked Tillie to marry him and that she had consented."

He sighed. "Rich ladies are always tempting prey for scalawags. I warned her about him, and about the Grogans, too, but she pooh-poohed me."

"Perhaps she liked the attention," I offered, "or found them entertaining."

"That's just what she said. Told me to mind my own business and to not spoil her fun."

"But you don't trust them."

"How could I? Nothing there for her. Everything for them. She's always needed protecting. Too trusting by half. Told her to make sure she locked up tight at night." A wave of distress crossed his face. "I'm not sure she listened. Her death still doesn't make sense to me."

"What about it doesn't make sense, Doctor?"

"Her falling down those darn stairs."

"You don't believe it was an accident?"

He shrugged and sighed. "Couldn't say it wasn't. No proof otherwise. But, Mrs. Fletcher, I tell you that Tillie Mortelaine was as steady on her feet as you and I. Yes, she was ninety-one. And yes, she'd had a spell or two when she overdid, but still . . ." His voice trailed off.

"Mrs. Goodall found her slipper at the top of the stairs," I said. "She could have caught her foot in the frayed rug. Or maybe she just tripped. That can happen to the steadiest of us. Accidents happen in the home all the time. That's common knowledge."

"I know the statistics," he said, staring down into his empty cup. "But I was her doctor for fifty years, and it just bothers me. I can't envision her tripping."

"What's the alternative?"

He glanced up at me but said nothing.

"You don't think someone killed her?" I asked, the chill I'd felt earlier coming back. Tillie was a small sparrow of a woman, barely a hundred pounds, if that much. It would not have been difficult for someone larger to pick her up and throw her down the stairs.

Dr. Payne ignored my question. "Mrs. Goodall called me right after she called 911, but I got held up at the hospital." He shook his head. "You can't walk out in the middle of rounds. By the time I got here, the police were finishing up. Another doctor had pronounced her, and her body had been taken away."

"Was there an autopsy?" I asked.

He gave a sharp nod. "At my insistence. The coroner and I are old friends. He did it more as a favor to me. The police were willing to let the body go straight to the funeral home. They had already decided it was an accidental death."

"What did the results of the autopsy indicate?"

"Inconclusive. Nothing you could hang your hat on."

"Have you mentioned your suspicions to anyone else?"

"I spent an hour questioning the people in the guesthouse. They'd be deaf and blind not to know that I suspected them of something nefarious. Pettigrew swore that Miss Tillie had locked up after them. I know for a fact that Mrs. Goodall checks all the doors before she leaves. Very reliable. You can set a clock by that woman."

"Did the Grogans add anything?"

Dr. Payne poked his fingers through his hair, causing it to stand on end again. "That fool told me that angry spirits have been known to push people. He said if Miss Tillie offended someone in life, they could have come back to seek revenge."

"And how did you answer him?"

Dr. Payne looked embarrassed. "I didn't beat him up, but it was a near thing. Could have taken him, too. He's soft around the middle."

"It's probably just as well you didn't."

"I'm hoping Rollie will boot those leeches out tomorrow."

We chatted for a little longer, then cleaned up our tea service. Dr. Payne walked me around the house, showing me the doors to the outside and checking that they were all locked—I doubted that the windows had been opened in years—and took his leave. I locked the front door behind him and turned around. My eye fell on the little lamp. I leaned down to see where the switch was and twisted it. It clicked, but no light came on. I unscrewed the tiny bulb and shook it to hear if the filament was loose, replaced it, and tried the switch again. Still nothing.

Giving the lamp one backward glance, I started upstairs to my room, passing a series of small mirrors framed in gilt as I climbed. Out of the corner of my eye, I thought I saw something move in the reflection. I turned sharply and studied the front hall below. I'd left an overhead light on. The floor was marble, and the painted walls held no fabric that could respond to a breeze, not that there was one.

Stop spooking yourself, Jessica, I told myself. *All this talk of ghosts and spirits has simply fired your imagination.* But I gave a little sigh of relief when I reached my room and could shut the door behind me.

Chapter Seven

The radium hands of the bedside clock read two a.m., and I sat up wondering why I wasn't asleep. The room was very dark. Earlier in the evening, all my attempts to open the painted-closed shutters had ended in vain and I'd eventually given up. Before bed, I'd placed the little flashlight that I always carry with me when I travel on the nightstand.

By my reckoning, the room's arch-topped windows overlooked the courtyard, but with no way to look out, I couldn't be certain. Any illumination from a streetlamp hadn't reached the slats. I listened, my ears straining to detect even the faintest sound, and my eyes focused on the shadowy outlines of furniture around me.

I was in a nineteenth-century carved mahogany four-poster bed, the silk tester above me tightly pleated around a center rosette. In the corner was an upholstered chair with matching ottoman. Between the pair of tall windows through which no light could seep was a Bombay chest with three drawers, topped by an oval mirror. Across from the bed was an armoire that must have been built in the room. Reaching almost to the ceiling molding, it would never have fit through the door.

Thinking of the Grogans and their electromagnetic theory, I tried to sense if I was being watched. There were a number of outlets and a small chandelier in the room. In addition, when I was unpacking that afternoon, I'd straightened a painting that hung askew and found that it hid the electrical panel for the second floor. Thankfully, none of these potential sources of electromagnetic fields were disturbing me, and I perceived no otherworldly gaze aimed in my direction.

I pushed back the covers, slipped off the side of the bed, and felt for my slippers on the needlepoint rug. Mrs. Goodall had left a cotton robe for my use draped across a corner of the bed, and I put it on. Standing on the rug, tying the belt of the robe, I cocked my head toward the door. What was that?

A gentle stream of air was coming into the room from beneath the doorjamb. In a house seemingly as hermetically sealed as an apothecary jar, that wasn't logical. All my senses went on alert. The sound of a door slamming somewhere made me jump, and the breeze at my feet petered out.

Was someone here? Or had someone just left? The room

suddenly felt stuffy. I groped around the nightstand for my flashlight, tucked it into the pocket of the robe, opened the door quietly, and stepped into the broad upstairs hall, my ears straining to hear any movement. Dim light from the fixture I'd left on in the downstairs foyer allowed me to peer into the gloom. All the second-floor doors were closed, except mine. The only sound was the ticking of a grandfather clock somewhere downstairs. I thought I remembered spotting one in Tillie's study when Dr. Payne and I were making the rounds of the house locking up, but we hadn't gone into that room since it had no door to the outside.

Where could that slammed door have been? It sounded too far away to be on the second floor. I went to the top of the stairs. The woven rug under my feet was worn through, the bare section a patch of loose strands of heavy warp thread where it had lost its weft. I remembered Mrs. Goodall's warning and stepped to the side, off the worn part. Gripping the banister, I descended the staircase, planting each foot carefully and slowly so as not to make the wood creak beneath my slipper. The small mirrors over my shoulder on the right-hand wall twinkled and I checked the reflection in them, remembering my earlier sensation of something moving. All was still.

As I reached the marble floor of the foyer, I began to feel foolish. Had I really heard a door slam in the house? Loud noises carry in the night. Could it have been a door in the guesthouse, or perhaps another home in the square? After all, many people kept late hours. Just because I preferred to get a good night's sleep didn't mean everyone else in Savannah went to bed before midnight. After all, this was a big city. There were restaurants and bars and nightclubs. Perhaps a neighbor had been out celebrating and the wind caught his front door before he could keep it from slamming. Or maybe a teenager broke her curfew and came home to an angry parent who flung the door closed behind her.

A loud crack sounded from the staircase behind me and I swung around with a gasp. Nothing was there. Now annoyed, I chided myself for being skittish. *Stop it, Jessica! This is no time to get jumpy. Mrs. Goodall told you it's an old house with a lot of noises. You'll have a difficult month if you let every sound rattle you. What you need is a good night's rest.*

Unfortunately, I was fully awake. If Tillie's resident spirits intended to disrupt my sleep, they had done a fine job of it. I decided a cup of herbal tea would be soothing and hoped the pantry held such a prize. I switched on the chandelier in the dining room, crossed to the butler's pantry, and descended the back stairs into the kitchen, turning on lights as I went. In the old houses in Savannah's landmark district, the kitchen was typically on the ground floor, the wealthy owners of centuries ago accustomed to having cooks and other servants ferry the food to the formal dining room above.

The back stairs fed into a hallway with wood paneling in a nested-squares design. To the left, the hall led to the room Mrs. Goodall used when she was in residence. To

the right, it went to the kitchen. Before the kitchen, however, there were two doors, one on either side. I checked
them both. The first had a simple lock. I slid the bolt to the
side and opened the door to rough wooden stairs leading
down into blackness. A chill raised goose bumps on my
arms. *That's for another day,* I thought, quickly closing the
door and relocking it. The door opposite had no lock, and
when I turned the knob, it revealed shelves of cans and dry
goods—the kinds of staples I had in my own kitchen in
Cabot Cove—and row upon row of hand-labeled jars of
pickles, fruits, and vegetables. But no tea.

I flipped the switch for the kitchen light, an old ceiling fixture that did not give off much light, and crossed
the black-and-white-checkerboard floor to the cupboard
where Dr. Payne had found the tin of loose tea, hoping
there might be a noncaffeinated version. A box of Sleepytime was tucked next to the tin. I silently blessed Mrs.
Goodall, took out a tea bag, filled the kettle at the sink,
and turned on one of the stove's gas burners. Mindful of
the watched pot never boiling, I sat on a chair at a small
wooden table and surveyed my surroundings.

The kitchen was a large rectangular room with windows
on two sides. In the center of one windowed wall was a
door to the outside, its glass top half covered by a pull-
down shade. From other visits to the kitchen, I knew
the door led to the courtyard and garden. The stove, dishwasher, and refrigerator were of recent vintage, but everything else in the room retained a century-old flavor, with
cupboards thick with paint, a heavy butcher's chopping

block on four legs, and two wooden tables: one, next to the stove against the wall, on which Mrs. Goodall kept her cooking utensils, a flashlight, and an electric coffeepot; the other, the small square at which I was seated.

The last time I'd visited Tillie, I don't believe I ever entered the kitchen. Meals were always taken in the dining room. To save Mrs. Goodall steps, Tillie had encouraged her to set a buffet on the sideboard, from which we all helped ourselves.

"There's a dumbwaiter you can use for that," Tillie had said to Mrs. Goodall when she carried in a large tray holding the dishes for lunch for three—Tillie, Charmelle, and me—during one of my previous visits.

"By the time I pull that thing down and haul it back up again, I be up and down the stairs twice," Mrs. Goodall replied.

"It's there for your convenience," Tillie said, "to save you the up and down."

"Only thing to help my convenience is if you put the kitchen on the main floor. That ain't gonna happen, so I manage the way I manage."

"I didn't know you had a dumbwaiter," I said. "How big is it?"

"Big enough to hold a Thanksgiving turkey and a suckling pig at the same time," Tillie replied.

Mrs. Goodall harrumphed.

"Or a small person," Tillie said with a twinkle.

"You didn't," Charmelle said, her eyes wide.

"I have to try it out now and then to make sure it works, don't I?"

"Near to give me heart failure," Mrs. Goodall said as she arranged plates on the sideboard. "I open that door and she says 'Boo!' and I almost dropped the jar of gingered peaches I was holdin'. Thought I'd be seeing my Maker directly."

"But you didn't drop it," Tillie said, smiling at her housekeeper. "And you're still here."

"No thanks to you," Mrs. Goodall muttered as she left the room.

"She shouldn't talk to you like that, Miss Tillie," Charmelle said. "It's not appropriate."

"Don't be such a stuffed sweater, Charmelle. Emanuela and I go back a long time. She can talk to me any way she likes. We're old friends."

"Well, the judge would never allow such talk in our house. The people who work for us know to maintain their decorum. And we are formal with them as well. That's as it should be."

"Your brother Frank is just as small-minded as you. It's a new world out there and if we don't welcome it, we'll become extinct, like the dinosaurs and the dodo birds."

"Well, I like things just the way they are," Charmelle replied. "And I don't know how you can talk about Frank like that after all he did for you."

"I am indebted to Frank O'Neill for life, but that doesn't mean I have to cheer on his provincial view of things," Tillie said, removing the stopper from a crystal decanter.

"Now, who would like a taste of bourbon to go with this marvelous ham?"

The whistle of the kettle interrupted my reverie. I glanced over to the hallway at the base of the back stairs and wondered where the dumbwaiter was, and if Mrs. Goodall still refused to use it.

A rattling of the doorknob caused me to wheel around the other way. The hair on the back of my neck rose as I stared at the knob being twisted, first in one direction and then in the other. Someone was at the kitchen door and trying to get in. I turned off the burner and waited. Would the person break the glass? I lifted the kettle and filled my cup. It would be terrible to scald someone with boiling water, but lacking another weapon, I would use what I had at hand.

At last there was a loud knock at the door, then a persistent rapping. "Mrs. Fletcher! Jessica! Are you all right?"

I let out the breath I was holding, dropped the tea bag into the water, and went to the door. I pulled aside the shade to see Artie and Samantha Grogan in their nightclothes. He had a camera slung around his neck; she carried a box with wires hanging down from the top. I pulled the key from its hook, unlocked the door, and opened it.

"We saw all the lights and thought something was wrong," Artie said.

"Are you okay?" Samantha asked.

"Perfectly fine," I said.

"May we come in?" Artie asked.

I held open the door. "I was just making myself a cup of tea," I said, turning back to the stove. I removed the tea bag from my cup and threw it away. I resisted offering the Grogans any tea. It would mean a long conversation and I was feeling tired again.

"It's two thirty," Samantha said. "Do you always get up in the middle of the night for tea?"

"Sometimes," I said, taking a sip of the Sleepytime. "When I can't sleep."

"What woke you?" Artie asked. "Did you hear anything? See anything? Spirits are most active at night. Did you feel a cold spot or see any lights?"

"I think it probably had more to do with a long day of travel and not sleeping in my own bed," I said.

"Oh." Samantha was clearly disappointed. "We thought perhaps you saw something and turned on the lights for comfort. The house is lit up like a Christmas tree."

"Since I wasn't sure of my way around, I left lights on as I came downstairs," I said. "I'll try to be more careful in the future so I don't alarm you, or waste electricity."

"I brought my equipment just in case," Artie said, shrugging.

"I see that."

"Would you mind if I took a stroll through, just to sort of check things out? Won't take too long."

"Perhaps another time," I said. "I think I would like to try to get back to sleep. It's going to be a busy day tomorrow—or rather, today."

"Nighttime is the best time for contacting them, you

know," he said, with a trace of a pout. "Less distractions and all that. You can pick up the sounds much better."

"I'll keep that in mind," I said as I ushered them to the door. "Thank you for your concern."

"See you at Richardson's office," Samantha said.

I locked the door behind them and shook my head. Would they ever have done such a thing to Tillie? Would she have allowed them to traipse through her home in the wee hours of the night, photographing elusive images and recording the silence?

I hung the key back on its hook and took the cup of tea with me as I headed for the stairs. My hand was on the kitchen light switch when I noticed the latch to the door opposite the pantry. It was open and the door was slightly ajar.

I know I locked it, I thought, pressing the door closed and sliding the bolt home.

Or did I?

Chapter Eight

Mr. Richardson had arranged for a car service to pick me up the next morning to take me to his office for the reading of the will. I was up and dressed far in advance of its arrival, and went downstairs to find a breakfast buffet laid out in the dining room by Mrs. Goodall, who'd left by then to collect Melanie. The Grogans were already at the table when I walked in; General Pettigrew showed up a few minutes later and sat next to me.

"Sleep well?" he asked.

"Not especially. I always have trouble the first night in a strange bed."

"Never bothers me," he said pompously. "An old military man like me learns to sleep under any conditions—on the battlefield, rocky terrain, you name it."

"I'm sure that's true," I said, concentrating on the bowl of fresh fruit I'd taken from the sideboard, along with coffee and a dry English muffin.

"Mrs. Fletcher had an experience last night," Artie Grogan announced.

"Oh?" said Pettigrew. "What sort of experience?"

"I simply had trouble sleeping and—"

Artie gave out with a knowing laugh. "I don't blame you, Jessica, for looking for a simplistic reason for your restlessness last evening. After all, you're not schooled in the supernatural."

"Saw a ghost, did you?" the general asked.

"No!" I said. "It's true I was restless, but—"

"The magnetic field was especially evident last night," Samantha said. "Artie and I could feel it all the way from the guesthouse."

"I didn't feel anything," said Pettigrew. "Slept like a log."

Aided by a hefty glass of Armagnac, I mused, then chided myself for unkind thoughts. The general, it seemed, could bring out the worst in me, his intentionally annoying comments irritating to say the least. I turned toward Artie, who was trying to get my attention.

"The aura was powerful, Jessica," Artie said. "We were drawn to the house by it."

"You said you'd come to the house because you saw lights on and wondered whether something was wrong."

Samantha smiled sweetly. "We didn't want to unduly upset you," she said. "Frankly, your presence here might be exactly what we need. You obviously have a sensitivity level conducive to coaxing spirits to reveal themselves."

I started to protest but thought better of it, finished my breakfast, and excused myself. Before I left the room, however, I addressed Tillie's three guests. "Mr. Richardson is sending a car for me. Would any of you like a ride to his office?"

"Special treatment for the best-selling author?" Pettigrew said.

Ignoring his comment, I said, "You're welcome to join me. I'm sure there will be room for everyone."

"No thanks," said the general.

I looked at the Grogans.

"We've already made other arrangements," Samantha said.

"Then I'll see you in a little while," I said, secretly grateful they would not be joining me, and went outside to await the arrival of the hired car. It pulled up a few minutes later, driven by an elderly African American gentleman wearing a black suit, white shirt, black tie, and jaunty little black cap. "Mrs. Jessica Fletcher?" he asked after coming around to open the rear passenger door.

"Good morning," I said.

"Good morning to you, ma'am. Lovely day."

I looked up into a milky sky and wondered if it would stay lovely.

The short trip took us down streets canopied by the arching branches of the city's signature live oak trees. Draping down from the branches were long skeins of wispy Spanish moss. I'd read that the moss is a member of the pineapple family, and takes its moisture and nutrients from the air, rather than from the tree itself.

"Don't touch it, Jessica," Tillie had warned me on my last visit when I'd bent to examine a clump of the moss that had fallen on the sidewalk.

"Good heavens," I said, pulling back my hand sharply and looking at her. "Why not? Isn't this the same material that florists use to decorate potted plants?"

"Yes. And some people use it to stuff pillows, too, but not until it's fumigated."

Tillie had gone on to inform me that tourists often bring bags of it home with them, much to their eventual chagrin when they discover that the soft gray moss is infested with chiggers, tiny red bugs of the mite family that cause intense itching. Fortunately, she had saved me from a similar fate.

Roland Richardson's law office was on the top floor of a renovated older, red brick building on bluff-level Bay Street, a block off and up from Savannah's famed River Street, which runs alongside the busy Savannah River. My driver ran ahead to open the building's front door, and assured me he'd be there when I emerged.

Richardson's receptionist/secretary, whose name was Amber Smith, was a pert, pretty young woman—I judged her to be in her late twenties—with a wide smile and a bubbly personality. As I waited in the attractive reception area for the others to arrive, she told me that her mother was a big fan of my books, then sheepishly pulled a copy from the desk drawer and asked if I would sign it, which I did, of course. I'd just closed the cover and handed it back to her when General Pettigrew arrived. He announced himself to the receptionist, stressing "General," then turned to me and said, "I don't require a private car. The local taxis are more than adequate for my needs."

"How nice for you," I said mildly, refusing to acknowledge the rudeness with which he seemed insistent upon addressing me.

Minutes later, the Grogans walked in, followed by other people, whose identities were unknown to me. Dr. Warner Payne arrived alone and greeted me along with the rest of the group. A man in a wheelchair, wire-rimmed glasses perched on his nose, was pushed into the room by a uniformed nurse, who announced his presence to the receptionist. "His Honor, Judge Francis T. O'Neill." That would be Charmelle's brother, who had represented Tillie more than sixty years ago when her deceased husband's family made a claim against her property.

"When is this going to start?" the judge asked. "I have a busy day ahead."

The answer was provided the next minute by Roland Richardson when he opened the door to his inner office and invited us in.

The office was spacious and flooded with light from huge windows facing Bay Street. Richardson's desk was large and covered with papers. An oval conference table with a dozen chairs around it occupied one end of the room, in front of floor-to-ceiling bookcases jammed with legal volumes. The attorney had arranged two rows of folding chairs to accommodate all the people who crowded into his office. He was in shirtsleeves when he ushered us in. "Please have a seat wherever it's comfortable," he advised, slipping into his suit jacket and checking his appearance in a mirror behind his desk.

"I hope this won't take too long," Judge O'Neill said as his wheelchair was positioned at the head of the table.

"I'll do my best to move things along, Your Honor," Richardson replied in his small, low voice. "Of course, Ah sometimes used to wish things moved a little faster when Ah was in your courtroom." He uttered a small laugh to indicate he was kidding. O'Neill didn't smile. He adjusted his large frame in the chair, tucked his chin down, and gazed over the top of his glasses at the attorney, his expression saying he wasn't in the mood for chitchat.

The receptionist joined us, a steno pad in hand, and sat next to Richardson. "Ms. Smith will record these proceedings," the attorney said. "For the record, present at this reading of the last will and testament of Miss Tillie Mortelaine are—" He held up a sheet of legal-sized paper and read off our names, including those whom I'd not met as yet. Seated at the table, in addition to myself, the doctor, and the three staying in Tillie's guesthouse—the Grogans and Pettigrew—were Judge O'Neill; Tillie's late husband's niece and nephew, Rose Margaret Kendall and Roy Richard Kendall, also known as Rocky; and a middle-aged man, Joseph Jones, who was identified as Wanamaker Jones's nephew. There were several charity officials who took seats in the first row of chairs, as well as old friends of Tillie's and half a dozen others whose IDs and affiliations I didn't catch as the attorney rattled off their names in his soft voice. Emanuela Goodall and her daughter, Melanie, were the last to arrive and apologized for their tardiness as they took chairs on the side of the room.

With the recitation of names out of the way, Richardson read aloud a lengthy bureaucratic introduction from the will, written in legalese, using such language as "the party of the first part," and similar phrases. I assumed this represented a legal requirement, but his slow, deliberate style quickly caused a great deal of throat clearing, yawning, and shifting in chairs.

"Can't we just get to the important matters, Richardson?" General Pettigrew asked during a pause when the attorney fumbled the turning of a page.

Richardson looked at him and frowned.

"Go ahead, Rollie," O'Neill growled. "Move on."

Which Richardson did. Eventually, he reached that portion of Tillie's will dealing with the disposition of her assets. "You were all invited here this morning because each of you is named in the will," he said.

There was a palpable increase in attention. People sat up straighter and leaned forward in their chairs.

"While the will assures that each person here will eventually receive something from Miss Tillie's estate, however large or small that may be," he continued, "she insisted upon including her evaluation of those mentioned— against my best advice, I might add."

"Just get on with it," O'Neill barked.

Tillie's bequests included donations to several charities with which she had been involved, among them the Georgia Historical Society, the Historic Savannah Foundation, and the King-Tisdell Cottage Foundation. She also remembered her church, and the hospital, for which she endowed a chair in the name of Dr. Warner Payne, as well as bequeathing a small amount to the man himself "to use to get a decent haircut." She left lump sums of money to several people with whom she had held longtime relationships, including Charmelle, "my oldest and dearest friend, who never learned to speak up for herself. She doesn't need any money but there's still time to acquire a little gumption. Remember I told you that"; her niece, Rose Margaret, "in hopes she will use it to improve her wardrobe," and her nephew, Rocky, "who never had the privilege of meeting his beloved uncle for whom he is named, and who would certainly have learned a great deal about handling money if he had."

"Is that all?" Rocky Kendall asked when the bequests to him and to his sister were announced. "That's not a lot for her only living relatives. Who gets the house?"

"Patience, please," said Mr. Richardson. "We have a long way to go." He peered over his half-glasses, looking around the room. "Mrs. Goodall, I believe you are mentioned next."

Mrs. Goodall and her daughter had sat quietly while the other bequests were announced. Now they looked at Richardson with some trepidation. "Miss Tillie didn't say anything bad about me, did she?" the housekeeper asked.

Richardson smiled at her. "No, Mrs. Goodall, she certainly did not. In fact, she went on at length about how much she appreciated your service and loyalty over the years. Let me find the pages on which she mentions you." He riffled through several sheets of paper and read Tillie's encomiums to her longtime housekeeper, to whom she left a large sum with which Mrs. Goodall could retire "or open that restaurant she's been threatening me with for the last twenty-five years," and an additional amount enough to cover the remainder of Melanie's college education. Melanie hugged her mother, then handed her a packet of tissues to wipe her streaming eyes.

"I'd like to take a little break to allow those who have already received their bequests the opportunity to leave," Richardson said, nodding at the people in the two rows of chairs, most of whom shuffled out of the room.

Melanie got up to leave, but Mrs. Goodall put a hand on her daughter's arm and she sat down again.

"I'm not leaving until I hear about the house," Tillie's nephew declared.

Samantha Grogan raised her hand timidly. "We didn't hear our names mentioned," she said.

"That's right," Pettigrew said, scowling at the lawyer. "You said we're all mentioned in the will."

"I suggest you three find alternative accommodations, as you may have less than a month to continue as guests of Tillie Mortelaine," Richardson replied. He removed his half-glasses and, taking in those who remained in the room, said, "That is all I can tell you at this juncture."

"What are you talking about?" Judge O'Neill demanded.

Richardson cleared his throat. "I'm afraid that there will still be some—how shall I say it?—there remain some unresolved issues."

"Like the house," Rocky put in. "Which of us gets the damn house?"

"Unresolved?" Judge O'Neill said. "How can there be unresolved issues? I'm sure Tillie Mortelaine's last wishes were clearly spelled out in her will."

"Oh, yes, sir, they certainly were," Richardson responded, "and I took special pains to see that her wishes were put in unequivocal language, the King's English, if you will. But as you all know, Miss Tillie had her own—how shall I say it?—had her own peculiar notions of how things should be done. In all my years of practicing law in this fair city, I have never represented anyone quite like her."

"What does all this mean?" Tillie's niece asked. "We're not going to learn who gets the rest?"

"In a sense, that is correct," said Richardson, replacing his glasses and looking down at the next page of the will. "Let me be specific." He looked over his glasses at me and asked, "Are you ready, Mrs. Fletcher?"

His question took me by surprise. "Ready for what?" I replied.

He turned from me and said to the others, "When Miss Tillie executed this latest version of her will—and there have been many versions, I assure you—she was explicit in her desire to see the murder of her paramour, Wanamaker Jones, solved." He peered over his glasses at Joseph Jones. "This should interest you, sir."

"It does indeed," he replied.

Richardson continued. "She wanted, however, for that to be accomplished only after her demise. Her instructions were for her friend Jessica Fletcher to come to Savannah after Miss Tillie's death and apply her—" He adjusted his glasses and read: " 'Apply her considerable insight into the criminal mind and her penchant for solving seemingly unsolvable crimes.' "

There followed a pregnant silence in the room when he finished reading. People looked at each other, the expressions on their faces testifying to their confusion. Not surprisingly, it was Judge O'Neill who interrupted the hush. "Miss Tillie was obviously demented at the time she made this request. You were a fool to let her get away with it, Rollie."

"And what does this have to do with the disposition of her estate?" Rocky asked.

"It has everything to do with it, Mr. Kendall," Richardson replied. "Mrs. Fletcher has one month to solve the murder of Wanamaker Jones. Should she succeed, one million dollars of Miss Tillie's estate will go to her, with specific instructions that Mrs. Fletcher use it to further the literacy program that these two fine ladies established a number of years ago."

"And what if she doesn't succeed?" Rose Kendall asked.

"Whether Mrs. Fletcher succeeds or not," Richardson

explained, "there is a sealed envelope that is to be opened, either upon her successful resolution of the murder or one month from today. It contains instructions as to how the remainder of the estate will be distributed, possibly including the house." He cocked his head at the Grogans and Pettigrew. "Miss Tillie instructed me that you may continue in residence until that day, and not a moment longer."

"This is outrageous," Rocky said.

"It certainly is," Pettigrew said. "Am I mentioned in that envelope?"

The attorney sniffed. "I'm not at liberty to say."

O'Neill turned in his wheelchair to face me. "This is why you've come to Savannah?" he demanded. "This is why you're here today?"

"Yes," I said. "I assure you that I was as surprised at Tillie's request as all of you are. I debated long and hard about accepting her challenge, and decided that the literacy project was important enough to pursue the million dollars. Frankly, I wish that Tillie had simply left the money to the project, but that isn't what she decided to do. And her wishes are to be respected. After all, it's her money and her right to have it distributed as she saw fit."

"She distinctly told me she was leaving me the Meissen figurines," Rose whispered to her brother.

"So we have to wait another month to find out if our aunt left us anything else?" Rocky grumbled.

"Unless Mrs. Fletcher solves the murder sooner than that," said Richardson. He had a tiny smile on his lips, and I suspected he was enjoying this.

Dr. Payne spoke up. "An interesting conundrum isn't it? If Mrs. Fletcher fails to solve the murder, there's a million dollars that might go to someone at this table—a good reason to hinder her investigation."

"An equally good reason to help her," Richardson said, "provided you believe in the literacy project that meant so much to Miss Tillie, and obviously to Mrs. Fletcher."

"What about the house?" Rose asked. "Surely that's not bound up in this ridiculous investigation Mrs. Fletcher has been asked to undertake."

"And the furnishings and her various collections?" Rocky added.

Richardson held up his hand. "I'm afraid that everything else is on hold until Mrs. Fletcher either identifies who killed Wanamaker Jones or fails and a month passes."

"And do we get them if she fails?" Rose asked. "I've already had an offer from the hotel next door."

"You mean *we've* already had an offer," her brother amended, shooting her an angry look. "They want to annex Aunt Tillie's house and make it part of the hotel."

Another silence engulfed the room.

"We're her only living relatives," Rose said, looking at the faces around the room. "It should come to us. It's only right."

Richardson held up a sealed envelope. "Who inherits the house is yet to be determined," he said.

Tillie's niece and nephew stood in unison. "There's no sense in sitting here any longer," Rocky said. "Frankly,

I'm disappointed in Aunt Tillie. She's always been a game player, but this borders on cruelty."

O'Neill signaled to his nurse, who was sitting along a wall, to come get him.

"I hope you'll give my best to your sister, Charmelle," I said. "We met when Tillie and I were putting together the literacy project. I understand she's not well."

"That's an understatement, Mrs. Fletcher," her brother answered. "Good day—and good luck!"

The judge's abrupt departure kept me from asking if I could stop in to see Charmelle. Before I discovered she was ailing, I had been counting on her to tell me about the relationship between Tillie and her fiancé and what important events, if any, may have led up to the day Wanamaker Jones was killed. I still had hopes of talking with her, even if only for a few minutes, but her brother's gruff attitude did not bode well for accommodating my request. Still, I'd gotten around obstinate people before. Perhaps I could find a way to convince the judge to allow me to pay a visit to his sister. I hoped so. My task was difficult enough without losing the few witnesses from that time who would be able to provide, if nothing else, a starting point for my investigation.

Soon, I was left in Richardson's office with only the attorney, Joseph Jones, and Dr. Payne.

Wanamaker's nephew, a man in his mid-forties, was dressed casually in neatly pressed slacks and a white polo shirt with a red collar. The thumb of his left hand was hooked under the collar of a sports jacket flung over one shoulder. Tillie had left him a small bequest, "a token in memory of my affection for his uncle." He came around the table to where I sat and extended his right hand. "Pleased to meet you, Mrs. Fletcher. I wondered why I would be mentioned in Miss Tillie's will to begin with. Frankly, I'm surprised that she left me anything, but maybe it's just because she wanted the family to know that she intends to succeed where the police have failed." He pronounced "police" in the Southern manner, with the emphasis on the first syllable. "Truthfully, the best bequest she could give us would be to solve his murder. I hope you find out who killed my uncle."

"I certainly intend to try," I said. "I understand he was quite a colorful man."

His nephew laughed. "That's what everyone in the family says. Anytime you want to talk to us about him, we'll be more than happy." He handed me a card with his contact information.

"Thank you, Mr. Jones. I'll probably take you up on your offer."

He said good-bye and left the office.

"Well, well, well. Looks like Miss Tillie was not the only one keeping secrets," the doctor said, stretching back in his chair and looking from me to Roland Richardson.

"I didn't feel at liberty to inform you of Tillie's requirement until it was made official this morning," I said.

"And quite right," Richardson put in. "Now, if you two will excuse me for a few minutes, I want to give Amber some instructions."

"You have your work cut out for you, Mrs. Fletcher," Payne said as Richardson left the room. "I don't envy you."

"I don't envy me, either," I said with a rueful laugh.

"I know where you might start."

"Please tell me."

"Get ahold of Sherry Buchwalter."

"She is?"

"It's a he. Sherry for Sheridan. Retired policeman. Sherry was a detective on the Wanamaker Jones murder case."

I noted his name on a small pad I'd placed in front of me at the start of the meeting. Dr. Payne gave me what he thought was Officer Buchwalter's address. "Sorry," he said, "but I don't have his phone number with me. He's a crusty guy, and smart. Sherry's been a patient of mine for years."

"I get the impression that you probably know just about everyone in Savannah I might need to talk to."

His laugh was gentle. "I've treated a few local folks in my fifty-some years as a physician. If you're suggesting that I might help you in your investigation, I'll consider it." He reached for the pad I'd been writing on and scribbled his number at the top of the sheet. "Call me anytime, Mrs. Fletcher. This promises to be more fun than when our Saint Pat parade's grand marshal fell off his horse thirty years ago. Damn fool was drunk. Lucky for him all he suffered was a whole mess of bruises and an equally bruised ego. Yes, do call me, Mrs. Fletcher. You and your literacy project are going to need all the help you can get."

Chapter Nine

I showed Melanie the address Dr. Payne had given me for Sheridan Buchwalter. "Do you think you can take me there?" I asked.

"Yes, ma'am. I kind of know where it is. It's an area called Southside. Does he know you're coming?"

"I hope so. Dr. Payne said Mr. Buchwalter was expecting us, but when I called for directions, I got his answering machine. I left a message telling him we'd be there this morning."

"Well, if he's not home, we can always go to the mall," she said with a twinkle in her eye. "There's a sale at Old Navy I wouldn't mind checking out."

Melanie was dressed in a short black-and-white-striped jacket with flared cuffs and a wide leather belt over a pair of black denim jeans embroidered in gold thread. Around her neck she had arranged a turquoise and gold scarf in a complicated bow that would have taken me a month to learn how to tie. In my serviceable taupe pantsuit that always traveled well, even with a favorite gold brooch I'd pinned on the collar, I was reminded that although I had no desire to dress like a teenage fashion plate, I seemed to have left behind my days of more elegant attire when I gave up the apartment I used to have in New York City. Perhaps some shopping was in order.

"If we stop at Belk's," Melanie said, seeming to read my mind, "I bet we could find you a nice red top to go with that suit. I'm guessing red is a good color for you."

"I do like red," I said, "and I'd enjoy shopping, but we have important business to attend to first."

As I sat back in Melanie's blue Honda, I thought about how I could organize this murder investigation. I hoped Detective Buchwalter would cooperate. He had worked on the case, but it had probably been relegated to the cold files even before he'd retired. Would he be resentful of interference, concerned that what I might find would show him up and make him look foolish? That was certainly not my intention. I only hoped that a fresh look at the murder from a distance of many years could yield new information. Perhaps people who were hesitant to speak up in 1967 would feel freed by the passage of time and be willing to share what had been hidden so long ago. I needed the detective's insights. Without them, I would be left adrift. There were few witnesses to begin with, and those who were around—with the exception of Dr. Payne—did not seem eager to help me.

My return to Tillie's house from the attorney's office the day before had been greeted with mixed reviews. Melanie had been excited and had offered to be my assistant. "I can drive you anywhere you want to go," she said happily. "I've lived here my whole life."

"I'm happy to take you up on that, Melanie, so long as your mother doesn't object."

"Oh, she won't. It's spring break. She likes it when I'm occupied."

I intended to get a confirmation of that from Mrs. Goodall, but she had largely avoided me. I'm not certain if it was intentional. She was preoccupied with a leak that had apparently developed while we were out and had left a large wet spot on the carpet in the study. Unsure of its source, she'd left a message with a plumber and hastened to find towels to soak up the water and a bucket deep enough to keep the drips from continuing to splash on the cream-colored Oriental. When I attempted to speak with her later in the day, she shooed me from the kitchen, citing dinner preparations and an imminent callback from the plumber for why she had "no time to chat."

Meanwhile, the Grogans had taken their month's notice as permission to speed up the pace of their paranormal investigations. When I went upstairs to wash for lunch, the door to the bathroom was blocked by an elaborate contraption on a tripod with wires extending in all directions.

"Don't touch that," Samantha screeched when I approached the door. "You'll reset the calibration it took Artie an hour and a half to tune."

I'd had to use the bathroom off Tillie's bedroom, passing by the gruesome painting *Judith Holding the Head of Holofernes*, which Mrs. Goodall had relocated to the wall above Tillie's fireplace.

I felt vaguely disoriented using Tillie's bathroom. All her personal items were still arrayed on a mirrored tray atop an antique cabinet next to the sink—bottles of perfume, jars of face cream, a comb, a medicine container, a silver cup in which she'd left a pair of earrings, even her toothbrush and a half-used tube of toothpaste. It looked as if she were still alive, had left only a few minutes earlier, and would be back shortly to straighten up. *Perhaps Mrs. Goodall couldn't bring herself to put these things away,* I thought as I washed my hands with gardenia-scented soap. *Perhaps she felt closer to her longtime friend and employer by leaving evidence of her daily life in place.* For me, it was as if I were invading Tillie's privacy—peeking into a part of her life that was intensely personal—even though she had invited me to do just that with her demand that I solve the murder of her fiancé.

On my way out, I deliberately turned my head away from the disturbing oil painting and noticed for the first time that there were several photographs on Tillie's bedside table. I stopped to look at them, thinking that those pictured must have been very dear to her if she kept them where she would see their faces every morning when she awoke. I picked up a silver picture frame. It held a shot of a very young Tillie and an equally young Charmelle, their arms twined around each other's waists. Tillie was grinning at the camera, and Charmelle's soft smile was directed at her friend. I've always felt that photographs reveal more about their subjects than the people posing ever realized. Here was a perfect example, with an extroverted, impish Tillie facing the world straight on, and a shyer, quiet Charmelle not quite ready to show her true personality.

Another frame held a picture of a young soldier in uniform, one foot resting on the running board of a car I gauged to be of 1930s or 1940s vintage. His head was cocked to the side and one hand was raised as if he were giving instructions to the photographer. This had to be the husband Tillie lost in the war. I smiled at the image. He had a sweet and open face, and I'd bet he had his hands full with a spunky wife like Tillie. And she had given him the greatest gift of love—she had never forgotten him.

The last picture was the one I'd been expecting. It was a professional portrait like those Hollywood photos that actors send to their fans and had even been signed: "To my darling Tillie, from your devoted W." I noted how handsome he'd been. Wanamaker Jones must have easily captured hearts with his thick, wavy hair, movie-star looks, and the devilish expression in his eyes. He had a small scar that intersected one eyebrow, adding a dash of rakishness to a face that was close to being pretty.

I put the silver frame back where I'd found it. If her

most cherished photographs were to speak for her, they would say there were only two men in Tillie's life, all her would-be beaus notwithstanding.

I had found myself alone for lunch, the Grogans upstairs with their experiments, Mrs. Goodall downstairs and not in a mood to talk. The general saw me sitting by myself at the dining room table and hastily headed for the door, a sandwich wrapped in a napkin stuffed in his pocket.

"I'd like to talk with you," I said before he made his escape.

"No time right now. I have to make alternative living arrangements before I'm booted out on my rear." He disappeared down the hall.

Why a perfectly healthy adult had thought he could impose indefinitely on an elderly woman's hospitality was puzzling. And why he resented that he would be asked to leave now that she was dead was a complete mystery to me. Tillie had had her secrets, but I didn't think her relationship with James Pettigrew, such as it was, was the one she wanted me to unveil. Or was I wrong? Pettigrew claimed she had accepted his proposal. Of course, she wasn't around to confirm or contradict his assertion, but I couldn't conceive that Tillie would agree to marry such an arrogant boor. But then, why had she taken him in and lodged him in her guesthouse? *No more, Jessica*, I scolded myself. Much as I wanted to know why Tillie tolerated the abrasive Pettigrew, that wasn't the mystery I was supposed to address.

I pulled a sheet of paper from my pocket. Mr. Richardson had given me a copy of his list of those attending the reading of the will, and his secretary, Amber, had provided telephone numbers next to each name. I put check marks in the margin alongside those I hoped to interview. But later, when I sat in Tillie's study and began dialing numbers, I ended up leaving voice mails, rather than reaching anyone directly. The sole exceptions were Dr. Payne, who invited me to dinner to talk over my *findings*—not that I had any findings yet—and Joseph Jones, Wanamaker's nephew, who had volunteered his and his family's remembrances if I needed them.

"My folks will be in town Saturday for the Saint Paddy's Day parade," he said. "Uncle Wanamaker was my dad's brother. He loves to talk about 'the prodigal son,' as he calls him."

We made a date to meet at a café close to the parade route, and I earnestly hoped we could find an undisturbed corner for the interview. Saint Patrick's Day anywhere is not known as a quiet holiday, and Melanie had told me Savannah's celebration draws upwards of half a million people to see all the floats and marching units, together with fifty or more bands.

As we drove out to Southside, Melanie gave me a brief tour of the city's preparations for the coming holiday.

"I thought I'd go by Forsyth Park so you can see the fountain," she said as she steered the car around a series of squares and up Bull. "Savannah sure likes to celebrate its Saint Patrick's Day."

"So I noticed," I said.

Along our way, we passed houses draped with bunting of green, white, and orange, the colors of the Irish flag. On others, ribbons of the same colors twined around gates or climbed up wrought-iron banisters. Irish flags hung side by side with the Stars and Stripes. And kelly green and gold garlands competed with the Spanish moss in the branches of the oak trees.

"Wait till you see this." Melanie slowed as she reached Forsyth Park so I could see the huge fountain for which it's famous. It reminded me of the kinds of tiered fountains I'd seen in Europe with its central figure at the top of a robed woman, her arm raised above her head. At the base, figures of tritons—half man, half serpent—held horns shaped like shells to their lips, and a little farther out four swans raised their graceful necks. However, unlike all the classical fountains with mythical creatures that I'd seen before, this one was spewing bright green water. The cast-iron figures, usually white, had a delicate green glow to them.

"They did the official Greening of the Fountain last week," Melanie said, driving around the park. "It was on television. The committee members all standing around the fountain with watering cans of green dye. Is this a crazy place, or what?"

"It's certainly a colorful one," I said, and we both laughed.

Melanie took Abercorn Street out of the downtown area—"Now you'll see my favorite part of the city"—so she could point out the mall. We passed shopping center after shopping center along the straight, flat road, until I began to look at my watch. But her promised knowledge of her hometown proved reliable when a half hour later, she pulled up in front of a redbrick ranch on a tree-shaded street some distance away from the city's major thoroughfare. A car was in the driveway.

"Looks like he's home," she chirped. "Can I come in with you?"

"You may," I said, "if you promise not to talk, just to sit and listen."

"Yes, ma'am. I'm a good listener," she said. "I *am*," she repeated when I raised my eyebrows. "You'll see."

We heard bells ring inside when I pulled on the trunk of what I thought was an elephant knocker. The door was opened by a solidly built African American man with a gray beard and a bald pate. He wore half-glasses, and an open newspaper dangled from his hand.

"Mr. Buchwalter?" I asked.

"Who wants to know?" he said, his gaze sliding from me to Melanie.

"I'm Jessica Fletcher. I left you a message on your answering machine. Dr. Payne said you were expecting me."

"And who is this?" he asked, indicating Melanie with his chin.

"I'm Melanie Goodall. My mama was housekeeper to Miss Tillie Mortelaine. I knew Miss Tillie all my life. I drove Mrs. Fletcher out here. She doesn't drive." She paused in her recitation. "Ooh, sorry. I'm not supposed to speak."

"Seems you don't follow instructions so well, young lady."

"No, sir. I guess I don't."

"Well, y'all come on in," the detective said, turning around and leaving the door open for us to follow him inside. He waved at a gray couch, swiping sections of the newspaper off the cushion. "The doc said you would be here, but I wasn't expecting a crowd."

"I can wait in the car if you really want me to," Melanie said, her eyes begging to stay.

"That won't be necessary," Buchwalter said, settling into a blue tweed recliner, "but I'll put you in the kitchen cleaning the birdcage if you talk too much."

"Ooh, you have a bird?"

He winked at me.

"Go on in and see. His name is Sunshine. He's a sun conure. Cage's just over there, next to the pantry. Now don't scare him, you hear?"

Melanie was around the corner and cooing at the bird a moment later.

"Always keeps the grandkids occupied, too," he said.

"Detective Buchwalter, I want to thank you for agreeing to see me."

"No problem, Mrs. Fletcher. Not sure what I can help you with, but I'll listen."

"I'm hoping that Dr. Payne has told you about the provision in Tillie Mortelaine's will."

"He did, but I already knew about it." He waved the newspaper back and forth. "It's in here."

"I beg your pardon. I'm afraid I don't understand."

"Take a look-see for yourself," he said, poking at the paper as he leaned forward to pass it to me.

I scanned the articles on the page he'd indicated. There was a piece on an auto accident, FATAL DAY ON 95, another on an upcoming concert, TELFAIR AND ALL THAT JAZZ, and a photo of several men standing in front of a building with the caption REAL ESTATE DEVELOPER PLANS HOTEL EXPANSION. But it was the headline of an article beneath the photo that took me aback.

FAMED WRITER HERE TO SOLVE COLD CASE

Mystery writer Jessica Fletcher is in town, but it isn't to promote her latest book. This newspaper has learned that the author from Maine, who helped establish this city's literacy program two decades ago, is back in town to solve a murder. A provision in the will of Tillie Mortelaine, one of Savannah's most popular hostesses before her death last month at 91, requires Mrs. Fletcher to solve, in less than a month, a crime that has stumped the Metro Police for forty years. According to sources who have requested anonymity, the will of Ms. Mortelaine, known to be eccentric at times, is holding up a million-dollar bequest to the Savannah Literacy Foundation until Mrs. Fletcher can name the murderer of Wanamaker Jones, a society bon vivant and then-fiancé of the deceased, who was shot dead in Mortelaine House on New Year's Day in 1967.

According to a spokesperson at Savannah-Chatham Metropolitan Police headquarters, the case hasn't been relegated to their cold files. "We don't ever close a homicide," she said. "If someone thinks they have new evidence, we'll be happy to take it under consideration. However, we don't encourage amateurs to pursue investigations that are clearly the jurisdiction of the police."

The article went on to detail Tillie's philanthropic activities in the city, with a quote from the director of the literacy foundation, who was "disappointed" that Miss Mortelaine would "play games" with such an important donation, and a recitation of some of the cases in which I played a part leading to the arrest of the perpetrator, and finally a promise that the paper would publish any news I came up with on the murder.

"Oh dear," I said, handing him back the paper. "This is not good."

"It'll certainly shake the nuts out of the trees," he said.

"That's what I'm afraid of."

"Then again, you might get a good lead."

"Or, I'll get more leads than I can possibly pursue in a month's time—and most of them apocryphal."

He let the newspaper fall into a pile on the floor and

linked his fingers over his stomach. "So now, what can *I* do for you?"

"Well, for a start, you can tell me a little about the case. I don't have any idea of what happened that night other than the fact that Wanamaker Jones was shot. I'm sure you can add to that."

"I can tell you that there was some cover-up."

"What do you mean by that?"

"I mean that wherever we went, people just clammed up, wouldn't talk, gave us as little information as possible."

"I'm surprised to hear that," I said.

"I was surprised to hear that Miss Mortelaine wanted the case solved, even after her death. She certainly didn't help our investigation at the time."

"What did she do?"

"It's not what she did, Mrs. Fletcher. It's what she *didn't* do. She didn't cooperate. She didn't answer questions. She 'forgot' to mention things. She lost track of the time. She couldn't find evidence we requested. Some of my colleagues thought she had an alcohol problem. Others thought she was crazy. Is any of this news to you?"

"I know that Tillie liked to take a drink now and then, but I never saw her overindulge. Of course, I can only speak of the few times I visited with her, and that was twenty years after the murder. As to her being crazy, maybe she was a bit eccentric, as the paper says. I think it was more that she liked to poke fun, play practical jokes, puncture big egos. Perhaps she had an odd sense of humor, but she wasn't irrational."

"I didn't say she was irrational. She was rational, all right. You know what I think? I think she was crazy like a fox. She was sly. Let people think she was nutty, all the while controlling everyone and everything around her. That's what I think."

"That's pretty harsh, Detective."

"Maybe, but she stonewalled me. I knew it, and she knew that I knew. Of course, just my being on the case may have had something to do with it."

"What do you mean?"

"Should be obvious. I'm a black man investigating a white murder. Didn't go over too well at the time. Savannah had eliminated segregated lunch counters only two, three years before I got here."

"Where had you come from?"

"Philly. Was a Philadelphia cop for fifteen years, but my wife missed her family. I applied here and they hired me. At the time black detectives worked only in black neighborhoods, but things were starting to change. We had the election of the first black sheriff since Reconstruction. Not here. It was over in Macon, in the center of the state. Still, my white partner used to make a production of wiping off the seat when I got out of the car. We changed in different barracks. The white officers had nice perks, card tables, pool tables. We got nothin'. You can bet that if a black officer had something on a white person in Savannah, he'd better have it buttoned up tighter than a snake wrapped around a rat's neck. Otherwise there'd be mighty big trouble." He paused, the expression on his face a reflection of those unpleasant memories. "Anyway," he continued, "that's neither here nor there. It's a lot better these days."

"Do you really think Tillie didn't cooperate because she was prejudiced against you?" I asked. "I confess I didn't know her all that well, but what little I did know about her would lead me to think that seems out of character."

"I wouldn't swear to it in a court of law," he said, sighing. "But at the time, there was so much tension on the police force it was the first thing we all thought of. All the colored guys, anyway. But the white guys on the squad didn't get any more out of her than I did, so maybe I'm wrong."

"What happened that night? Do you remember? I'd like to get a feel for the sequence of events."

"You'll need to get the file from headquarters for the details, but I remember it was New Year's Eve, and Miss Mortelaine had hosted a big party. Every big shot in the city made an appearance. Didn't make our job any easier. Must've been a hundred people at her house earlier in the night. I know we questioned that many people later on. But when we got there, there was only about a dozen of them left, maybe not quite that many. There was your friend, Miss Tillie, her sister-in-law and brother-in-law. Then the lawyer and the judge." He counted on his fingers. "The judge's sister. Doc Payne was there. He's the one pronounced the victim dead. The pastor who gave him last rites. And then the folks in the kitchen. The housekeeper and two guys they hired on to help serve. It was around three in the morning when we got the call . . ."

"Good evening, sir. We're Officers Buchwalter and Hadleigh. We got a report of a shooting. Is that right?"

Frank O'Neill's nostrils flared when he eyed the two uniformed policemen, one black, one white, but his expression was otherwise impassive. "That's right. I called. Come this way, officers. The body is upstairs."

"Don't I know you, sir?"

"I'm Judge O'Neill."

"Thought I recognized you. We brought a perp up on burglary-one before you last week. Remember, Buchwalter?" Hadleigh elbowed his partner.

"That's possible," the judge said. "I see a lot of cops in court." He crossed the marble foyer, striding past the door to the parlor without looking in on the people who were sitting in front of a fireplace, sober expressions on their faces, drinks in their hands.

A housekeeper in a uniform placed a tray on a table in the hall and started collecting the empty champagne glasses that littered every flat surface.

"Excuse me, ma'am," Officer Buchwalter said, stopping to speak to the woman. "We'd rather that you didn't clean up just yet."

"Oh, heavens!" The woman jumped at being addressed and accidentally pushed the tray against a small lamp with a mushroom-shaped shade. The lamp teetered on the edge of the table and fell onto an umbrella stand.

"Oh, no!" she wailed. "I've broken it!" She bent to lift the lamp with shaking hands and placed it back on the table.

"No. I think it looks okay," Buchwalter said. "Sorry to startle you."

"Oh, Lord. I'll lose my place if it's broke. I just started here. I can't lose my place."

"Buchwalter, what's keeping you?" Hadleigh called. He was halfway up the stairs.

"I'll need to speak with you later, ma'am." Buchwalter said. He heard a voice from the parlor call out.

"Emanuela, get someone to help you with those glasses. I can't do everything myself."

The lights in the upstairs hallway were dimmed, but the officers could see the body sprawled on the rug. Someone had turned the man onto his back, or else he'd fallen that way, his arms akimbo, a dark stain surrounding a hole in his pale blue silk shirt right above his heart. There was blood on the fingers of his right hand as if he'd grabbed his chest where the bullet had gone in, and on his forehead where he'd used his bloody fingers to push away his wavy blond hair. Hadleigh knelt by his side and put two fingers on the man's neck. "He's dead," he said, looking up at Buchwalter.

"Of course he's dead," the judge said, plainly irritated. "The doctor confirmed that an hour ago."

"You found the body an hour ago, and we just get the notice?" Buchwalter said.

"Took you a while to get here," O'Neill said.

Or took you a while to call, Buchwalter thought.

"Who's this doctor you mentioned, Judge?" Hadleigh said, pulling a pad from his back pocket.

"Dr. Payne. He's downstairs."

"Did you call him before you called the police?" Buchwalter asked.

"No. He was a guest here."

"Do you know this man?" He waved a hand toward the body.

"Of course. He's Wanamaker Jones."

"Does he live here? I mean, *did* he live here?"

"I believe so."

"Age?"

"I don't know. You'll have to ask Miss Mortelaine. He was her guest, or rather her fiancé."

"Who was the last person to see him alive?"

"I haven't the vaguest idea."

"Well, then, who discovered the body?"

"I believe it was the children."

"Children! Where are they?"

"Their parents took them home. We thought it best. Didn't want them upset any further. Plenty of time for you to talk to them tomorrow."

Buchwalter and Hadleigh exchanged glances.

"We'll need their names and address, sir," Hadleigh said.

"Miss Tillie can give you that. They're her niece and nephew, her brother-in-law's children."

"Big party tonight, Your Honor?"

"Obviously."

"How many people were here?"

O'Neill wiped a hand across his brow and sighed. "I

don't know. Too many. You'll have to ask the hostess." He looked over to the landing at the top of the staircase where the housekeeper was hovering. "Yes, Emanuela?" he said wearily.

"There's some other policemen at the door, Judge."

"That'll be our backup," Buchwalter said, turning toward the stairs. "Don't touch anything up here, please," he instructed the housekeeper.

"No, sir, I won't."

"Hey, Harry, get up here with the camera," he yelled down to one of the men in a group that had already filed into the marble foyer.

"I'll be in the parlor if you need me," O'Neill told the officers, and left without looking back at the body.

Buchwalter turned to Emanuela. "Where can I find you later?" he asked.

"In the kitchen. I got a lot to clean up."

"Don't leave until I speak with you."

"No, sir. I be here. I live here."

"See you later, then." He winked at her in hopes he could set her mind at ease, but she was still nervous, wiping her trembling hands on her apron skirt. She hurried down the hallway toward what Buchwalter assumed was the back staircase to the kitchen. *Didn't these old houses all have separate stairs for the help? Heaven forbid the wealthy owners touch the same banisters as their servants. Never thought I'd miss Philadelphia so much.*

An officer carrying a large camera with a flash attachment brushed past the judge on the main stairs. O'Neill hugged the wall as he descended, leaving room for the other policemen who were jogging up the stairs, one carrying a briefcase. Buchwalter watched the judge cross the marble floor and disappear into the room where the other guests, and presumably the hostess, were doing their best to forget that a dead man lay on the floor above their heads.

"When we walked in, we thought it was going to be a smoking-gun situation," Buchwalter said to me, running a hand over his bald head. "One of those easy-to-solve cases where you got the victim, the murder weapon, and someone admitting to the crime. But we didn't have the gun, and it turned out no one knew anything or heard anything. It was a noisy New Year's Eve, they said. Teenagers had been setting off firecrackers in the square all night. Inside, they were popping champagne corks. A hundred people talking, trying to be heard over the loud music. No one noticed anything that sounded like a gunshot. No one went upstairs."

"And you never found the gun?" I asked.

"Never did. Searched the premises. That was a job. It's a big house to start with and they were in the middle of some construction upstairs, so a couple of the rooms were a mess. Came up empty. We knew from ballistics it was from a small pistol, the kind of gun a lady might buy for protection. But Miss Mortelaine and her friends all denied owning a weapon. No, that's not entirely true. The judge had one handgun. But his was back in his bedside table, hadn't been fired, and was a different caliber altogether."

"Did Wanamaker Jones have any enemies?"

"Couldn't find anyone to say a bad word about him. Handsome, beautiful dresser, a real charmer. The men seemed to like him, the ladies liked him even more. He knew how to golf, dance, play the piano, tell a story, mix a cocktail—tailor-made to fit into Savannah society."

"Was he from Savannah?"

"We didn't know where he was from. Then, anyway. And we put a lot of effort into it. Took prints from the corpse, but he didn't have a record—at least not in Georgia. 'Course, it's not like today, where computers let you compare fingerprints from anywhere in the country. Back then, we had limited access to information. And with a name like Jones, it isn't easy to track someone down."

"But 'Wanamaker' is certainly unusual. Didn't that help?"

"Might have if it was his real name, but it wasn't. His real name was Joseph Adam Jones, Jr."

"I met Wanamaker's nephew at the reading of Tillie's will yesterday."

"We found the family several years later when they filed a missing-persons report. He'd been a drifter, but he usually checked in with his brother every few years. When the family went a couple of Christmases without hearing from him, they started to worry." Buchwalter leaned forward in his chair. "I'm getting a bit dry. Want a Coke or something else to drink?"

"Anything is fine," I said.

I followed him into the kitchen, where Melanie sat cross-legged on the floor in front of a white metal cage, making kissing sounds to a beautiful yellow and green parrot with an orange head.

"Look at this bird, Mrs. Fletcher," she said, crooning. "Isn't he beautiful? I'm teaching him to say 'hello.' I already got him to say it once. Say 'hello,' Sunshine."

Buchwalter gave out a hearty laugh, which turned into a cough. He pulled a white handkerchief from his pants pocket and wiped his mouth. "That bird has a bigger vocabulary than I do," he said. "He's just stringing you along so you'll keep talking to him. That's how he entertains himself."

"Oh," Melanie said, disappointed. "You naughty bird." She shook her finger at the bird, which cocked its head to the side, looking contrite.

"What kind of bird did you say it was?" I asked.

"A sun conure," he said, washing his hands at the sink. "From South America. My daughter bought it for me after my wife passed on. She thought I needed something to keep me company. He's good company all right. Funny bird. Squawks all the time. Only problem is he'll probably live longer than I will." He opened the refrigerator and removed a six-pack of Coca-Cola. "I imagine you want a glass."

"Yes, please."

Buchwalter handed me a glass, then pulled three cans of soda from the plastic collar, passed one to me and another to Melanie. "Would you like some chocolate syrup for your Coke?" he asked her.

"No, sir, but thank you anyway," she said.

"It's a Southern thing," he said in response to the surprised expression on my face. "Kind of a nice combination, but Doc Payne said it's not good for my blood sugar."

"Nor anyone's, I imagine," I said.

We popped open our cans and sat at a small round kitchen table, sipping soda.

"You were telling me about Wanamaker Jones," I said. "Or Joseph Jones. I'm surprised he was able to move so easily in Savannah society. Tillie once told me that she knew the heritage of every one of her friends. I know she prided herself on the fact that her family had been here for more than two centuries. How did Wanamaker get past that requirement for acceptance?"

Buchwalter chuckled. "It's not just the society folk who have that attitude. My mechanic boasted to me that his great-great-great-grandfather used to change the wheels on the wagons for the Confederate Army."

"But Wanamaker was able to come into this established class and make himself a part of it. How?"

"Near as we could make out, he just turned up one Wednesday night, their regular stag night, at the Forest City Gun Club."

"Gun club?"

"I know what you're thinking, but they only fire shotguns. Skeet. Clay. It's a real high-society-type place."

"Then how did Jones get in?"

"He claimed to be a cousin of Rufus Symington. Symington, who was an officer in the club, had just died—it was a big story in all the local papers—and his widow was, well, let's just say she was not all there. Probably had Alzheimer's, but we didn't know that name then. We just called her senile."

"So Wanamaker applied his charm and convinced the widow that he was a relation of her late husband?" I asked.

"Must be what he did."

"And everyone believed him."

"People see what they want to see, Mrs. Fletcher."

"But Tillie—she was always so sharp."

"Miss Mortelaine liked the idea of having a fiancé, I guess. Especially one welcomed by her friends. She must have been in her fifties by then. Not a lot of prospects at that age."

"I don't know about that," I said, thinking that there were still a few gentlemen who paid attention to me, and I was older than Tillie had been back then.

"Didn't mean to offend."

"No offense taken," I said. "Does the Forest City Gun Club still exist?"

"Oh, yes. Far as I know, it's still goin' strong. They might have a lady or two as a member now. Back then it was all male."

Melanie and I thanked Mr. Buchwalter for his hospitality and his time. I asked, and he agreed to call headquarters to help me get access to the original murder file. On the ride back downtown, Melanie was quiet, in contrast to her voluble personality earlier in the day. "Are you all right?" I asked at one point.

"I didn't mean to eavesdrop, ma'am."

"You weren't eavesdropping, Melanie. There wasn't anything Detective Buchwalter talked about that you shouldn't have heard. At least I don't think so."

"Do you remember when he was talking about the two men who helped my mother serve at the party that night?"

"Yes, I remember."

"Well, one of them was my father."

Chapter Ten

"Water travels, you know. Just because the ceiling is leaking over here don't mean that's where the pipe is at." The plumber tucked his hands behind the bib of his overalls and rocked back on his heels.

Melanie rolled her eyes and made a face at her mother.

"I just want to know can you fix it?" Mrs. Goodall asked.

"I reckon. Might take a bit of time, though. And I charge by the hour."

"How much time you talkin' about?"

"Don't know yet. Got to trace that leak back to the source."

"I'm not about to let you pull down every ceiling in this house till you find it."

"No need, ma'am. I got me a camera. It can travel two hundred feet, if there ain't nothin' in its way. Just need a small hole to start."

"And how much is that goin' to be?"

"Won't know till I get up there and look around."

"Mama, just let him fix it," Melanie said. "Mr. Richardson said he trusts you to take care of it. He'll pay the bill."

Mrs. Goodall frowned at her daughter. "I'm not wasting Miss Tillie's money any more now that she's gone than I would when she was right here."

"Better make up your mind," the plumber said. "After today, if'n I get busy, you may not see me for a week or more."

"I'll take that chance or find me another plumber," Mrs. Goodall said, her arms crossed.

"This weekend's Saint Patrick's Day, you know."

"What's that got to do with a leak?"

"Could be lots of work on account of, you know, people celebratin' and maybe damagin' their pipes."

Melanie snickered. "Hoo boy, that's a stretch," she said, just loud enough for all of us to hear.

"Hush up, Melanie," her mother said. "I don't like that sass. You apologize."

"Yes, ma'am. Sorry, sir."

Mrs. Goodall turned to the plumber. "You write me out an estimate and I'll let you know."

"Okay. I'll give you one this afternoon. That soon enough?"

Mrs. Goodall grunted, but she seemed pleased with the results of her negotiation.

The plumber picked up his tool kit, and started for the door. "Now, you keep in mind, I'm bringin' in some high-tech equipment," he said. "That's to save your ceiling. Best there is. But it will cost you some. I got to pay for that thing and it ran me a lot of money."

"You give me the estimate. Then we'll talk."

"I can start tomorrow if you let me know early enough."

"I'll call you."

Mrs. Goodall escorted the plumber out.

"Where is she taking him?" I asked Melanie.

"To the back door. She's not about to let him go out the front entrance. Plus, she just washed that floor." She perched on a chair in front of the desk in the study and used the toe of her metallic leather wedge to adjust the placement of the pan that was catching the drips from the ceiling.

It was Friday morning and I had been sitting in Tillie's study reviewing my list and trying to set up appointments to talk with people who could shed light on the murder of Wanamaker Jones. Mrs. Goodall had promised she would give me some time "later." I knew Melanie was trying to pry information from her mother, and I was pretty sure Mrs. Goodall was not going to accommodate her daughter, but I hoped she'd be more forthcoming with me.

Messages left with Rose Margaret Kendall and her brother, Rocky, had gone unanswered. Tillie's niece and nephew were angry that the house and its contents had not been left to them outright, and of course, I couldn't guarantee that they would get their inheritance if they co-operated with me. I had no idea what Tillie's plans were for the house, or what other instructions she had placed in that sealed envelope.

"Where are you going to dinner with Dr. Payne to-night?" Melanie asked

"I think he said the Olde Pink House," I replied.

"Oh, yeah. On Reynolds Square. That's a Savannah in-stitution. It's in all the guidebooks. They have a ghost, you know."

I gave a mock sigh. "Not another one."

She giggled. "I bet Savannah is the most haunted city in America."

"Who is the ghost in the Olde Pink House?"

"James Habersham. He built the place. They have his portrait hanging right there, so you'll recognize him if he materializes in front of you." Melanie pursed her lips and hooted, "Ooooooooooh," her version of a ghost sound.

I laughed.

"Our architectural history class took a tour there once," she said. "The upstairs is a formal restaurant. Downstairs, they have the original tavern, stone walls and all. Actually, I think that's where most of the ghost stories come from."

"If I see any ghosts, I'll give them your regards," I said.

"No, please. Don't mention my name. I don't want 'em to know who I am." She shivered. "It's bad enough those crazies in the guesthouse are trying to raise the dead."

"But you said you and your friend went looking for the ghosts here yourself."

"We did, but we had all the lights on."

I started to laugh. "I see. And the Grogans work in the dark."

"Yeah. It's creepy. I don't want to be around if they find something. They have cameras going everywhere. And I don't want anything to come looking for me."

"Are you going to the Saint Patrick's Day parade?" I asked.

Melanie snorted. "You can't escape it if you're downtown."

"Mr. Richardson invited me to view the festivities from his office, but I'm supposed to get together with Wanamaker's nephew." I rummaged in my purse to find the slip of paper on which I'd written the name of the café where I was to meet the Jones family.

"Mr. Richardson's office is right on Bay Street," she said. "That'd be a cool place to watch the parade, plus you'd be up off the street, out of harm's way."

"Harm's way?"

"Just a figure of speech."

I showed Melanie the paper with the name of the café.

"That's smack in the middle of the celebration. You'd better get there early if you even want a seat."

"Oh, dear," I said. "It doesn't sound like the best location for an interview."

"You'll be lucky if you can hear them shout 'hello,'" she said. "Savannah will be toasting its Irish heritage all day and all night. If you like crowds, it's great. The streets will be jammed with out-of-towners drinking green beer. In fact, if you don't need me to drive you somewhere tomorrow, I think I might grab Tish and go uptown to get away from it. We still have to write up our report on Mortelaine House."

"Don't worry about driving me," I said. "I can always walk or take a cab if I need to go somewhere. And I'm very interested in seeing that report when you've finished it."

"You are?"

"Of course. Why are you surprised?"

"It's just an old house. Nobody famous ever lived here."

"But a murder took place," I said. "Doesn't that make it unique?"

"Yes, ma'am, but we don't have anything about that in the report. We do say who the owners were, but other than that we just talk about architectural stuff, like who designed it, when it was built, whether we found the original colors of the walls, and what renovations were done."

"Sounds fascinating to me. What kind of renovations were done? Tell me a little bit about it."

"I can do better than that," Melanie said. "I can show them to you."

"Wonderful!" I said. "Let's start downstairs. There's a door I want to ask you about."

Chapter Eleven

D r. Payne had suggested that we meet in the Planters Tavern at the Olde Pink House before going upstairs for dinner. He'd told me that under ordinary circumstances he preferred to dine in the tavern, but because I was visiting Savannah, he thought I would enjoy the ambience of the upstairs rooms. "The Olde Pink House is reputed to be one of the most haunted buildings in the city," he'd said, echoing what Melanie had told me. "With any luck, you'll end up in a conversation with James Habersham himself." Habersham, he explained, was an extremely wealthy merchant for whom the house was built on the northwest corner of Abercorn and Bryan streets in the late 1700s, and who makes an occasional appearance to make sure things are going well. I'd laughed, but the good doctor didn't join me. He seemed perfectly serious.

As the day progressed, I found myself flagging, and considered canceling my dinner with Payne. I needed some time to relax and to try to put into perspective what I'd learned to date, which I admit wasn't much. But the pressure to solve Wanamaker Jones's murder in thirty days, and by extension save the million dollars for the literacy project, weighed heavily on me. Dr. Payne seemed to know everyone involved. Not only had he been present the night Jones was shot, but he'd pronounced him dead. I couldn't pass up any and every opportunity to question him.

Despite an aching knee, I decided to walk to Reynolds Square, where the Olde Pink House is located. The injury to my knee had occurred that afternoon under circumstances better left for explaining a little later. Suffice it to say that while I hadn't injured any of my knee's internal workings, I'd ended up with a nasty gash that necessitated a sizable bandage.

It had been overcast all day, and quite humid. I walked slowly, favoring my knee and stopping now and then to take in the wonderful old houses I passed and to admire the other squares. Savannah is such a lovely city, but like any place, large or small, there are always darker sides that few visitors encounter. Forty years ago, the murder of Wanamaker Jones was big news. Now, because of Tillie Mortelaine's quirky last will and testament, his killing was about to be resurrected, and I was smack in the middle of it.

I arrived at the Olde Pink House a few minutes before I was scheduled to meet Dr. Payne and stood in front of the building that once had been the home of one of

America's richest men. It's a splendid example of Georgian architecture, and as its name promises, it *is* pink. Originally it was constructed of brick made from red clay; the red bled through the white stucco that had been applied over it, turning it pink. Mr. Habersham, a war hero during the Revolutionary War, wasn't about to live in a pink house and had it painted white. The red clay continued to turn the walls pink until the 1920s, when a woman who ran a tearoom there decided it was folly to continue trying to cover up the pink and had it painted—pink. *Real* pink.

I hobbled down a narrow set of concrete steps to the tavern level and walked into a lively room filled with convivial people, many at the bar enjoying drinks, others seated at tables having dinner. The crowd at the highly polished bar was boisterous, and I judged them to be mostly locals who found the tavern to be a home away from home, Savannah's answer to Cheers. Velvet couches at either end of the large, low-ceilinged room faced fireplaces whose brick hearths reached from floor to ceiling. Payne had secured a small table with two chairs in a far corner, and I joined him. He graciously stood and held out a chair for me. "You're limping," he said.

"Yes. I'm afraid I took a tumble this afternoon."

"Oh, my dear. How did that happen?"

"A long story, Doctor. Nothing major, just a bruise and a cut." I swiveled in my chair to take in my surroundings. "What a charming spot," I said.

"One of Savannah's better watering holes," he said. "Good food, too. If you want a rumor to get around Sa-

vannah, pass it along here. I understand from Sherry Buchwalter that you had a pleasant visit."

"Yes. He's a nice gentleman."

"Helpful?"

"I think so, although I haven't quite figured out how."

"So," he said, "how has the rest of your day gone?"

"It's been—interesting."

He laughed. "I always enjoy that answer, Mrs. Fletcher.
It can mean so many things."

"You're right," I said. "And please call me Jessica."

"Some of my patients resent me calling them by their
first names," he said, "while they're expected to call me Dr.
Payne. I suppose they're right. Jessica it shall be, and I'm
Warner. So, tell me about your *interesting* day, Jessica."

I recounted for him the tour of Tillie's house I'd taken with
Melanie Goodall that afternoon.

Melanie and I had used the back stairs to get to the
ground floor, and she led me down the wood-paneled hall
to her mother's bedroom. "When she started working here,
this is where she lived," she said, opening the door. "When
my father finally convinced her to marry him—she was a
reluctant bride—they moved to our house uptown."

The room was small but nicely furnished, with a high
window that gave it natural light. An upholstered armchair had a matching ottoman, similar to the one in my
room upstairs. The bed had an elaborately figured cast-
iron headboard with swags and curlicues, a beautiful antique that would have fetched a small fortune—or maybe

a large one—at an auction. It was covered by a patchwork quilt in a log cabin design around a blue center square.

Melanie ran her hand over the quilt to smooth its surface. "This was my grandmother's. Do you know the significance of quilts in our history?"

"I remember reading that they were used as signals for those traveling the Underground Railroad."

She smiled. "That's right. It was a secret code. Quilts were hung out with the laundry or over the porch railing of a 'station' in the Underground Railroad. If runaway slaves saw that the center square was blue or black, it meant the coast was clear and it was okay to come in. But if the center square was red, it meant that wasn't a safe time to knock on the door. Look!" She lifted the bottom of the quilt to show me the red center square on the reverse.

"You have a piece of history there," I said.

"I know. It's so exciting."

"You should make sure to include the history of the quilt in your report on Mortelaine House," I said.

A cloud passed over her features. "But the quilt doesn't belong to Miss Tillie," she said. "It's my mother's."

"Of course, it's hers, but your mother herself is part of the history of Mortelaine House and her quilt has been here—how long?"

"As long as she has."

"You see?"

"Ooh. I never thought to put my mother in the report. Thanks!"

Melanie continued our tour across the hall in the laun-

dry room. It was a spare, undecorated space with two anti-
quated machines and an equally ancient sink. I wasn't sure
if I wanted to try my luck with this equipment, and made
a mental note to find a local launderette.

"I understand Tillie put in a dumbwaiter, but I haven't
seen it," I said. "Do you know where it is?"

"I do, and you could look day and night and never discover it."

"My goodness! Now I'm even more eager to see it."

She took me back in the hall and paused next to the
staircase. "Can you find it?"

The walls in the hallway were paneled in maple squares
within squares, each square trimmed with molding. Now
that I knew the dumbwaiter was nearby, I searched for
where the panel pieces met, looking for a place where the
joining might show a gap, but there wasn't one. I ran my
hand across the wall in search of a stream of air that might
indicate a secret opening.

Melanie laughed, and leaned forward to push one of
the squares. There was a whoosh of dank air and the panel
popped open, revealing a shaft cut into the wall and a series of ropes on pulleys. Melanie tugged on a rope, hand
over hand, until a wooden box descended into the opening.
"See? The top and bottom slide up and down, and voilà!
the dumbwaiter. You put in the food, close the doors, and
use the ropes to pull it up to the next floor. It goes all the
way up to the third-floor hall. They have electric motors
for these now, but since my mother refused to use it anyway, Miss Tillie never had it upgraded."

"How long has it been here?"

"All my life and probably a lot longer."

"And you can't see it when it's closed."

"No, ma'am. When I was a kid, I used to think of it as a secret passage, and my friends and I used to send coded messages up and down to each other. We tried to climb into it once, but my mother came after us with a broom."

"What are you two up to?" Mrs. Goodall called from the kitchen. She was elbow-deep in flour and didn't look up from her culinary task when we walked in.

"I'm giving Mrs. Fletcher a tour of the house," Melanie replied.

"Miss Tillie used to give tours," her former housekeeper said, "during one of those weeks when lots of houses were open. People paid a handsome fee to see how the well-to-do lived. All went to charity, as I understand it."

"We have charitable house tours in Maine," I said. "It's always fascinating to see how people have decorated and furnished their homes."

"Never did like it much when they trooped all over the house," said Mrs. Goodall. "I told Miss Tillie somebody'll come through with a hook hand and steal you blind."

Melanie gave me a look that said we'd best be going. I wished the housekeeper a good day and followed her daughter into the hallway where the pantry was located, opposite the mystery door, the one that I was sure I'd locked during my nighttime sojourn for a cup of tea. I pointed to the door with the lock. "What's down there?" I asked.

Melanie's face turned serious. "I don't know, and I don't want to know. Just stairs leading to someplace. My mama told me that if she ever caught me going down there, she'd whup me good. Of course, that was when I was just a little kid. She wouldn't do it to me now." She giggled. "Too big for a whuppin' these days. But I've never gone down. Probably full of dead bodies."

I laughed. "I certainly hope you're wrong," I said. "Well, show me the rest of the things you and your friend have cataloged about this magnificent old mansion."

We spent the next forty-five minutes going into room after room, poking our heads into every nook and cranny. Melanie showed me where the new bathrooms had been installed—the only twentieth-century improvements made to the mansion. She was a delightful, enthusiastic, and knowledgeable guide, and I learned a great deal about the history of Mortelaine House. When we were finished, she said she had to run some errands for her mother but would be back in an hour in case I needed to be driven someplace.

I went to my room, peered between the slats of the shutters on one of the windows—Mrs. Goodall had shown me the trick to opening them—stepped out of my shoes, and sank into the armchair, resting my feet on its ottoman. It was a gray day in Savannah, which was okay with me. I certainly wasn't intending to go sightseeing. I had a few hours before I was scheduled to meet Dr. Payne for dinner, and decided a nap was in order. I closed my eyes, but couldn't sleep. I tried lying on the bed, but kept sitting up every time a new thought struck.

I remembered Seth's displeasure with my coming to Savannah to accept Tillie's challenge, and wondered if he'd been right. He so often was. I thought of the people I'd met, especially General Pettigrew and Artie and Samantha Grogan. The gruff Judge O'Neill was a formidable man, to be sure, and I wanted to spend time with him and his sister. Like Dr. Payne, O'Neill had been at the party the night Wanamaker Jones was shot, although based upon what former detective Buchwalter told me, the judge hadn't been particularly forthcoming the night of the murder. I hoped he would be more open with me.

Once I realized that sleep was eluding me, I gave up the attempt, got up, put my shoes back on, and wandered downstairs. I checked the kitchen in case Mrs. Goodall had some time to spare. It was empty. I turned to leave, but the door leading downstairs stopped me. Its bolt was secured; I turned the knob to test it anyway. Nope. Still locked. *Ignore it, Jessica,* I told myself. Seth Hazlitt always says that my natural sense of curiosity will get me into trouble one day, and he's been proven right on more than one occasion.

I blotted out his sage advice, slid the bolt open, and allowed the door to squeakily, slowly swing toward me. I found a wall switch, and a low-wattage light came on. I remembered having seen a flashlight in the kitchen, and fetched it. Training its beam down the stairs, I took a few tentative steps onto the wooden landing just inside the door, which creaked beneath my weight. I used the flashlight to examine the walls on either side of the steep staircase. They were concrete and appeared to be damp. Closer examination revealed a layer of greasy mold.

I redirected my attention to the bottom of the stairs. Should I go down? There was a slender piece of wood strung down the left side of the staircase that served as a banister. I placed my left hand on it and slowly began my descent. The railing was flimsy and undulated each time I moved my hand on it.

I reached the bottom and stopped to acclimate myself to the darkness, and to allow my nose to get used to the heavy, musty smell of mold and foul water. I looked down. The concrete floor beneath my feet had a film of rancid water, and I silently reminded myself to step carefully should I elect to go any farther.

The beam from the flashlight illuminated a narrow room with stout wooden shelves along one side. A thick layer of dust covered the few items still left on the shelves and gave evidence that this storage room had not been used in years, probably decades. I swung the light around to the opposite wall to reveal a passageway, whose height I judged to be slightly lower than my own. I leaned into the opening and aimed the light ahead. The ceiling was cement, as were the walls, but the length went beyond the reach of my flashlight—a tunnel.

I started into it, aware of the floor's wetness and careful to lower my head to avoid banging it. The air became increasingly oppressive, not hot but cool and damp, as though the molecules became denser with each step.

I tried to judge which way I was headed—toward the

front of the house, to the side, or in the direction of the rear of the property. I gave up. I was hopelessly disoriented.

I proceeded another fifteen or so feet before stopping and looking down at the floor. The concrete was stained beneath the wet, greasy layer of water. I directed the flashlight's beam to the walls, which were also stained—large, irregular patterns of darkness and light, some of it so foul that patches of green hairlike fuzz grew from it. The temperature had dropped precipitously, raising goose bumps on my arms. An image flashed through my mind of tunnels like this functioning as morgues during Savannah's yellow fever epidemic, physicians working in this unfriendly atmosphere, candles burning, the air thick with the odor of death.

I winced and shuddered, rubbing my arms to bring some warmth back into them. I considered turning back, but up ahead I saw what appeared to be a dim line of light, and decided to check out its origin. I advanced another ten feet or so, my body crouched over and my eyes on the ceiling to ensure that no beam or other protuberance would knock me silly before I reached my destination. That's when my toe caught on something and sent me sprawling forward, my knees slamming painfully against the floor. The flashlight went flying from my hand and I extended my arms to keep from going facefirst into the cement.

"Gorry!" I exclaimed. It's an old Maine expression meaning just about anything you want it to mean. Tears stung my eyes as the pain from my injured knee reached my brain. I got to my feet and groped for the flashlight, which hadn't gone far. I picked it up and shone the light on my knee, now oozing blood. I also looked at what had caused me to trip. It was a length of heavy, rusted chain coiled into a pile.

I pulled a handkerchief from my sweater pocket and used it to stem the blood. For some reason I wasn't cold anymore. I looked back down the tunnel and decided that the shaft of light was closer than the stairs leading back to the house.

When I reached the light, I saw that it came from beneath a door at the top of a flight of stairs similar to the ones leading down from the house. I grimaced as I went up them and reached a small platform. I directed the light at the brass doorknob and grasped it. It turned, but the door wouldn't open. I tried again, and again. No luck. Then I heard a sound from the other side of the door. A voice. A man. I balled my right hand into a fist and rapped with my knuckles. Harder now. Another voice, this time female. I was about to use the flashlight to more loudly announce my presence when I heard the sound of a sliding bolt. The door opened a crack, then wider.

"Careful," Samantha Grogan commanded. "Don't disturb the wires and equipment."

"Mrs. Fletcher," Artie Grogan said, sounding as surprised as if he were looking at someone who'd been dead for ages. "What are *you* doing here?"

My nonresponse was, "I fell." I shone the light on my wound.

"Good gracious," Artie said. "Come in and—"

"Don't upset the equipment," his wife repeated, ignoring my bloody knee.

I carefully came through the door, deftly navigated the maze of wires attached to their meters, and realized I was in the kitchen of the guesthouse in which I'd stayed on previous visits. Holding the handkerchief against my knee to avoid dripping blood on the floor, I limped to the nearest seat, a hard black straight-backed chair hand-painted with little red and yellow birds.

"How long have you been down there?" Samantha asked.

"I don't know," I said. "A half hour maybe."

"We were monitoring our equipment," Artie Grogan said. "We do it every hour whenever we feel there's an unusually strong spirit presence somewhere in the house or on the property. The meters indicated an especially strong field within the past half hour coming from the tunnel."

"You're aware of the tunnel," I said.

"Oh, yes," Grogan responded.

"Have you been down there yourselves?" I asked, taking a peek at my damaged knee and pleased to see that the bleeding had stopped. My handkerchief, however, was a wet red mess.

"Of course we have," his wife snapped, extricating a memory card from a camera, labeling it and tossing it on a pile of other cards. "There isn't a corner of this property that we haven't personally visited. We'd be derelict in our duties if we didn't."

"Of course," I said, having had enough with her. "If you'll excuse me."

I went to the sink, rinsed out my handkerchief, squirted it with dishwashing soap, and washed off my cut, gasping at the sting of the soap on the open wound.

"Do you want me to find some first-aid cream?" Samantha asked, finally recalling her manners.

"I think it will be fine for now," I said and started for the door leading to the gardens, beyond which sat the main house.

Artie followed me outside. "We'd like to know what you saw down there," he said.

"I'm sure nothing that you haven't seen," I said.

"The aura coming from the tunnel is always powerful," he said, walking beside me toward the house, "but today is unique."

I forced a laugh. "Maybe your meters are especially sensitive to mystery writers from Maine," I said.

"No. No. It was more than that. I mean, we've been in the tunnel when the meters were on, so it wasn't just you."

"By the way, Artie, I tripped over chain down there. Yours?"

"Chain? I don't remember a chain. No, not ours. Are you suggesting that—?"

"I'm not suggesting anything," I replied, "except a hot bath and some antibacterial ointment for my knee. Good seeing you."

He stopped walking, and I was aware that he continued to watch me limp up to the house and through a back door. I immediately acted on my intentions. I ran a hot tub and soaked in it before getting into a robe and ministering to my knee. Content that the wound was superficial, I dressed and headed off for dinner with Dr. Warner Payne.

"Quite an experience," Dr. Payne said after I'd recounted my afternoon in the tunnel. I had told him my tale over a glass of white wine. The doctor had a bourbon and water.

"One I can do without repeating," I said. "How well do you know the Grogans?"

"Not well at all. Their pseudo-science amuses me, but each person to his own madness. Why do you ask?"

"No special reason. But I know now that the guesthouse is connected with the main house by that tunnel, which means that anyone could have entered and left the house by way of it."

He nodded. "Wanamaker Jones's murderer," he said flatly.

"Possibly. I know it happened forty years ago, but do you happen to remember anything about that night that could point me in the direction of who might have killed him?"

He sat back and smiled. "My memory's not as keen as it once was, but I happen to have that evening clearly in mind. I suppose you don't easily forget a New Year's Eve when someone is gunned down in cold blood as part of the festivities."

"I know I wouldn't forget it," I said.

He was about to recall that fateful evening when a couple came to the table to greet him. I'd noticed that he was the recipient of numerous waves from people at the bar and at other tables. Payne was well-known, and I assumed beloved, after all those years of providing compassionate medical aid and advice to Savannah's residents. He introduced me and they chatted for a moment about the upcoming parade.

"We'll see you tomorrow, Dr. Payne. Nice to meet you, Mrs. Fletcher."

"No wonder you like coming here," I said. "You're obviously a popular fellow."

"If you live long enough, you get to meet just about everyone," he said. "Now, where were we?"

"You were about to give me your recollections of the night Wanamaker Jones was killed."

"Ah, yes. As you know, it was New Year's Eve. Savannah likes to party, as you'll see tomorrow. That holiday was no exception."

The New Year's Eve party at Tillie's house was as grand and festive as all the previous ones had been. Tillie was known as a gracious hostess, and invitations to her parties were zealously coveted. A six-piece Dixieland band provided spirited music throughout the evening, augmented by a singer imported from New Orleans for the occasion. More than a hundred guests took part in the festivities, and the champagne flowed freely. By the time the countdown to midnight and the New Year had begun, many partygoers were drunk, which provided a few problems. Some inebriated guests took the opportunity to embrace and, in some cases, fondle female objects of their desire, which prompted a few arguments and threatened fistfights between husbands and overeager male celebrants.

It was close to two in the morning when Tillie made it known that the festivities were officially over—at least for the majority of guests. Earlier in the evening, she'd quietly asked a select few to stay after the others left, which she often did at her parties, bestowing VIP treatment on those she favored. Included in that privileged group were Wanamaker Jones, Dr. Payne, Roland Richardson III, Judge Frank O'Neill and his sister, a pastor from the church Tillie attended now and then, and Tillie's brother-in-law and sister-in-law. In addition to the hostess and her guests, three members of the household staff were on hand. The regular staff had been augmented to handle the demands of such a large gathering. A bottle of rare aged bourbon was produced and served in snifters by a uniformed black man to the remaining guests, some of whom settled in the drawing room, their sighs mirroring their fatigue at the end of a long, spirited party.

"Tell me about the group that stayed on," I said after Dr. Payne had set the party scene for me.

"As I recall," he said, "the pastor, whose name was Bradford Penny, promptly fell asleep in his chair." He chuckled. "Pastor Penny was well-known around Savannah as having a direct connection with the devil—devil-rum, that is. At any rate, the mood was subdued, especially in contrast to the noisy, sometimes raucous goings-on earlier in the evening."

"A welcome quiet time," I suggested.

"Exactly."

"Who else was in the room?" I asked.

Payne frowned in thought. "Me, of course. Miss Tillie's brother-in-law and sister-in-law—brother to her late husband, that is." He ran his fingers through his hair. "They were not among her favorites, but they'd brought their kids—that's Rose Margaret and Rocky Kendall. You met them at the reading of the will. The children had been put to bed upstairs. The plan was for them to stay overnight, so Miss Tillie could hardly leave her in-laws out of our elite little group."

"Are her in-laws still living?"

He shook his head. "They passed away some time back, within a few years of each other."

That news was disappointing, but I hoped their children would remember something of that evening when I had a chance to talk with them.

"Did you say Roland Richardson was there? I wonder why he never mentioned that to me."

"Probably wanted to see if you discovered it on your own."

It began to appear that Tillie was not the only game player among her friends. Did everyone put the skills of their friends and colleagues to the test? General Pettigrew had been challenging me since I arrived. Now I learned that Richardson was being less than forthright.

"Anything else you can recall from that gathering?" I asked.

"The judge was having a tiff with his sister. I remember that."

"Why?"

"Oh, something about her flirting with someone during the evening."

"Is that so terrible?"

"Frank has always been a bit of a prig. After their parents died, Charmelle moved in with him. Frank was overprotective. Made it a little difficult for her to have any beaus."

"Was Wanamaker Jones there?"

He shook his head. "I'd seen him a lot during the party, though. Wanamaker was a restless sort, Jessica, one of those men who never seem to be able to sit still for any period of time, always in motion. I suppose that contributed to his slender build, burning up calories by constantly moving about."

"Did you like him?"

"Jones?"

"Yes."

"I—I never really thought about him," he offered, although I wasn't convinced he was telling the truth. "He was charming, of course," he went on smoothly. "No one without charm would ever have attracted Miss Tillie's attention. He was accepted by the others."

"Are you a member of the Forest City Gun Club?"

"Me? No. No time for that sort of thing."

"*Were* you ever a member of the club?"

"This is beginning to sound like an interrogation." He squirmed in his chair, his shoulders hunched.

"My apologies," I said, "but if I'm going to meet that deadline, I need more details about Wanamaker Jones and the people who knew him, socialized with him. You said you would help."

"Well, I knew him," he said. "Not well, but we ran in the same circles—or at least he ran in mine."

"How long had he been around?"

"That I can't remember. A year or two, maybe more. You're talking forty years ago, Jessica."

"Okay. What about Tillie?" I asked.

"What about her?"

I could see his shoulders relax a little.

"On that night, after the party, did she sit and join you, or was she too busy playing the hostess?"

Payne laughed a little. "Tillie Mortelaine and Wanamaker Jones were kindred souls, Jessica. She was as fidgety as he was."

"And slender."

"And slender. She was a little bitty thing. He was a head taller. The two of them seemed to be in perpetual motion at times, light on their feet, dancing their way through life. They cut quite a figure on the dance floor, you know."

"I didn't know. I never saw Tillie dance."

"Right up until the end. A few weeks before she died, she picked up again on ballroom dancing lessons at a studio in town."

I sat back and smiled at the inspiring vision of this ninety-one-year-old woman doing the fox trot or waltz.

"Ready to go upstairs for dinner?" Payne asked.

"Yes, but before we do, tell me something about Tillie's brother-in-law and sister-in-law. Now that I've met their children, Rose Margaret and Rocky, I'm curious about their parents. Rose and Rocky were the ones who discovered Wanamaker's body."

"That's right."

"I believe you indicated to me that the relationship between Tillie and her husband's family was less than cordial."

"Right again."

"So why were the parents and their children invited to the New Year's Eve party at Tillie's house? This was well after Tillie had become widowed. Did she remain in touch with her deceased husband's family despite the bad feelings that existed between them?"

"Tell you what, Jessica," he said, motioning for the bill. "Let's get upstairs before they give away the prime table I've reserved. I'll answer that question, and all the others I'm sure you have, over some good food and wine."

We ascended the concrete stairs and entered the historic building, where a young man greeted Payne warmly. The interior was surprisingly spare, even severe, with stiff-backed chairs and floors of bare Georgia pine. It reminded me of buildings I'd visited in Colonial Williamsburg.

We were led up a rickety, winding staircase to the second floor and into a small room.

"It's called the Office Room," Payne explained after we'd been seated by a window. "Has a lovely view of Reynolds Square, wouldn't you say?"

"Very nice," I agreed.

"We'll start with she-crab soup," he said.

"I was going to suggest that," I said. "I've always meant to try it when in the South but have never gotten around to it."

"More indigenous to South Carolina than Georgia," he said, "but we've adopted it nicely here in Savannah. I tend to believe that the Scots introduced it to the area back in the seventeen hundreds. They called it *partan bree*, crab and rice soup. Of course, being part Scottish might color my thinking. At any rate, hope you don't mind some history."

"I always enjoy history."

"A passion of mine. She-crab soup really gained popularity after the mayor of Charleston, South Carolina, a chap named Rhett, entertained William Howard Taft, our twenty-seventh president, at his home. Legend has it that Rhett wanted his cook to jazz up her she-crab for his distinguished guest, make it less pale, more colorful. This chef added crab roe, which imparted an orange color and enhanced flavor. They lace it with sherry here at Pink House. As good as I've ever tasted."

After we placed our order for the soup, and Payne ordered a bottle of his favorite wine, I again raised my question about why Tillie had invited her late husband's family members when she disliked them.

"Let's just say that Miss Tillie was a bit of an imp,

Jessica. She enjoyed stirring the pot and seeing what came of it. There was another reason why she kept in touch with them. She viewed them as enemies, and it was her belief that by keeping your enemies in sight, you can avoid being broadsided by them."

"I never realized that she was quite so manipulative," I said.

His raised eyebrows indicated surprise at my statement. "*I'm* surprised that *you're* surprised," he said, mirth in his voice, a twinkle in his eye. "After all, consider the reason you're here."

I had to laugh. He was right, of course. Only an incorrigible imp, as he labeled Tillie, could have come up with the scenario that had lured me to Savannah following her death. It occurred to me during dinner—roast duck with wild berry sauce and hoppin' John (black-eyed peas and rice) for me, crisp, scored flounder with apricot shallot sauce for him, and a shared Caesar salad—that this might all be a practical joke on the part of Tillie. Was she giggling from her grave at how I'd risen to the bait and was about to learn that the joke was on me? If so, I wouldn't be joining the laughter. What brought me back from this possibility was the fact that her fiancé, Wanamaker Jones, *had* been murdered in her house. That was no joke.

We changed the subject from murder to tales of Payne's life in Savannah, the changes he'd seen as a physician over the past fifty years. He was a charming storyteller with an easy way of speaking, not so much Southern as stemming from his personality. He was a delightful dinner companion, although I must admit that as we finished our entrées and debated having dessert, I found myself anxious to get back to Wanamaker Jones's death.

"When the children discovered Wanamaker's body," I said after he'd convinced me to share a trifle with him, "where were you?"

"In the parlor."

"Who else was with you at that moment?"

"I have a pretty good memory, Jessica, but not *that* good. I do know that Pastor Penny was there, fast asleep in the chair next to me and snoring loudly."

"Anyone else you can remember?" I asked.

"Let me see. Yes, Frank O'Neill had just entered the room. I believe Tillie was with him."

"Did they stay?"

"Only for a moment. Once we heard the children yelling, we all fled the room and went to the stairs."

"Did you go up right away?" I asked, hoping I wasn't pushing for details that he probably couldn't remember and thus becoming an annoyance.

"I did."

"Who went up with you?"

"Everyone, as I recall. No, I take that back. The children's parents remained at the foot of the stairs. I remember that quite vividly because I found it strange. When one's children call out in anguish, a parent usually charges to the rescue. Agreed?"

"Certainly."

"Well, they always were an odd lot."

"That would have been quite a crowd around the body in the upstairs hall," I said.

"Not really. We shooed the children downstairs right away. Frank ushered Charmelle into one of the bedrooms. She was hysterical and was making matters worse. Rollie was worried about the police and Miss Tillie's reputation. As soon as I knew there was nothing we could do, I got Pastor Penny to say a prayer over him."

"And Tillie. How was she? This was the man she was going to marry."

"Presumably. Miss Tillie was upset, of course, but she was in control. I think Rollie's concerns may have been hers as well."

The trifle, as with every other course, was wonderful, as was the rich, dark coffee.

"This has been a wonderful evening," I said after he'd paid the bill and we walked downstairs to the street.

"I enjoyed it, too, Jessica," he said. "I hope I was helpful. Forty years ago is a long time."

"Your recall is remarkable," I said. "I'm sure I could never do as well. I hope I can talk with you again about that night."

"Whenever you like."

"Mind one more question?"

"Of course not."

"Who do you think killed Wanamaker Jones?"

"I haven't the slightest idea," he replied. "Besides, even if I had a notion, I wouldn't want to step on your toes.

After all, Tillie expects *you* to solve the murder, not me. Come, I'll drive you back to Mortelaine House."

I found his comment to be strange, but didn't challenge him on it.

We pulled up in front of Tillie's house and Payne turned off the ignition. "Invite me in for a nightcap?" he said.

"Oh, I'm afraid not. Thank you for dinner, and for sharing what you know about the murder."

"May I give you a kiss good night?"

"A kiss—? No, but thank you again for the evening."

I left the car and walked to the front door. I turned and saw that he still sat in the car, looking at me. I waved, opened the door, and went inside.

This was a complication I didn't need.

Chapter Twelve

I was surprised to find Mrs. Goodall there when I entered the house.

"I've fallen behind in some of my chores," she said in response to my query, but her eyes seemed to avoid mine. "Thought I'd catch up. Did you have a good time?"

"Yes, very pleasant, thank you," I replied, wondering if something was wrong. She hadn't stayed late since my arrival.

The bandage on my knee caught her attention. "Now how in the world did that happen?" she asked.

"I tripped and fell," I said. "Clumsy me."

"I imagine a nice cup of hot tea would go a ways to soothing that knee," she suggested.

"You know," I said, "I believe you're right, but I don't want to interfere with your chores."

"I'm all but finished, Mrs. Fletcher. A cup of tea will suit me fine, too."

I settled at the kitchen table and we chatted.

"Did you have a good meal at the Olde Pink House?" she asked.

"Excellent. I had my first taste of she-crab soup."

"Never cared much for it, although I fix it for guests sometime," she commented as she placed two cups of steaming tea on the table and joined me.

"Dr. Payne is an interesting gentleman," I said, and sipped. His suggestion that we kiss good night had stayed very much with me. Was he married? Widowed? Divorced? Had he ever married?

I asked.

"Oh, I don't think so," she replied. "At least not that I know. To be honest, he was smitten with Miss Tillie."

I suppose my expression reflected my surprise. "He was quite a bit younger than she," I said.

"Would make no difference with Miss Tillie," was the housekeeper's response. "Lots of younger men took a fancy to her." She scowled. "Looking for her money is the way I see it—like General Pettigrew."

"The general said he proposed to her and she accepted. Did she tell you that?"

"I should hope she'd know better than that. He's just a loafer, that one. Hangs around all day, doing nothing."

"Was Wanamaker Jones the same, also after her money?"

"Now, I don't know about that Mr. Jones. Maybe he

was different, but he was years younger than her, could have been her son."

"I didn't realize that," I said, mentally filing that information away for later. "You say Dr. Payne was romantically interested in her. Did they ever have a relationship of that sort?"

"If they did, they kept it a secret from everyone." Her face softened as she reflected on a pleasant memory. "If I'd had my say," she said, "I'd have voted for Dr. Payne over Mr. Jones. But you can't never vote on such things, can you?"

"No, you can't. Why do you feel that way?"

"Because he's a good and decent man. I don't remember much of the night Mr. Jones got hisself shot to death, but I do remember how Dr. Payne comforted Miss Tillie. My goodness, poor thing, she was about to have a heart attack right on the spot. But Dr. Payne took her aside after the policemen were done and Mr. Jones's body had been taken away and calmed her right nice. She always listened to him, him being a medical man and all. She once told me that he was the smartest man she'd ever known—and she'd known a few in her lifetime, believe me."

"As you say, a fine man. Where were you when the children discovered Mr. Jones's body?" I asked.

"Oh, that I remember like it was yesterday. I was in the kitchen cleaning up. I had me a staff for that night."

"Including your future husband?"

"How'd you know about that?"

Had I said something I shouldn't? "I believe Melanie mentioned it to me."

"That one lets her mouth overload her tail, Mrs. Fletcher. But it's true. Andrew, he was a skilled carpenter—he did a lot of the fine work in this house—but he wasn't too big in his boots to turn me down when I needed extras to serve at the party. A good man, he was, loved to read. Melanie, she favors him. He was right there alongside me in the kitchen when the little ones started yelling and crying upstairs. Sends a chill up my spine just thinkin' about it."

"It must have been a traumatic night for everyone involved."

"Yes, ma'am. It was that. But like I said, when Dr. Payne whisked Miss Tillie away to where they could be alone, things got better, at least for her. She come out of that room all calmed down and more like her usual self."

"We always need a calming influence when bad things happen to us," I offered.

"It was a bad night, all right. The police, they questioned Andrew for hours, the other help, too. Looked like they was trying to pin the killing on a black man. But they didn't even know the man. I was the only one knew him."

"Did the police question you?"

"Yes, ma'am, but they didn't keep me long. There was a black officer and he wouldn't let them put the pressure on. And Miss Tillie, she flew into a rage when they took me off. Must have had the judge call someone. They let me go pretty quick. I was real glad to get back to my kitchen. There was still a mess left from the party and the policemen had turned everythin' upside down looking for the gun."

"But they never found it."

"Never did."

"Was Wanamaker Jones living here at the time?" I asked.

"He was a guest that night, but mostly not. Miss Tillie, she was careful of her reputation in that regard."

"Did Tillie keep a gun in the house?"

She shook her head. "I would have seen it if she had. The judge, he tried to give her one for protection," she said with a chuckle, "but she said she might shoot him on purpose if she had a gun in her hand."

"Why would she say that?"

"They was always arguing over Miss O'Neill. Miss Tillie, she thought he was keeping his sister down, not letting her get out in the world. 'Overbearing,' that's what she used to call him," she said as she took our cups to the sink. "Still the case," I heard her mutter.

"By the way, have you heard any news about Charmelle? Is she any better?"

She gave a soft snort from where she rinsed the cups. "Hard to know," she said. "Since Miss O'Neill fell and hit her head, she stays mostly to home. That brother of hers sees to that."

I walked over to the sink to ask, "Did you ever visit her after her accident?"

"Wasn't allowed to."

"What do you mean?"

"The judge, he's a powerful big shot here in Savannah, goin' to be grand marshal tomorrow for the parade."

"My goodness!" I said. "I'd forgotten about the Saint Patrick's Day parade. I gather that the judge is very protective of his sister."

"Keeps her under his thumb like she was in some sorta prison."

"Why? I would think that having visitors could be therapeutic for her."

"Can't say why he does a thing, Mrs. Fletcher. I just know enough not to cross the man." Mrs. Goodall dried her hands on a towel and turned to face me.

"The tea was delicious," I said. "Just what I needed. And thank you for talking to me about the night of the murder. I hope I haven't interrupted your plans for the evening."

"Mrs. Fletcher," she said, then hesitated.

"Is something wrong, Mrs. Goodall?"

"Not exactly, but we been getting a coupla calls since that piece 'bout you was in the paper. Not nice calls."

"Ahh," I said, understanding immediately. That article was starting to shake the nuts out of the trees, as Detective Buchwalter had predicted. "I'm sorry if you were inconvenienced."

"No trouble to me," she said, "but there were some threats. 'Yankee go home,' that sort of thing. You need to be careful while you're here. Some folks don't take to someone from up north interferin' in their business."

"Did you get any names?"

"People like that don't leave their names. They just say something ugly and hang up." She shuddered.

"I'm so sorry you had to listen to that."

"No need to apologize. I've heard worse. Just worry about you, that's all. Wanted to let you know to be on the watch. The world isn't always a nice place." She shook her head.

"I appreciate your staying late to tell me," I said. "I promise I'll be careful."

She smiled.

I had other questions to ask, but they would wait for another time.

"Now, you be sure and lock up once I'm gone," she said. "Check the front door, too."

"I will," I said.

"If you go in the study, watch out for those buckets we set for the drips. Hope that darn leak don't get worse," she muttered as she scooped up her oversized purse from where she'd left it on a battered church pew next to the door. "Can't get the plumber to come back till all the Saint Patrick's Day silliness is over. Hope it don't get worse before he does. Good night, Mrs. Fletcher. You sleep tight."

Chapter Thirteen

I wish I could have accommodated Mrs. Goodall, but I spent the night tossing and turning, more awake than asleep, my eyes constantly going to the bedside clock, which seemed to be operating in extreme slow motion. 12:35. After what seemed an hour, it read 12:40. And so it went for most of the night.

There were more people at breakfast than on previous mornings. The usual group—the Grogans and General Pettigrew—had been augmented by Tillie's niece and nephew, Rose Margaret Kendall and her brother, Roy Richard "Rocky" Kendall. I issued a pleasant good morning, but the only person to reply was Artie Grogan. Nevertheless, I was pleased that Rose and Rocky were present. I'd left messages for them and hoped they had come to talk with me.

It was after I'd gotten a bowl of fruit and an English muffin from the sideboard and retaken my seat that I learned I'd been mistaken.

"Making any progress in solving a forty-year-old murder?" Pettigrew said sarcastically.

"Not yet," I replied. "But perhaps I'll get some help this morning." I smiled in the direction of Rose and Rocky, but they were busy eating.

The general guffawed. "Silliest damn thing I've ever heard," he said. "Miss Tillie must have been out of her mind when she came up with *that*. It's a shame you two have been made a victim of her whim." He nodded at the sister and brother. "But I'm sure she'll do right by you eventually. Are you planning to live here?"

Rose looked around the dining room. "Oh, I don't think so. This place is so—I don't know—old-fashioned."

"What I don't understand," Rocky burst out, "is what that murder has to do with the disposition of this house. It should be a simple matter of passing it on to Aunt Tillie's remaining relatives—namely us." He looked to his sister, and they both glared at me.

"What happens to this house is really no concern of mine," I said. "I'm here because Tillie Mortelaine created a situation in her last will and testament that calls for my being here."

"Well, you allowed yourself to be drawn into this mess," Rose said to me. "If you hadn't agreed to going on this fool's errand, we'd already know who she left the house to and none of us would have to sit around on pins and needles."

I was surprised when Samantha came to my defense. "She's trying to save the donation for the literacy center," she said. "You've already received a lot of money from Miss Tillie, and you stand to get more. I'd be more patient if I were you. Attacking Mrs. Fletcher just makes you look greedy."

Rocky gave out with a hoot. "Do go on! Look who's talking about greedy," he said. "You must be thinking of yourself. What are you doing piddling around here? Miss Tillie didn't leave one penny to you. And nothing Mrs. Fletcher comes up with will change that."

"We are here under legitimate circumstances," Artie said sternly. "We are conducting a scientific research project, and Miss Tillie was our sponsor. In fact—"

"Sponsor, my eye," the general growled. "You were here for her amusement only."

"You want to talk about amusement?" Samantha said. "I never heard Miss Tillie refer to you as her fiancé as you claim to have been. Perhaps amusement is the function you provided."

"Ladies and gentlemen," I said, "there really is no need for this type of unpleasantness."

Rocky dabbed at his mouth with his napkin and stood. "Excuse us. Rose and I have an appointment with a reporter from the newspaper."

"Mrs. Fletcher isn't the only person with a stake in this circus," Rose said, also rising. "The reporter who wrote about her wants to interview Rocky and me to get our views."

"Why would anyone be interested in your views?" Samantha asked, looking pleased with herself that she'd gotten in a jab.

"Because they represent common sense and decency," Rocky snapped, and led his sister from the room.

"Please wait!" I called after them. I could see my own interview of the pair disappearing and got up to go after Rose and Rocky. But Samantha grabbed my arm. "They're irrelevant," she said. "Arthur and I have something extremely important to report."

"This better be good," Pettigrew said.

I sat down again, and the general and I waited for her announcement.

Samantha held up her hand until she heard the front door close behind Tillie's niece and nephew. "We saw Wanamaker Jones last night," she whispered.

There was silence at the table. I broke it. "I'm not sure I understand," I said.

"We saw Wanamaker Jones," Artie Grogan said, sounding gleeful. "He was here in the house, upstairs, right where he was shot."

"Yeah, right! One of your fantasies, I'm sure," Pettigrew said.

"I'd like to hear more," I said.

Artie gave Pettigrew a satisfied look.

"It happened at precisely midnight," Samantha said. "Artie and I had sensed a powerful aura in the house for the past two days and felt we might be able to identify and document it."

"I was in my bedroom at midnight," I said, "right off the second floor landing. I didn't hear anything. And I was wide-awake." I left out that I was having difficulty sleeping. I didn't want to give the general any more fodder for his nasty comments.

"Of course you didn't hear anything, Mrs. Fletcher," Artie said smugly, taking a small notebook from his pocket. "When confronting a ghostly presence like Mr. Jones, one must tread softly so as to not alert the spirit to *our* presence."

"Go on," I said, wishing Pettigrew would stop grimacing and rolling his eyes. I might not have bought into their claim, but I wanted to hear what they had to say, every bit of it.

"We positioned ourselves at the end of the hallway with our portable EMF meter—that's the smaller one—and our custom infrared digital camera," Artie said.

"What time was that?" I asked.

Artie flipped through several pages in his notebook. "We arrived at eleven thirty-one—we always keep precise notes as to time and place—and waited."

His wife picked up the narrative. "Everything was calm and normal," she said, "until a few minutes before midnight. That was when cold air suddenly came rushing down the hallway, absolutely frigid. And then there was this faint orb of light, glowing and growing brighter."

"And?" I said.

"And there he was, all bloodied and obviously very unhappy."

"Angry is a more apt description," her husband chimed in. "His face was set in this vengeful expression, as though he was ready to attack."

"Attack *us*," Samantha added.

"What happened next?" I asked.

"He looked to me as though he was searching for something," Samantha said. "He seemed desperate. Then, he was gone as quickly as he'd appeared. Vanished. Of course, that's not unusual. Spirits, especially those who met their death in a particularly brutal way, seldom stay for more than a few seconds."

"But," Artie said proudly and loudly, "he remained long enough for me to grab this." He reached down into a backpack resting next to him on the floor and came up with a camera.

Now Pettigrew's blatant dismissal of their tale changed to interest. He leaned forward and said, "You have his picture?"

The general and I left our places and came around behind Artie. He turned on the camera, and the screen on the camera's back came to life. Pettigrew and I leaned in as close as possible to see what the image contained.

"It's all a bunch of shadows," Pettigrew said.

"No, it's not," Artie said. "Look closer. See that streak of light running vertically down the center of the screen?"

"I see it," I said. "What is it?"

"Wanamaker Jones," Samantha proclaimed.

"Looks like nothing but some kind of light to me," Pettigrew grunted.

"Spirits emit an aura of light, never their whole being," Artie said by way of explanation. "It's very rare to see features or details in a camera image. It has happened, of course—there's a picture of the ghost of a monk standing in a church balcony, and others—but it's very rare. However, you can make out the shape of his head, here." He pointed to a blob of gray. "And here are his legs."

Samantha sat back with a sigh. "We think now that he's let us photograph him once, we may be able to capture more the next time."

"Rubbish, pure rubbish," said Pettigrew, walking out of the room.

"I detest that man," Samantha said.

"This is going to save us a lot of time," Artie said, patting his wife's hand.

"Why's that?" I asked.

"With this one, and if we get another good image in the next day or so, we may be able to do our report on Mortelaine House without having to study all the other photos we've made."

"We must have hundreds of hours documented," Samantha said. "We expected to spend all spring and summer analyzing the film."

Artie started to return the camera to his backpack.

"May I see it again?" I asked.

He handed the camera to me, and I examined the image more closely. I saw what I'd thought I'd seen on the first pass. A unique piece of Victorian furniture in the upstairs hallway was discernible in the picture. There was no doubt that Artie had taken the photograph where he said he had. What had caused the streak of light to appear at that moment? I wondered. It obviously hadn't originated from any lighting fixture in the hallway. Had they artificially created it? If so, I was at a loss as to how. It wasn't light as we know it. It was a gray light, fuzzy and ethereal.

"Thank you," I said, handing back the camera.

"At least you're open-minded," Artie said.

"I try to be," I said. "Thank you for showing it to me. It's interesting." I thought of Dr. Payne's comment about terming something "interesting," and had to smile as I excused myself and headed for my room.

I paused on the second-floor landing near the piece of furniture seen in the Grogans' photo and looked around the area, paying special attention to lighting fixtures. As far as I could see, none of them—wall sconces and two table lamps—would have cast the quality of light seen in the photo.

Amazing that I didn't hear them, I thought. Age had certainly affected my eyesight; I've needed reading glasses for several years. But my hearing has always been acute. That Artie and Samantha could enter the house, creep up the stairs, and take photographs without my sensing their presence or detecting any sound to indicate that someone was in the hallway outside my room—well, that was more disturbing to me than the idea of a ghost haunting Mortelaine House.

Perhaps it was disappointment in my failing senses that made me listen harder, but my ears picked up a noise

I hadn't heard before. It came from behind the wall between my bedroom and the next one. I pressed my ear to
the striped wallpaper. Running water? I hadn't noticed
that previously. I opened the door of the other room
and peeked in. There wasn't a bathroom or even a closet.
Could it be that someone had turned on a sink or flushed
a toilet downstairs, and I was hearing the echo of it upstairs? I waited to hear if the water stopped. But it didn't.
And it didn't sound as if it were coming from far away. It
was quite close. Obviously, something was wrong behind
the wall. Perhaps a pipe had developed a pinhole leak. Or
maybe the solder where two pipes were joined together
had cracked. Could this be the cause of the wetness downstairs beneath where I stood? It was a good possibility. I
hoped it wouldn't get any worse before the plumber could
return on Monday morning and find and repair the problem. I vowed to alert Mrs. Goodall to this new symptom
when I saw her next.

Melanie had admonished me to get to the parade route
early in order to secure a decent vantage point. Given what
she'd said, it was probably already too late to accomplish
that, but I decided to make for the west side of town anyway. I had a lunch date with Wanamaker Jones's nephew
and his parents at the City Market and hoped that learn-
ing more about Tillie's fiancé from them would help fill in
some of the puzzle pieces.

    I stepped outside and looked up. The parade sponsors
were fortunate; the sky was cobalt blue, with only a few

streaks of white to mar its beauty. It was cool and breezy. I breathed deeply and set off at a brisk pace. I needed a good walk to dissipate the cobwebs in my brain from a fitful night's sleep.

I didn't get very far. I stopped in front of the hotel that had been erected next door to Tillie's mansion and admired the lovely gardens decorating its facade. The hotel appeared to be a series of ocher-colored stucco Savannah houses, no more than four stories high, joined together to form one long building. All the classic details were there— tall, multipaned windows with sunburst pediments and dark green shutters, wrought-iron balconies painted to match, and at the entrance, a broad concrete staircase with huge pots of flowers—all green and white for the occasion—set on either side of the landing and flanking double doors with leaded-glass inserts.

I decided to go inside to see if the interior was as impressive as the exterior. At the reading of the will, Rose and Rocky had let slip the fact that the hotel had already contacted them regarding Tillie's house. Would the hotel's owners want to buy it only to annex it and extend the hotel's size? While I'm certainly not against progress, too often commercial interests trump historical considerations, and I hoped that the hotel's intentions to expand wouldn't include Tillie's fine old house. Besides, the hotel already looked big enough to me. I had to admit that whoever designed it had tried to make it blend in with the primarily residential neighborhood. Of course, in the historic district, there were quite a few hotels of modern vintage constructed to emulate their antique neighbors.

The lobby was nicely decorated and inviting. A fountain provided rippling background sound, and large, colorful, modern paintings on the walls to either side of the reception desk added to the overall ambience. To the right were a concierge's desk and the bell captain's station. To the left was an entrance to a restaurant. I went to the door and perused the menu posted next to a podium. The entrées it listed were simple, with a few typical Southern specialties offered as well. Dinner there might provide a welcome respite from the heavy meals I'd been enjoying. I stepped inside and looked around. A few of the booths were occupied, as were some tables. If I decided to grab a quick bite away from the house during my stay, I would certainly give it a try.

As I admired the graceful decor, a booth in a far corner of the not very large room caught my attention. Seated at it were two men in dark suits, one who looked to be in his thirties, the other middle-aged. With them was General James J. Pettigrew. A bellman holding a silver tray spoke to the younger man, who immediately rose, said something to his colleagues, and headed for the door. I turned my back to the table so as not to be recognized by the general. The younger man walked quickly past me, excusing himself as he did so, and I followed him out of the restaurant. Lingering in the lobby, I saw him confer with one of the clerks at the reception desk. She handed him a clipboard, which he glanced at, then wrote something on it, handed the clipboard back to her, and returned to the restaurant.

I went to the reception desk. "That gentleman you just spoke with," I said. "I think I know him."

"You probably do if you've stayed with us before, ma'am," she replied through a wide smile and in a heavy Southern accent. "He's Mr. Dailey, our general manager and one of the hotel's owners. Is there anything I can help you with? Did you need to speak with Mr. Dailey? I can call him back."

"Oh, no, thank you. I wouldn't want to disturb him again. Would you happen to know the other gentlemen he's dining with? One of them looks familiar, too."

"I don't," she said, looking truly sorry that she couldn't answer my question.

I thanked her and had turned to leave when she called me back.

"I did see Mr. Dailey this morning talking to our real estate consultant, Mr. Pettigrew. Perhaps that's the man you recognized."

"Yes, that's probably who it is. Real estate consultant, you said?"

"I believe he's the one in charge of the expansion plans."

I thanked her again and stepped outside, taking a deep breath of the cool refreshing air. It looked as if Tillie's "fiancé" had ulterior motives behind his courtship of her. I fervently hoped she hadn't been fooled by the general. I hoped she'd seen through any wiles he may have practiced on her and hadn't fallen for a line of sweet talk. But most of all I hoped that the sealed envelope in Mr. Richardson's possession didn't give General Pettigrew the right to annex Tillie's family home and make it part of a hotel.

Chapter Fourteen

Melanie had provided me with a map of the parade route, and I was going to have to cross it twice in order to reach the west side of the city, where I was to meet the Joneses. The alternative was to walk uptown twenty or more blocks to the far end of Forsyth Park, continue west several blocks, and then find my way back downtown an equal distance. If I took that course, I would definitely be late for my appointment. Crossing Abercorn Street, where the parade would start, would be my first challenge.

Two blocks away, I heard drums and the roar of approval from the crowd as it spotted the first of the parade vehicles. I hurried forward, trying to skirt throngs of people as they ambled along waving Irish and American flags. There were many parents pushing children in strollers bedecked with green ribbons—one baby was sucking on a bottle of green milk. Everyone was arrayed in green. They were either clad in green clothes, carried green balloons, had ropes of green beads around their necks, or wore green hats. Some had shamrocks painted on their cheeks. A few had dyed their hair green or covered their heads with green wigs. Houses sported green bows on their door knockers. Green ribbon was twined around railings and hung from the trees. It looked as if a paint store had exploded and covered everyone nearby in bright kelly green.

I looked down at my outfit. I'd worn a black woolen pantsuit—it was still chilly in mid-March—and I'd paired it with a pale blue shirt, but my scarf was green and blue, and I'd pinned a silver shamrock on my lapel. I hoped that would pass muster with the Irish celebrants. I could claim appropriate ancestry after all; my mother was born in Ireland.

A man in a soiled, once-white robe and holding a sign that read THE END IS NEAR stepped in front of me. "The end is near, sister," he intoned, shaking the long wooden pole to which the sign had been affixed. "Are you ready to meet your Maker?"

"Excuse me," I said, trying to dodge around him.

He matched my moves, preventing me from passing, and shouted, "Ladies and gentlemen, the end is near. The world is about to explode. You are all sinners." He waved one arm in a wide arc, then shoved his face into mine. "All sinners must repent. I repeat: Sister! Are you ready to meet your Maker?"

"Not at the moment," I muttered, growing irritated as he continued to block my way. A small crowd had started to surround us, laughing, pointing, and jeering at the man. I looked around in distress.

"Sinners! Laugh if you will, but you are all going to spend eternity in flames," he screamed, pounding the pole on the ground.

A man in a KISS ME, I'M IRISH T-shirt, walking by with his girlfriend, grabbed the sign holder by the shoulder and pushed him aside. "Get out of the way. I'm trying to get to the parade."

"Brother, you are going to burn for your sins."

"Maybe so, but I'll see the parade first," the man replied.

"If you'll excuse me," I said, squeezing around the two. The man in the T-shirt had drawn attention away from me; for that he deserved to be kissed, Irish or not. Instead, I pushed through the circle of spectators, only to find myself staring at the backs of more people inching their way toward Abercorn.

I stepped off the sidewalk into the street, where the throng was slightly less thick, and wove my way in and out until I reached the intersection. The first marchers were passing by, a color guard with green (of course) uniformed soldiers holding an American flag, an Irish flag, and the state flag of Georgia. A young woman wearing bright red lipstick broke from the crowd, ran up to one of the flag holders, and gave him a big kiss, leaving a red mark only a little more vivid than the blush staining the soldier's cheek. She returned to the sidelines, laughing and raising her fist in victory, then pulled a tube of lipstick from her pocket and refreshed the color on her lips. As more soldiers passed by, I noticed quite a few young men bearing red kiss marks—a Savannah parade tradition, I would later learn.

Following the soldiers was a group of dignitaries walking behind two Girl Scouts holding a banner, and behind them an open car in which sat the grand marshal and two attendants. All three men were wearing dark green blazers with kelly green sashes fringed in gold and medals hanging from green, white, and orange ribbons. I recognized Judge Frank O'Neill immediately. He sat in the middle and waved to the people on both sides of the street, and they responded with polite applause. Many of them, I was sure, had no idea who he was.

If memory serves, grand marshals usually walk in the parade that is honoring them. But Judge O'Neill's age and infirmity made that impossible. I admired the parade organizers for their sensitivity in allowing their honoree to ride. Of course, he could have been pushed in his wheelchair while others walked, but my guess was that Frank O'Neill wouldn't want the public to see him as anything other than the vigorous jurist who had served his jurisdiction for more than forty years. He would have seen the wheelchair as a sign of weakness.

A drum corps followed the grand marshal's car, and then came a series of open cars bearing former parade grand marshals. A flower-covered float featured three beautiful young ladies, Miss Saint Patrick's Day and her two runners-up. A group of men in kilts played bagpipes, the shrill sound of their instruments drowning the noise of the vendors loudly hawking their wares and the hordes of cheering people.

I peered up Abercorn, trying to spot a break in the parade where I could sprint across the street, my fingers crossed that the police didn't give me a ticket or arrest me on the spot. It didn't look as if there would be a gap for quite a while. Another group of flag bearers neared my location; behind them came a bugle and drum corps and after that a group carrying a banner from the Hibernian Society. The flags were carried by four people on horseback. There were two palominos, followed by a pair of white horses whose hides had been dyed for the holiday. I shook my head, grinning at the silliness. Were the green horses proud of their colorful coats or did they consider it, as I did, an indignity? I wondered what the other horses in the stable thought of their now green companions. Was there snickering among their equine neighbors? Jealousy over the attention? Or were horses color-blind? Could they recognize a change in color on themselves or on others? Would it matter if they did? I'd have to look it up. One of the things I like best about being a writer is the opportunity to research all manner of strange, wonderful, and even ridiculous questions.

The horses were almost at my side when people in the crowd pressed forward, knocking against me, throwing me off balance. Angry voices were raised.

"Hey, cut that out."

"I was here first."

"Who do you think you are?"

Events transpired so quickly, I couldn't prepare for what happened next. I felt two strong hands shove me from behind. I fell forward into the flank of one of the palominos, which whinnied and sidestepped away from me. I tumbled to the pavement, stunned. A sharp pain pierced my consciousness. My already injured knee had taken yet another blow. I twisted onto my hip to ease the discomfort, only to see the startled green horse rear up, its frightened neigh louder than the notes from bugles in the band. I looked up. Its two front hooves were flailing in the air, right over my head. I cringed, shut my eyes, and put my arm up to shield my face from the iron-shod feet that would certainly crack my skull when they made contact. Later, I would be told that the rider, a woman of uncommon skill, pulled the reins sharply to the left and managed to keep control of both the flag and her green horse, which staggered back two steps and twirled to the left before dropping down onto all four legs.

As the horses nervously danced away from my crumpled form, hands came under my arms and knees, scooping me up and pulling me back into the crowd on the sidewalk.

"Are you all right?"

"Who did that?"

"Stop pushing. Didn't you see what can happen?"

"She's okay."

A woman retrieved my bag, which had flown from my shoulder when I fell. I hope I thanked her. I was dizzy with the pain in my knee. Was it an accident? I wasn't sure. Someone pushed me. I knew that. Was it inadvertent, a result of the jostling mob? Or was it intentional?

"Jessica! Jessica! Are you all right?" Dr. Warner Payne's face swam in front of mine.

I shook my head to clear the cobwebs, and realized I was sitting on the curb. Warner helped me to my feet, and I brushed off the seat of my pants, trying not to look as humiliated as I felt.

"Take it easy with that knee," he said, offering me his arm to lean on. "We should find a place for you to rest. Can I get you a drink of water? That could have been a nasty accident."

"How?" I started to say, then stopped. "I don't understand. How did you know I was here?"

Warner stabbed his fingers through his hair, leaving it standing on end. That was a familiar gesture to me by now. "I was walking in the parade with the Hibernians," he said. "We were right behind the drum and bugle corps. I saw it all happen as if in slow motion. Of course, I would have helped out right away if there had been an injury. But there didn't appear to be one. And then I realized it was you and I came rushing over."

I don't know why I doubted his story. He had on the same dark green sports jacket that so many of the participants were wearing. Even so, I would have thought that I could pick him out of the crowd. He had that distinctive shock of white hair. How could I not have noticed him with the marchers? I knew what he looked like. We'd had dinner together only last night.

It would have been rude to turn to some of those around me to confirm what he'd said, to ask them if they'd seen him walking in the parade or if, in truth, he was hanging back, hiding in the crowd behind me, waiting for the perfect opportunity, the exact moment to thrust me in front of the horses, knowing that I could be gravely injured—or worse.

But why would he have any reason to put me in danger? I asked myself. *What motive could he possibly have? He was flirting with me last night. He wanted to kiss me. Didn't that indicate that he had some kindly feelings toward me? Could I have misjudged him so badly?*

"Jessica, did you hit your head when you fell? You seem a little disoriented."

His voice was filled with concern, and I felt ashamed that I had doubted his account of how he'd found me. "It's the pain," I said, grimacing. My knee was throbbing.

"You must have reinjured the joint when you fell. Would you like me to take a look at it?"

"Certainly not here," I said, forcing a smile.

"What were you doing standing with the spectators anyway?" he scolded. "Rollie told me he offered you a perfect view of the parade from a comfortable chair in his office."

"He did," I said, thinking that if I'd wanted to watch the parade, sitting in front of the picture window in

Attorney Richardson's office was certainly preferable to fighting for a space on the parade route along with thousands of others. I explained that I'd considered walking all the way around the parade, but it was too far, and that I was simply trying to find an opportunity to cross the street. "I have an appointment at the City Market." I looked at my watch. "I'm afraid I'm going to be late."

"There is such a thing as taxicabs in this town," he said gently. "And with your bad knee, that would have been a wise decision."

"I'm embarrassed to say it didn't occur to me," I said.

"If you're okay walking, I'll show you how to get across Abercorn now."

"I'll be in your debt," I said, gingerly placing my weight on the injured knee.

Warner hailed one of the vendors, peeled off a few bills from a roll in his pocket, and shortly presented me with a beautiful shillelagh. I would have rejected a cane, but the gnarled stick was right in keeping with the festivities, and I gratefully leaned on it. Warner waited until a group of marchers bearing a banner from the Shenanigans Society came in sight. When they drew abreast of us, he stepped into the parade with me on his arm. Nodding and smiling at other marchers, he maneuvered so that we took an angled path starting from one side of Abercorn, arriving a block later at the other. At the next intersection, he waved to his colleagues and deftly guided me out of the parade, past a police barrier, and onto the street heading west.

"Now why didn't I think of that?" I said. "I was worried the police would give me a ticket if I tried to cross."

"And they would have," he said. "The trick is to look as if you're one of the marchers and leave the parade the way you would a bus when you reach your destination."

I laughed. "You're a devious fellow."

"I've been called worse," he said.

We found a hotel on the next corner, arriving just as a cabbie pulled up to deposit his passenger. Warner held the door for me and gave the driver my destination. "Put up your foot when you get back to the house and have Mrs. Goodall give you an ice pack. It should help."

"I will," I said, and thanked him.

"And please call me if you need anything for the pain." He blew me a kiss as the cab pulled away from the curb.

I sat back against the leather upholstery and ran my hand over the knobby wood of the shillelagh. A line from a Gilbert and Sullivan operetta floated into my mind. "Things are seldom what they seem. Skimmed milk masquerades as cream." I hummed the refrain. "Very true, so they do."

Chapter Fifteen

The African American driver wore a green straw hat. He dropped me in front of the City Market and wished me a good day, which I returned. The famed historic market once was just that, a place to which, more than two centuries ago, farmers and fishermen hauled their produce and brought in the day's catch to sell to the city's residents. At the time, the market was the commercial and social center of life in eighteenth-century Savannah. Today, the popular destination draws tourists and natives alike to the art galleries, boutiques, and restaurants that crowd either side of a pedestrian walkway. I walked with difficulty down the center of the market, leaning on the shillelagh Warner Payne had given me and trying not to trip over all the youngsters around me. A Dixieland band was playing down the street and several children were dancing, their parents clapping hands in time to the music. Other children licked big green puffs of cotton candy. Still others chased each other around the easels set up outside by artists who were making charcoal sketches or pastel portraits of Saint Patrick's Day visitors.

I'd visited the market on previous trips to Savannah but had never eaten at the café. A long line snaked out the door into the public space. I limped around the waiting diners and pressed my way into the restaurant. The young man greeting me looked at his watch and said, "It'll be about forty-five minutes till I can seat you. Want me to put you down for lunch for one?"

"No, I'm meeting some people," I said. "I believe Mr. Jones made a reservation."

He consulted his reservation list. "Your party is already here."

Joseph Jones, Wanamaker Jones's nephew, was at one of the tables in the lovely outdoor section framed by a green hedge. Sitting with him was an elderly couple who, I presumed, were his parents. The alfresco location was the perfect place to watch the city's enthusiasm for its Irish heritage played out in the costumes and makeup of the people who'd dressed up for the occasion. Those who had chosen not to brave the throngs along the parade route still gave a nod to the holiday by wearing something to indicate they were in tune with the festivities. But I was more interested in what Joseph Jones's parents had to say than in the expressions of Hibernian allegiance that Savannah had on display. Fortunately, although there was much animated conversation around me, it was easy to hear Joseph Jones, who stood as I approached on my game leg and extended his hand. "So glad you could make it," he said, "but what happened to you?"

I took a seat and forced a laugh. "Wrong place at the wrong time," I said.

He introduced me to his mother and father, John and Mabel Jones. John was of medium height and trim in build, a handsome man who was not without a measure of vanity—the orange tint in his curls was probably a result of hair dye. His angular face was pleasant, his smile quick and natural. His green eyes belonged to a man who missed little. His wife, Mabel, appeared to me to be a high-energy woman—not unlike myself—and as lunch progressed, her mentions of the activities in which she was involved confirmed it.

"Your brother had an unusual name," I said to the father.

He grinned. "Yeah, but Wanamaker wasn't his given name."

"So I understand," I said. I turned to Joseph, who hadn't said anything after the introductions. "Are you named for your uncle? I understand his real name was Joseph."

His mother answered. "That's right. We named him after John's brother, although I admit I wasn't for it."

Her husband laughed as he said, "She and my brother, Joe, didn't always get along. He was sort of a wild type, always getting into some scrape or other."

"Fights?" I asked.

"No. Joe was a lover, not a fighter, as the saying goes. But he often seemed to get involved with the wrong type—gamblers, con men, people like that. Still, he could usually charm his way out of trouble. There weren't too many times I had to bail him out of a mess."

Mabel raised her eyes and slowly shook her head.

"How did he come up with the name Wanamaker?" I asked.

John shrugged. "It was memorable, and different enough to please him, I suppose. He always needed to be different from other people."

"That was important to him?" I asked. "Being different from others?"

"Oh, yes," John Jones said. "Joe could never stand conformity or routine. That's why he left home when he did and lived his way."

"What way was that?" I asked.

The answer was interrupted by a waitress seeking our order. We quickly took up our menus and scanned the list of dishes offered. Joseph opted for the New Orleans–style fried oyster poor boy, and we all fell in line except for Mabel, who preferred a grilled cheese sandwich with artichoke hearts. John ordered a beer; the rest of us chose Hank's Philadelphia Root Beer.

"You were saying, Jessica?" Mabel said.

"I was asking how Wanamaker Jones lived his life. You see, I'm here in Savannah to—"

"Oh, we know why you're here, dear," she said. "It was in the papers."

"And Joseph has told us all about it, too," John said. He snorted. "That Miss Tillie was some character. Doesn't surprise me at all that she included something like this in her will."

Joseph said, "She must've been a good match for Uncle Joe, or rather Uncle Wanamaker, although I don't think of him with that name."

"Because they were both different?" I asked.

He nodded. "I liked his style. I was only a little kid when he died, but I remember hearing the stories about his adventures. He'd come to visit driving the biggest car in the world, always sharply dressed, and loaded with gifts." He turned to his mother. "Remember, Mom?"

"I certainly do. He did have style. I'll give him that."

Our lunch was served and our conversation was put on hold as eating took center stage. The poor boy was delicious, a spicy Creole mayonnaise adding zest to the sandwich.

"Where were you and your brother brought up?" I asked John.

"We bounced around a little. Our dad was in the oil business, a pipeline worker, so we moved to where the jobs were. We were living in Oklahoma when Joe left home. He was eighteen."

"And did you leave, too?"

"I was more of a homebody. I got a scholarship to a little college in Tulsa and put in four years there, graduated with a degree in business. I've been sort of a glorified bookkeeper ever since."

His wife scolded him. "Don't say that, John. You've done very well."

"My biggest fan," he said, patting her hand on the table.

"As it should be," I said. My knee ached, and I quietly rubbed my fingertips over it beneath the table.

"Here we are talking about ourselves," Mabel said, "and you're a famous writer. We should be listening to you."

"Actually," I said, "I wanted to meet you because you knew the true Wanamaker Jones. I need your help. I'm determined to carry out Tillie Mortelaine's wishes in her will and find out who killed your brother-in-law, Mabel."

She fiddled with the food on her plate, then raised her eyes to mine. "We'd all like that to happen, too," she said, her voice soft. "A murder. It's such a lowering thing. Joe could be irresponsible—lots of times he disappointed us. He was always broke, couldn't hold on to a penny for more than a few minutes, but when he had money, he was the most generous man around. I can't see why someone would want to kill him."

Her husband laughed. "You wanted to kill him plenty of times yourself," he said.

"Did you know Tillie Mortelaine?" I asked.

"Not at the time," John replied. "We didn't even know Joe was in Savannah until we learned that he'd been shot. Last time he'd gotten in touch with us, he'd been up in New England, romancing some lady in Newport, Rhode Island."

"What happened with that relationship?" I asked.

He shrugged. "He never told us, but my guess is she got wise to him. She was older than Joe, a *lot* older."

His wife's expression turned stern.

"I know what Mabel's thinking, and she's right," her husband said. "Joe liked older women with money, lots of money. He studied them, knew what they liked. He could be whatever was needed at the moment, a good dancer, poker and croquet player. He was a lot more sophisticated than me." He winked at his wife, who sighed.

"John's always putting himself down," she said, "but he has what Joe never had. Integrity. And that stands for a lot more than being good at golf or playing the piano."

John laughed. "I got a tin ear, anyway." He turned to me. "Joe told me he learned to play piano by working in some houses of ill repute down in New Orleans. Of course, I didn't swallow all of his tales whole. He was very entertaining, but he had a habit of stretching the truth now and then."

"More often than that," Mabel muttered.

"Right," said her husband. "Anyway, after the police found us, they told us Joe had been engaged to Miss Tillie Mortelaine. We called her up to introduce ourselves and console each other over Joe's death. Miss Tillie confirmed they were planning to get married. I was relieved his fiancée wasn't the one who'd shot him. It had happened before."

"Oh?" I exclaimed.

Mabel picked up the thread. "One of those poor rich ladies he got involved with tried to get even."

Joseph, who'd sat passively while his father told tales out of school about his uncle, sat back, shook his head, and laughed.

"It wasn't funny, Joseph," his mother chided. "The poor woman lost most of her money to someone she knew as Gimbel Jones, and she almost killed him. The bullet grazed his face, made a path right through his eyebrow. Frankly, I can't blame her."

"Where did that happen?" I asked.

"San Francisco," John answered. "They charged her with attempted murder, but when the judge heard Joe's background, he threw out the case, said he considered it justified attempted homicide."

"I must admit," I said, "that your brother was fascinating, if in a somewhat negative way."

The younger Joseph said, "My uncle was always the topic of conversation at every Thanksgiving dinner. That's the way it is, isn't it? The black sheep of the family gets the most attention."

"For the wrong reasons," said his mother.

"I know, I know," her son said, "but you have to admit it's true."

"What do you do for a living?" I asked him.

"I'm an accountant, like Dad. Not an especially exciting way to live your life."

"But honest," said his mother.

"You don't know some of the accountants I know," he said playfully.

I insisted upon paying the check, and thanked Joseph

for getting me together with his parents. "The more I can learn about Wanamaker," I said, "the better my chances of solving his murder."

Joseph offered to drop me at the house on his way to bringing his parents to their hotel. In the car, I voiced what I'd been thinking during our conversation: "I wonder if there might have been others who were vying for Tillie's attention?"

"And money?" John said, rubbing his chin in thought. "Wouldn't surprise me. Before the woman in San Francisco shot my brother, I remember him complaining that there were scoundrels after her money." He laughed heartily.

Mabel added her editorial comment. "He should talk."

I thanked them all again as I got out of the car in front of Tillie's elegant house.

"We'll be in town for another few days," John Jones said. "You're welcome to call anytime if you think of more questions we can answer for you."

I assured them I would and waved good-bye as they drove off.

Mrs. Goodall was polishing the dining table when I came through the front door. I stopped to talk with her.

"Any chance of getting a bag of ice from you?" I asked.

She looked at the shillelagh in my hand, then down at the leg of my slacks, which had a smudge of dirt and an unsightly tear from the incident at the parade. I was more aggravated about that than the knee, which by now was sure to be turning a gruesome black, blue, and purple. The knee would heal, but the slacks of my favorite pantsuit would need to be repaired.

"What in the world?" she said.

"A silly accident," I replied.

"Do you need help getting upstairs?"

"No, thanks. I'm sure I can manage."

"You get on up to your room. I'll be there with the ice in a minute."

I sank gratefully into the upholstered chair in the corner of my room, slipped off my shoes, and gingerly lifted my leg onto the ottoman, raising the pant leg to expose a nasty bruise surrounding the original gash.

Mrs. Goodall walked in a few moments later with a tray holding the ice pack, a cup of tea, and two cookies cut in the shape of a shamrock and sprinkled with green sugar. She arranged a towel on the ottoman, draped the ice pack across my knee, and lectured me about the need not to move for twenty minutes, when she would be back to draw me a hot bath, which she said was a necessity if I didn't want to be sore tomorrow.

To make certain I didn't get up, she took my book from the bedside table and dropped in it my lap. I thanked her for her consideration and promised not to budge from the chair until she returned.

Since I'd just finished lunch, I didn't need a sweet, but the tea was welcome. I set the book aside, sat back and sipped contemplatively, allowing the events of the day to run through my mind.

So Wanamaker Jones had been a rogue, romancing

wealthy older women. No surprise there, given the age difference between him and Tillie. Although there have been some famous and long-lasting marriages between younger men and older women—and vice versa, for that matter—more often than not, people view a large age gap as a signal that the younger partner is a social climber or, worse, a gold digger. Not that Tillie was naïve by any means. She was a pretty shrewd judge of character. And not that she wasn't capable of charming men of all ages. Hadn't Dr. Payne been "smitten" as well, according to Mrs. Goodall?

John Jones had said that one of Wanamaker's inamoratas had tried to kill him. Perhaps there were others. Could another former lover have sought and found revenge during a New Year's Eve party at Tillie's house?

I shifted in my seat and felt a twinge of pain that reminded me I'd now fallen twice on that knee. The first time, in the tunnel, had been my own fault for keeping my eyes on the ceiling and missing the obstacle on the floor. Had someone deliberately pushed me at the parade? It seemed so unlikely, and I tried to erase it from my consciousness. But I couldn't. One thing was obvious. If someone *had* tried to harm me, it could only be because that person didn't want the murder of Wanamaker Jones to be solved. Who that might be was a question beyond my ability to answer at the moment.

I chided myself for my lack of progress. Time was going to run out before I knew it, and I was no closer to a solution than the day I arrived. I resolved to visit the police to see if the original report held any clues, assuming the authorities would let me take a look at it. *And you'd better step up the interviews of those who were at the fatal party,* I told myself. *No more allowing them to avoid your questions.* There were pieces of the puzzle that I needed to get filled in. And I was going to find them, sore knee or not.

By the time Mrs. Goodall returned, my teacup was empty and somehow the cookies had disappeared along with the beverage.

Chapter Sixteen

lthough I'd vowed to talk to all the people I could find who might be able to shed light on the killing, I spent the next two days with my leg elevated, per Dr. Payne's instructions. Mrs. Goodall had taken one look at the expression on my face in the morning and insisted upon calling him. Despite my protestations that even a doctor deserved a day of rest, Warner had stopped by to check out my injury, prescribing what he called "RICE," rest, ice, compression, and elevation. He had wrapped my knee in an Ace bandage and left a cardboard sleeve with little yellow pills in foil pockets in case the pain required medicating. Even though the day was a wash as far as my investigating the Wanamaker Jones case, I did get him to promise that he would call his friend Judge O'Neill and pave the way for an interview.

Mrs. Goodall spent Sunday and Monday hovering over my discolored leg, fussing with pillows for my back, and admonishing me not to rise from my seat for any reason and to call her for assistance. She plugged in an intercom right next to my chair—an action that had the Grogans squawking that it would interfere with their equipment and tarnish their data, but the housekeeper prevailed. All my meals were brought in on a tray. I finished the book I'd brought with me as well as another that Mrs. Goodall fetched from the library, and started reading the report on Mortelaine House that Melanie and her friend LaTisha were working on for their architectural history class.

After two days' rest, my knee was much improved and I was itching to get moving again. I'd telephoned the police station, and was granted an appointment for an interview with Captain Mead Parker. In the meantime, I would visit Charmelle, and see if she or her brother could contribute to my understanding of the murder.

"Melanie will drive you," Mrs. Goodall said when I came into the kitchen to announce my intention to visit the O'Neills. She was washing the breakfast dishes, even though a dishwasher was next to the sink.

"That's really not necessary," I said. "It's only a short walk. I looked it up on the map."

"You put too much pressure on that knee, it's goin' to swell up again."

"But if I don't exercise it, it will stiffen up even more," I countered.

"I can see I'll be callin' Dr. Payne again for more medicine," she said with a sniff. "But you suit yourself."

"I'm very grateful for all the care and consideration you've given me these past few days," I said. "I hope I've thanked you."

"You have."

"And I certainly don't want to do anything that will lead me to impose on you again."

"I'm not sayin' you imposed."

"I know. You're just concerned and I appreciate it. How's this? I promise to bring along the shillelagh for support, and to call Melanie to pick me up if the pain starts up again."

Mrs. Goodall wiped her hands on a dish towel and eyed me with suspicion. "I expect you know how to sweet-talk the bees out of the flowers, don't you?"

We both laughed.

"Go on. Get out of my kitchen. And make sure you say how-do to Miss O'Neill for me when you see her."

"I will."

I was happy to have the opportunity to get outside, even given the chill in the air, or perhaps because of it. It was still cold at home. March in Cabot Cove, as the snows melt, heralds the beginning of mud season, not our most attractive time. But everyone loves it all the same because it means that spring is on the way. I'd been cooped up in Tillie's house with its dark rooms, stuffy furniture, strange sounds, and leaky ceiling, not to mention the trying presence of Tillie's guests—or "tenants," as Mrs. Goodall insisted upon calling them—but turning my face to the sun and taking a deep breath, I could feel the tension ebb away. I reviewed the tourist map Melanie had given me and set off, sure that this day would bring something helpful.

The O'Neills lived on another of Savannah's famed squares, this one a simple park shaded by live oaks with crisscrossing paths leading to the surrounding streets, and benches on four sides of a low flower bed. Their house was an imposing edifice with a whitewashed cement facade and black shutters framing the tall windows. It had a stern, no-nonsense appearance, an apt reflection of its owner, or at least of one of them. Its only softening feature was a pair of curved staircases with delicate wrought-iron rails leading to either side of the stone portico, which was supported by simple tapered columns. I knocked at the front door. It was opened by a middle-aged lady wearing a white uniform, white shoes, and stockings.

"I'm here to see Judge O'Neill," I told her. "I believe I'm expected. My name is Jessica Fletcher."

The nurse, if that's what she was, invited me in and waved toward a straight-backed wooden chair against the wall. "The judge just got a call," she said. "If you'll wait here, I'll let him know you've arrived and see when he'll be available."

I thanked her, placed my shoulder bag on the chair along with a book I'd brought as a gift for Charmelle, and looked around the formal entrance. Except for the chair and its match on the opposite wall, the area was devoid of furniture or artwork. A staircase ahead on the right led up to an intermediate landing before continuing on both sides to the second floor. The walls of the stairwell and the hall were covered in ocher paper with a moss green fleur-de-lis pattern. The wallpaper provided the only spot of color in the otherwise unadorned entry.

I watched as the nurse walked down the long hall, the rubber soles of her shoes squeaking on the marble tile floor. She stopped before a carved wooden door, knocked, and slipped inside the room, leaving the door ajar.

"Dammit, Warner, you had no right to say I would talk to that woman," I heard the judge shout.

Apparently Dr. Payne had forgotten to telephone until now. He'd assured me he could talk his friend into seeing me and I'd come on the assumption that he'd been successful. Perhaps not. I edged down the hall, cocking my ear to catch more of the one-sided conversation.

"You give me one good reason why I should cooperate with that pen pusher," the judge was saying. "The Savannah detectives spent months on the case, followed procedure, and they had the full facilities of the department behind them. If they think there's nothing more to find, then that's all right with me. Jones was an interloper to begin with." There was a pause, and then I heard, "Don't tell me some amateur from up north is going to know more than our Savannah police."

He had a point, of course. Had she been alive, I would have told Tillie the same thing, perhaps phrased a bit differently. She'd put me in this prickly situation by threatening to disinherit a program we'd established together, and at the moment I was feeling quite annoyed with her. If I was able to make headway where the police had been stymied, the newspapers would have a field day. My efforts would publicly embarrass the professionals in the department, who would be rightfully indignant, and I would appear to be an egotistical know-it-all. If I failed to find anything new, a valuable program I believed in would lose out on an important donation, and I would be made to look foolish for having taken a bite of something that was too big for me to chew. Either way, my reputation would suffer. What could Tillie have been thinking? She was playing with people's lives and this wasn't a game. What could *I* have been thinking? Rose Kendall had put her finger on it. I was on a fool's errand. It would serve me right if the judge refused to talk to me.

Irritated for allowing myself to be drawn into such a no-win predicament, I walked back to the chair and shouldered my bag. I would leave the book for Charmelle, of course, but I needed to rethink this whole situation.

"Mrs. Fletcher?"

I turned at the nurse's voice.

"His Honor will see you now."

"Nuts!" I muttered to myself.

I strode down the hall and through the door into a well-appointed legal library. The nurse hovered in the doorway behind me. Judge O'Neill was sitting in a black leather wing chair behind a large walnut desk. His wheelchair had been pushed into a corner next to a gun case with a glass front. It held three shotguns. Tall bookcases behind him were filled with volumes of lawbooks with colorful leather bindings.

"Mrs. Fletcher, please excuse me for not rising," he said, extending his hand for me to shake.

"Of course," I said, leaning over the desk to take his hand and wincing slightly when his fingers crushed mine. "It was very kind of you to see me. I know what an imposition this is."

"Not at all. Have a seat. You're welcome in my home. May I offer you some coffee or tea?"

"No, thank you," I said. "I won't take up too much of your time."

"Bring us some iced tea, Beverly," the judge said. "And some of those praline cookies."

"Yes, sir," the nurse said and closed the door.

The judge nodded at me.

"How is Charmelle?" I asked.

He seemed surprised at the question. "Sister is as well as can be expected," he said cautiously. "She's been failing for some time now. Doesn't have as strong a constitution as mine. She suffered a shock when she was told Miss Tillie had passed on, both emotionally, of course—they'd been friends since childhood—and physically. She injured herself falling against a table."

"I'd heard that."

"The doctor says at her age she's lucky to have survived the fall. Knocked herself unconscious for several hours. Hospital released her two days later. Said there wasn't any more they could do for her. Her thinking hasn't been the same since."

"I'm sorry to hear that. Is there a chance I could see her?"

"I just told you that she's not thinking clearly. I doubt she'd recognize you. She barely knows me."

"That's all right. I'd just like to give her a book, maybe keep her company for a little while."

"She doesn't read anymore."

"Perhaps I can read to her."

"She's not accepting visitors. Sister never liked anyone to see her unless she was in good health and dressed properly. I don't want to upset her. She's still grieving."

"I don't want to upset her either," I said. "I just thought she might appreciate a visitor, a little distraction from her grief. She might take comfort in talking with someone instead of spending her days alone."

"She's not alone. She has her nurse."

"But—" My next argument was interrupted by the arrival of Beverly with a tray holding two glasses of iced tea and a plate of glazed praline cookies with half a pecan pressed into each.

"Best in Savannah," the judge proclaimed, reaching for a cookie. "Now, I understand you have some questions about the death of Wanamaker Jones. I didn't know the man very well, but I'll be happy to answer your questions as best I can." He looked at his watch.

The subject of Charmelle was obviously closed. I took a cookie and immediately regretted it. If I didn't stop eating all the good food that was either placed in front of me or selected from a menu, I soon wouldn't fit into the clothes I'd brought.

"Can you tell me how you met Wanamaker Jones?" I asked.

"Met him at the gun club. He was supposedly related to one of the board members who'd just passed on. Not a bad eye, too, when it came to shooting. Later, it turned out everything about him was a lie. But in the beginning he seemed like a charming fellow. Not very good at poker, which made him popular until he started winning. Scratch golfer. I invited him to attend a dinner the local bar association was giving in my honor. He had to pony up a hundred bucks for the ticket, which was pricey at the time, and he did it, no questions asked. Sister told me later that he flirted with her, but that he had an eye for Miss Tillie from the start. At least that's how I remember it."

"Jones, I'd like to introduce you to two lovely ladies of my acquaintance. This is my sister, Charmelle."

"Miss O'Neill, it's a pleasure."

Charmelle offered her fingertips to the gentleman. He was slender, of medium height, and wore a navy pin-striped double-breasted suit with a red-dotted bow tie. She thought he was quite good-looking, even with his wavy blond hair a bit too long, but it never paid to let a man know he was attractive. It gave them an ego and encouraged them to take advantage.

"And this is our old friend, Miss Tillie Mortelaine," the judge said, turning to Tillie.

"Not so old at all," Jones murmured as he took Tillie's

hand. He gave her a wink, and darned if she didn't wink back.

"I'll be sitting on the dais," said the judge, "so I'll leave them in your capable hands."

"Why, thank you, Your Honor. I will take extra-special care of them," Jones said, settling in the chair between Tillie and Charmelle. "How lucky can a man be to sit between two such beauties?"

Tillie leaned forward to talk around the new visitor. "Psst, Charmelle," she said in a stage whisper. "Look out for this one. He's too handsome for his own good—and ours."

Jones laughed heartily. "May I court you, Miss Tillie?"

"Why, I'd be offended if you didn't."

Jones thought he detected a slight pout on the lips of Charmelle O'Neill. "Now, Miss O'Neill," he said, leaning into her shoulder and putting his lips close to her ear. "I do love blondes. Do you think you can give me a little bit of encouragement?"

Charmelle felt a little stirring, but she tamped it down. "Looks to me as if you've already chosen, Mr. Jones."

"Come on, Charmelle," Tillie said, a twinkle in her eye. "I'm willing to share if you are."

"For a while they went everywhere together, the three of them," the judge said to me, his fingers playing with the gavel he kept on his desk. "I told Sister not to let him get too close, till it became clear Jones had a preference for Miss Tillie anyway. Even though she was probably old enough to have borned him. At first I thought he was her walker."

" 'Her walker'?" I'm afraid I don't know that expression."

"Her walker. Someone who escorts her around. Takes her to concerts, parties. Lots of Southern women have walkers. Most of them gay, I imagine, leastwise if the women have husbands. Anyway, I thought Jones was Miss Tillie's walker. Then they announced their engagement. Could have knocked me over with a feather."

"Was Charmelle surprised, too?"

"Sister?" The judge looked uncomfortable. "Why, I don't know. Never asked her."

"You never asked her if the engagement was a surprise to her?"

He shook his head. "Maybe I should have. She moped around for a while. I expect she was worried about being left behind. But then she was fine. They included her in all the social engagements. She was the same old Charmelle."

"And the night Wanamaker Jones was killed?"

"The children found him lying on the floor in Miss Tillie's upstairs hall. The boy thought he was asleep. Shook him to see if he would wake. That was when he saw the blood. Both of them started in to yell, and we all ran up the stairs to see what the commotion was about."

"All of you?"

"Pretty much. Sister was frightened by their screams. She and Miss Tillie ran out of the parlor. I followed. So did Warner—and Richardson. He was there, too."

"Their parents—did they go upstairs as well?"

"Don't rightly remember. I think they called up from the bottom of the stairs. It's been my experience that parents are less concerned about their children's screeching than those of us who have not been blessed with offspring."

"Was anyone else there?"

"Mrs. Goodall, but she wasn't Mrs. Goodall at the time. She stayed in the kitchen with the other help."

"Didn't she hear the screams?"

"Would've been hard not to, but I don't remember seeing her in the upstairs hall until the police came. Never did see the others. Mrs. Goodall swore they were in the kitchen washing up with her. But the police took them all down to headquarters and interrogated them for a long time. Had to let 'em go. No proof of anything."

"Do you suspect one of them killed Wanamaker Jones?"

"Probably not."

"I understand you and Charmelle had a disagreement that evening. Do you remember what it was about?"

He frowned and set the gavel down with a thump. "I don't like rumor and innuendo, Mrs. Fletcher."

"Nor do I," I said. "I'm just trying to get a picture of all the currents swirling around that evening to see if any of them have a bearing on the case."

He shifted in his seat and thought for a long time before answering. "To be honest, Mrs. Fletcher, I don't know what we argued about. It was all such a long time ago. And it's irrelevant. I trust the police. They did a fine job investigating. They had some problems. You know the murder weapon was never found?"

"Yes, I did know that."

"Well, without concrete proof, you cannot convict. There was no one with a motive that we knew about. 'Course, once we learned the truth about Jones, we understood. But at the time, no one knew he was a liar and a fraud."

"How was he a fraud?"

"Had no money. Lived off money Miss Tillie gave him. Later we found out there were others."

"Others?"

"Other women he tried to swindle."

"Who told you about them?"

"Must've been the police. I told them I wanted to know everything they could find on him."

"Why did you do that?"

"I suspected there was something up with Jones from the beginning. Told Sister to steer clear. Let Miss Tillie make a fool of herself, not her."

I cleared my throat. "So you suspected Wanamaker Jones was not what he appeared to be right from the beginning."

"Well, perhaps not from the very beginning. But what right-thinking man is interested in a woman old enough to be his mother? Seemed strange to me."

"Never heard of May-December weddings?" I said with a smile.

"Sure, but it's the man who's older and the woman younger."

"Ah. And how did Tillie and Charmelle react to the murder?"

"How do you think they reacted? They wept and wailed in each other's arms. But then they got over it. Nothing they could do about it. He was gone, and they went back to their lives as usual."

"Thank you so much for your time, Judge O'Neill."

"It was nothing. Now, you don't quote me, you understand?"

"I'm not writing anything. I'm just trying to understand what happened."

He grunted but said no more.

"Judge O'Neill, I brought a book for Charmelle. I'd really love to give it to her, even if she doesn't read. I won't keep her more than a minute. Just so she knows I'm thinking about her."

"Leave it here. I'll make sure she gets it."

I had no choice. I left the book on his desk and showed myself out. The nurse was nowhere in sight when I opened the front door and closed it softly behind me. I went down the stairs, taking a deep breath of the cool, fresh air, and crossed the street to the little park in the square. I sat on a bench and thought about Tillie and Charmelle and the engaging man they both had a crush on. He must have made them feel young again, attractive and admired. Was that such a bad thing? Why did the judge think it impossible for a young man to be attracted to older women, women who are confident in themselves, know a bit about the world, and accept it for what it is? What is the price for happiness? Had they paid it?

A little girl chasing a ball ran past me. A woman

standing some distance away called out to her. Beverly, the nurse, was standing with the woman, who I assumed was the little girl's nanny. I looked back at the child. The ball had come to rest against the shoe of an old woman sitting on a bench, a shawl wrapped around her frail shoulders. She leaned down, and with one manicured finger pushed the ball toward the child. When she looked up I was able to see her face. It was Charmelle.

Chapter Seventeen

I knew she was eighty-six, and although the years were etched into her face in fine lines across her cheeks and brow, Charmelle's features remained strong and beautiful, the skin taut around her jaw, her eyes very blue with a faraway look in them. Her hair had turned snow white, but she still pinned it up in a chignon. And someone—I assumed it was Beverly—made sure her nails were nicely manicured.

The little girl had run back to where her nanny and the nurse were standing and the three of them had ambled to the other side of the square.

I sat by Charmelle's side and took one of her hands in mine, studying the ringless fingers and the almost translucent skin under which the veins and sinews formed a delicate tracing.

"Do I know you?" she asked.

"Yes, Charmelle," I said. "It's Jessica Fletcher. You and I met many years ago. Tillie Mortelaine introduced us."

Pain flashed in her eyes at the mention of Tillie's name, and she withdrew her hand.

"I'm so sorry for your loss, Charmelle. I know what Tillie meant to you, and what you meant to her."

"Do you?"

"She had a photograph of the two of you on her nightstand, a daily reminder of your friendship. It's still there. I think that must have been a sign of her love for you."

She turned to me, eyes filling with tears. "What am I going to do without her? She . . . she . . ." Her voice was hoarse, rusty, as if she hadn't used it in a long time. Her hands lay fisted in her lap.

"We all think that way when we lose someone we love," I said, feeling not only the losses in her life but also those in mine. "Somehow, one day follows another and we cope, we endure, we wait for the pain to subside. It never goes away, that pain. I won't tell you it will. It's always there. But it loses the razor sharpness that you're feeling now."

She pulled a handkerchief from her pocket, wiped her eyes, and shook her head. "I don't know why I'm so weepy. She wasn't always nice to me, you know. She could be mean, play tricks, always teasing." She dabbed at tears that coursed down her cheeks. "But I haven't spent a day of my life since I was a little girl without seeing her or speaking to her. Even when she married Roy, we talked every day, laughed—until now. I don't know what to do." She rocked back and forth on the bench.

Charmelle was surprisingly coherent considering the description her brother had given of her mental state. I wondered why the judge wanted to keep people away from her. Perhaps she floated in and out of consciousness, in and out of awareness of who and where she was. People who do that are said to be in a fugue state. Maybe Charmelle was subject to fugue episodes and I'd just happened to catch her in one of her more lucid moments.

"Jessica?"

"Yes?"

"Are you the writer Tillie brought down to help with her literacy campaign?"

"Yes. I'm flattered that you remember."

"You live in New England somewhere."

"I live in Maine. You have a good memory."

"I do. I remember one Christmas we hired a man to fix up my study." Her voice drifted off, but I could see her visualizing the scene in her mind. "So handsome."

"Who?"

"The painter."

"Was that the man fixing up your study?"

She nodded and a small smile played around her lips. "Miss Tillie was batting her eyes at him, distracting him from his work." She waved her damp handkerchief around. "He spilled paint all over my desk."

"What a mess that must have been," I said.

"She always claimed I was man-hungry, but she was the worst flirt of all."

I was glad to give Charmelle an opportunity to

reminisce about Tillie. She needed to talk about her friend. It would help her face the loss. Yet her mind seemed to jump around from one thing to another. I wondered if she was falling into a fugue state.

"That's why, you know."

"Why what, Charmelle?"

"Why I stopped sending you Christmas cards."

"Because of the painter?"

She looked at me now. "He spilled paint all over my address book."

"Oh, my goodness."

"It was such a loss. I could have kept the pages that weren't ruined, but I just threw the whole thing away, in the garbage. I stopped sending cards to everyone. I hope you weren't angry."

"Not at all," I said. "People get busy with their lives and lose touch with acquaintances all the time, especially when your address book is covered with paint."

I glanced across the square to see Beverly and her friend wandering back in our direction. I turned my back on them, hoping Beverly wouldn't recognize me. At that moment, a movement in the O'Neills' house caught my eye. The judge, holding a telephone to his ear, was walking back and forth in front of the window that overlooked the park. *Walking!*

"Charmelle, do you mind if I ask you a question about something that happened a long time ago?" I asked. I knew I had limited time to question her.

"I suppose so. I don't remember things the way I used to. Things seem so—so fuzzy sometimes."

I tilted my head and looked at her sideways. "I think you're sharper than you let on, Miss O'Neill."

She tried not to smile. "You're very kind to say that. It isn't true, but go ahead and ask me what you want to. I'll try to remember."

"I understand the judge is a member of the Forest City Gun Club. Did you ever go there with him?"

"Not really. It's for gentlemen. They only let the ladies come for a Low Country boil or other some such occasion."

"Is your brother a good shot?"

"Very good, yes. Took the skeet prize one year."

"And what about you?"

"I used to beat him in target practice when we were children." She smiled at the memory.

"Do you still keep a gun?"

She frowned. "Not anymore. It was always just for protection."

"What happened to your gun?"

A tear trickled down her cheek. "I lost it a long time ago. I lost it."

"Do you recall the night Wanamaker Jones was killed?"

She nodded solemnly.

"Can you tell me what happened?"

Her lower lip began to tremble. "Why do you want to know *that*?"

"I'm trying to find out who killed him."

"Why? It was so long ago. And he was a bad man, a liar and a cheat. Why do you care?"

"Because Tillie did. It was in her will. A donation to the literacy foundation depends on my finding the murderer."

She gasped. "She's going to blame me, isn't she?"

"Who?"

"Tillie."

"Why do you say that?"

She buried her face in her hands. "Oh, God, I knew she'd get even. I've been dreading this day."

I put my hand on her shoulder. "Why would she blame you for Wanamaker's death, Charmelle?"

"Why? Because—because he was in love with me, not her."

The walk back to Tillie's house was not as easy as the one I'd taken to the O'Neills'. My knee was protesting its exercise and I leaned harder on the shillelagh than I'd needed to earlier in the day. Mrs. Goodall would say "I told you so." And she'd be right. Seth would say I was stubborn. And he would be correct, too. I was looking forward to a relaxing bath, a good soak to relax my aching joint and let my mind get around today's revelations.

Beverly, the nurse, had been across the square during most of my conversation with Charmelle. When she caught sight of me talking with her, she hurried over to rescue her charge, but not before Charmelle had let me know that she and Wanamaker Jones had been lovers. The more I learned about this man, the more I understood why someone would want to kill him.

He had insinuated himself into a tight-knit society, courted the most popular—and wealthy—woman he could find, then betrayed her with her best friend. Anyone in Tillie's house that night—assuming they knew what I now did—would have had a motive to kill him. Anyone who loved Tillie, from her housekeeper to her lawyer to her best friend's brother, might have gone after the man who'd broken her heart. *That was assuming, of course, that her heart was broken,* I told myself. *That was assuming that she even knew about the affair at the time.* Even if she'd been ignorant of Jones's duplicity, she'd had a lot of other beaus waiting to console her.

Mrs. Goodall had told me that in Tillie's moment of grief, she'd found solace with Dr. Payne, who had taken her aside into a private room after the police had left and presumably calmed her. I couldn't help but wonder why he hadn't mentioned that to me. What had he said to her? Did he know more about Wanamaker's past than she did? The housekeeper also indicated that the good doctor had had a crush on Tillie and had pursued her romantically. Had *he* killed her fiancé in order to get rid of his competition for her affections? Whatever the content of their conversation that night following the discovery of Wanamaker's body, it had soothed her. It had also shored up her determination not to cooperate with the authorities. Was she protecting someone? Dr. Payne? Charmelle? Judge O'Neill? Her deceased husband's relatives who'd been invited to the party along with their two children, Rocky and Rose? From what I'd learned, the relationship between Tillie and them was anything but cordial. She wouldn't want to protect them, would she?

The list was growing.

I limped across the square toward Tillie's house, where a white van with OGLETHORPE PLUMBING CONTRACTORS, ELLIOT BASKER, PRESIDENT painted in large blue and gold letters on its side partially blocked the entrance. The rear doors of the vehicle had been left open to expose a jumbled assortment of pipes, wrenches, ladders, and other metal materials piled on the floor. A tall tool cabinet leaned against one side, its drawers partially open. A plumber's helper in white overalls and work boots—not the man I'd seen the previous week—skipped down Tillie's front steps and rummaged in the back of the van. He pulled out a black box that looked like some sort of electrical equipment—didn't Artie Grogan have something similar?—slammed the doors shut, and jogged up the stairs.

"You get any dirt on my floors, I'm going to send *you* a bill," I heard Mrs. Goodall say to him.

I climbed the stairs, hoping my face didn't reflect the twinges I felt in my knee, but Mrs. Goodall was too preoccupied with her workmen to notice my entrance. There were heavy cables draped across the floor and plugged into the wall. The cord from the little hall lamp had been pulled from its outlet and lay curled on the table like a molting snake. I stepped around the wires, aware that if I tripped, I could do permanent damage to a joint I had taken for granted up to this point in my life.

I hobbled over to Tillie's study and poked my head in

the door. Mrs. Goodall, Melanie, the plumber, the plumber's helper, and Samantha and Artie Grogan were clustered around an aluminum case balanced on the box the helper had brought in. They were all peering at a flickering screen. A tall ladder was set up, its heavy legs resting on terry-cloth towels to protect the carpet. Dangling over the ladder from a hole in the ceiling was a long cord attached to what looked like a hose reel on the floor, next to which a huge toolbox lay open.

"Mrs. Fletcher," Melanie called, detaching herself from the huddle. "Come look. You can see inside the ceiling."

I joined the group scrutinizing the monitor, and tried to make sense of the dim picture.

"See, here's the water," the plumber said, pointing a grimy finger at a streak of light. "And that there's where it's coming from. Jason, git up that ladder and move the camera closer to the drip. Be gentle now. It ain't paid for yet."

"Great piece of equipment," Artie said. "Mind if I ask you where you got it?"

"Plumbers' supply. It's usually used for lookin' into pipes, but I find it handy for this kinda thing, too."

Jason, who appeared to be no more than sixteen, shot a glance at Melanie, climbed up, and wrapped his hand around the dangling cord.

"Not so fast, dang it," the plumber yelled when Jason, his eyes still on Melanie, pushed the cable deeper into the recess overhead and the picture on the screen jumped around. "That ain't no fishing line you're holding. Git on down now."

"But, Mr. Basker," the boy said.

"Don't 'Mr. Basker' me, boy. Quit cuttin' a fool, and pack up them tools." He shook his head. "A body cain't get good help no more."

Mr. Basker turned the monitor so he could see it from the ladder, clambered up himself, and delicately maneuvered the tube through which the camera cable ran closer to where the water was leaking down from the second floor. Then, eyes trained on the ceiling, he came down and stepped off the distance to the door and into the hall. "My best guess is right about heah," he said, pointing to the second floor.

"That looks to be under where you said you heard the water, Mrs. Fletcher," Mrs. Goodall said to me.

"Yes, it does," I replied.

Mr. Basker disconnected the pieces of the camera, laying them in a foam-lined case. Leaving Jason to patch the hole in the ceiling, he hauled all the equipment to the second floor. Mrs. Goodall, Melanie, Artie, Samantha, and I followed like ducklings in his wake.

Mr. Basker stalked back and forth in the upstairs hall, trying to get his bearings.

"You gonna make another hole?" Mrs. Goodall asked.

"Gotta. Cain't fix a leak if you cain't see it."

"This is where I thought I heard water running the other day," I said, tapping on the wall between my room and the adjacent bedroom.

Mr. Basker pressed his ear to the place I'd indicated, just as I'd done, and held his hand up for silence. We all held our breath.

"Oh, man," he said. "Somethin' just started happening in there. Take a listen."

We didn't have to move closer to the wall to hear what he was referring to. A sudden sound of rushing water could be clearly heard from wherever we stood.

Mrs. Goodall's eyes widened. "It sounds like a waterfall," she exclaimed.

Basker went to the top of the stairs and bellowed to Jason to bring up the saw. But he didn't wait for his young assistant to follow his orders. He reached down, picked up a small sledgehammer that was on the floor next to him, and opened a hole in the wall four inches across. He pulled a flashlight from his tool belt, and shone it inside. "I'll be," he said.

"What is it?" Mrs. Goodall demanded. "Can you fix it?"

Basker turned to us with a confused look on his face. "There's a damn shower running in there," he said.

"That can't be," Mrs. Goodall said.

"I bet it's from when they were constructing the new bathrooms," Melanie said. "They must have covered up an old one."

"That they did," said the plumber.

We continued to watch as Basker, using the saw Jason had handed him, cut a much larger hole, exposing a showerhead protruding from an inner wall. He reached through the opening, and with considerable effort twisted one of the on-off valves to turn off the flow of water.

"Good thing I was here when it come on," said Basker.

"I'll second that," I said. "If it had been allowed to run full force like that, the entire house would have been flooded."

"What would have caused it to start runnin'?" Mrs. Goodall asked.

"Beats me," Basker replied. "That on-off valve was real tight. Took plenty 'a muscle just to turn it off."

"But *somebody* turned that shower on," I said.

"Who could it be?" Melanie asked.

Artie and Samantha Grogan looked at each other and smiled.

"You aren't suggesting that some spirit turned on the shower, are you?" I said.

"Do you have a better explanation, Mrs. Fletcher?" Samantha asked smugly.

"No, but—"

I went to the hole that the plumber had bashed and cut in the wall and tried to look through it. I asked him for his flashlight, which he handed to me. Using it, I moved its beam around in an attempt to find some reasonable explanation for this bizarre event. I heard Mrs. Goodall behind me bemoaning the damage to the house, and Melanie trying to quiet her mother.

I was about to abandon my efforts when the flashlight's beam came to rest on something. I squinted to see what it was, without success. I turned to the plumber. "Mr. Basker," I said, "there's something in there I'd like to see. Do you think you can reach it?"

He joined me at the wall and looked to where I directed

the beam. He pushed his heft against the wall and strained to extend his beefy arm far enough to grasp what I'd referred to. "Got it," he said, and pulled his arm out of the opening.

We all stared in shock at what he held.

It was a revolver.

Chapter Eighteen

I asked Mrs. Goodall—who was still in shock—to call a taxi for me. It arrived five minutes later, and with the handgun in my purse, I asked the driver to take me to the Savannah-Chatham Metropolitan Police Department. Police captain Mead Parker had told me when I called for an appointment that I could walk there, but with my bruised knee and the sense of urgency I felt, I wanted to get there as quickly as possible.

As the cab pulled away from the curb, I caught sight of General Pettigrew leaving the hotel next door. He came down the stairs and walked in the direction of Tillie's house. Behind him on the landing were the two men I'd seen with him the morning of Saint Patrick's Day. I wondered what the general would make of the discovery of the shower. He'd made no bones about his skepticism regarding paranormal activities in general and the Grogans' research in particular. But would evidence of a ghost increase the value of Mortelaine House to the hotel owners? Tourists had been known to flock to buildings with a ghostly past. Savannah offered many tours of haunted houses.

The Grogans had been crowing ever since we'd found the gun, crediting Wanamaker Jones with pointing the way toward the missing murder weapon. Whether or not it *was* the murder weapon remained to be seen, but I tended to agree with their assessment on that point. As to Wanamaker Jones aiding the investigation, well, I can't say I was convinced, but it certainly was an odd occurrence. What, or who, had caused the shower to suddenly come on?

My driver came to a stop sign at the corner of Habersham and Oglethorpe. Immediately to my right was a small, tranquil park in the large median separating the two lanes of Oglethorpe. Just beyond it was police headquarters.

"This will be fine," I said, handing the fare over the back of his seat. "Thank you."

Although I was consumed with getting inside the stationhouse and delivering the weapon found behind the wall in Tillie's house, my watch said I was a few minutes early for my meeting. I lingered a while in the park to put my thoughts in order. It seemed a perfect place to accomplish that.

Just off the street, a statue of a police officer in uniform stood atop a large base. *How appropriate having it right here*, I thought and walked over to read the plaque on the monument: ABOVE AND BEYOND, LEST WE FORGET. Erected to honor police officers who gave their lives in the line of duty, the memorial contained the names of the fallen, beginning with the first, Harry L. Fender, in 1901, and going up through 1993. I suffered the same sense of sadness that I always do when visiting such memorials, including the much more expansive one in Washington, D.C. What a shame that good men and women have to die while trying to keep us safe from the criminal element.

Sufficiently pulled together, I crossed the street and approached the Habersham entrance to the three-story redbrick building that had once been a police barracks erected back in the late 1800s. I climbed the few steps to the front door, using a black iron railing to avoid tripping, and stepped through the glass door. To my right was a desk staffed by two uniformed female officers. "Yes, ma'am?" one said.

"My name is Jessica Fletcher," I said. "I have an appointment with Captain Parker."

She picked up a phone and called the captain. "She'll be with you in a few minutes," I was told.

As I waited for her, I inspected the police memorabilia displayed on shelves in a glass case in the lobby: hats and uniforms of other police units, batons, and tools, not all of them familiar to me. I looked around at the officers coming in and going out. I was acutely aware of their holstered guns and of the handgun weighing down my purse. It didn't seem to be very large, although I admit to not having had a lot of direct hands-on experience with weapons. I'd considered giving it to one of the officers on desk duty the moment I entered the building, but was afraid that pulling out a weapon might bring about an unfortunate response. Better to give it to the captain once inside her office, where I could explain before retrieving it from my bag.

A minute later, a door opened and a tall, attractive African American woman stepped through it. Her salt-and-pepper hair was braided close to her head, the braids gathered into a swirl in the back. She had an angular face with chiseled features, which could have made her look severe had it not been for the plum-colored lipstick she had applied that matched the pantsuit she wore, and the large drop earrings in the form of cats dangling from her ears. A silk shirt, a Native American necklace, and black pumps completed her outfit.

"Mrs. Fletcher," she said, extending her hand. "I'm Captain Parker."

"I appreciate your taking the time to see me," I said.

"Come on. We'll talk in my office."

We walked through the door from which she'd appeared and down a long hallway to where a sign outside an office read CAPT. MEAD PARKER. As we did, I silently hoped we wouldn't pass through a metal detector.

Her office was large and nicely furnished. A color photograph of her with a man and two teenage children sat on a credenza behind her desk. She slid off her jacket and hung it on a clothes tree. Her shirt was short-sleeved, exposing surprisingly muscular arms. *She must be a weight lifter*, I thought, and my immediate reaction was that this was a formidable woman who could handle herself in any situation.

She dropped into a leather armchair behind her desk, and I took one of the pair facing her, resting my shoulder bag in my lap.

"It's a pleasure meeting you," she said once we were both seated. "I'm well aware of your career as a mystery novelist, although I must admit I don't get to read much fiction."

"I'd be happy to send you a book when I get back home," I offered.

"I'd appreciate that," the captain said. "So, you're here in Savannah to try and solve a forty-year-old murder case."

"You've read the paper."

"Yes, I have. And I've spoken with former detective Sheridan Buchwalter, who worked the case. Frankly, I'm afraid this mission you're on will turn out to be futile."

"I hope you're wrong," I said. "You do know the circumstances that brought me to Savannah?"

"Miss Tillie Mortelaine's will. She was quite a character."

"I certainly wouldn't argue with that. Captain Parker, before we discuss my being here, I must give you something."

"Oh? What's that?"

I explained how recent events at Tillie's house had led to the discovery of a handgun behind the wall. She sat up straight and leaned forward in her chair. "What did you do with the gun?" she asked.

"I have it with me."

I could see the wheels spinning in her head. Was I some

crazed mystery writer from Maine who was about to pull a gun and shoot up Savannah police headquarters?

I headed off that speculation. "Why don't you remove it yourself, Captain?" I suggested, using two hands to transfer the bag from my lap to the end of her desk. "I would feel more comfortable that way and I suspect you would, too."

"Where is it?"

"In here, in a plastic bag," I said, indicating my purse.

"Did you touch it?"

I sighed. "I didn't. However, the plumber who found it did."

"We'll have to get his prints."

I got up from my chair while she came around the desk and retrieved the plastic bag. She held it up to light coming through a window behind her desk. "A thirty-eight revolver," she said to herself. "And loaded!"

I resumed my seat, and so did she. She placed the plastic bag so that the weapon pointed away from both of us.

"I'm assuming that's the weapon used to kill Wanamaker Jones," I said.

"I don't deal in assumptions, Mrs. Fletcher," she replied, picking up her phone and calling for someone to come to her office. A uniformed officer arrived, and Captain Parker gave him the weapon. "Get this placed in the evidence locker. It may be linked to the Wanamaker Jones murder case from forty years ago," she said. He looked at her strangely, but said nothing and left.

"I suggest that the next time you discover a potential

murder weapon, Mrs. Fletcher, you call the police instead of taking it upon yourself to deliver it."

"I knew I was coming here and thought it made sense for me to bring it," I said. "But I'll remember your advice if I ever end up finding a possible murder weapon again. Hopefully, I won't."

"Was this the only reason you made the appointment with me?" she asked. "To bring in the gun?"

"Heavens, no. I didn't know about the gun when I called."

"Well, then, what can I do for you?"

"I read the paper, too," I said. "The reporter quoted someone from the police saying your department never closes a murder case. I would really appreciate being allowed to review the file on Wanamaker Jones."

She immediately slid a thick manila file folder across the desk to me.

"This is it?" I said.

"That's it. When I knew you were coming in, I had it sent in from the Georgia Crime Information Center. That's where we store the records. We barely have room for so much as an additional scrap of paper here at headquarters, much less the multiple file cabinets the records require."

I lifted the cover of the file and let it close. I didn't want to be rude and read in front of her. She must have sensed my hesitation, because she rose and said, "Why don't I let you have fifteen minutes with the file? You can't take it with you, and I want your word you won't remove anything from it."

"You have it."

"I'll be back." She put on her jacket and left the office, leaving the door ajar.

I scooted my chair closer to the file on the desk, and pulled open the cover. The file contained typical case material: a copy of the death certificate, the initial report by officers Buchwalter and Hadleigh, numerous updates by the investigators, photos of the crime scene, the autopsy report, ballistics results, background checks. There was far more information than I could absorb in fifteen minutes. I took out a pad and pen so I could make notes and concentrated on the crime scene photos and the eyewitness reports. I quickly scanned the autopsy, then looked at pictures of the deceased.

The children had found Jones facedown, but by the time the police arrived he was lying on his back. Surely a child of eight or nine couldn't have turned the body over. I'd need to ask Dr. Payne if he'd been the one to move the victim. When a person dies, gravity causes blood to settle in the lowest part of the body. It's one of the signs that investigators use to determine the time of death. If the body has been lying somewhere for hours, the settled blood will leave a permanent mark. However, if the body had been turned over shortly after death, the settled blood would not have had time to leave the permanent mark and assessing the time of death could have been compromised.

Captain Mead returned in precisely fifteen minutes. She must have been keeping an eye on her watch. I thanked her for the opportunity to scan the file, and thought for a moment before saying, "Now that you have in your possession the possible murder weapon, will you reopen the case and pursue it again?"

"Possibly. Why is that important to you?"

"I wouldn't want to get in your way."

She laughed, showing very white teeth. "I can assure you, Mrs. Fletcher, that I won't allow you to get in our way during a murder investigation."

"I have no doubt of that," I said. "For my own edification, what's your procedure in investigating a murder, even one that's forty years old?"

She gave me a knowing smile. "Is this for your investigation of Mr. Jones's murder, or for a book you're writing?"

"A little bit of both," I said, returning her smile.

"Well, Mrs. Fletcher, our procedures these days will be very different from when Sherry Buchwalter investigated. By the way, he called and said you were a very nice lady."

"That was kind of him."

"He's a good man. Let me answer your question. The weapon you delivered is on its way to our forensic unit as we speak. We have the bullet that killed Mr. Jones. I'll assign one of our homicide investigators, probably a sergeant with considerable experience, and . . ."

"Yes?"

"I'll expect you to cooperate."

"Of course I will."

"According to what I understand, you wouldn't be happy if we reopen the case and solve it before you do. You have a million dollars riding on it."

I'd expected this from her. She was right on the surface, and I nodded my agreement. But I was hoping that the effort I'd already expended, along with having discovered the gun, might qualify me as having played a role in identifying the murderer, and by extension deserving the million dollars for the literacy center even if I wasn't the first to point a finger at the killer. Tillie hadn't been that specific as far as I knew, and in any case, it was Roland Richardson who probably would have the last word should the murderer be named by someone other than me.

"I really don't consider this a contest, Captain."

"And I didn't mean to imply that you did. The gauntlet that Miss Mortelaine laid down for you is challenging, and I have to admit it's amusing. But the end result is certainly admirable, and I wish you well, Mrs. Fletcher. I assure you that I'll cooperate with you to the extent that I can."

"I can't ask for anything fairer than that," I said. "I hope you'll share with me the forensics tests on the weapon."

"I will. Some of my investigators will want to go to Mortelaine House to document where and how the weapon was found."

"I'll be happy to answer any questions they may have," I said, standing and picking up my purse, which was now a little lighter. "I appreciate your time, Captain, and your candor."

She escorted me to the lobby and we shook hands again.

Once outside, I drew a series of deep breaths and returned to the small park. I sat on a bench to collect my thoughts. The discovery of the gun behind the wall in Tillie's house was unexpected, to say the least, and obviously significant. Was it the weapon that someone at the New Year's Eve party used to shoot Wanamaker Jones to death? It had to be. The question was, Who used it to murder him and discarded it behind the wall? Detective Buchwalter had told me that construction had been under way at the house the night of the murder. That would have provided the killer a place to secrete the weapon, although I couldn't imagine that the detective and his colleagues hadn't checked out any open walls or sifted through any construction debris that was there.

I allowed my mind to drift to my chance encounter with Charmelle O'Neill. She'd had an affair with Wanamaker Jones. If that had gone sour, she had a motive to shoot him. And so did her brother, whose virtual imprisonment of her was hard to fathom, unless he was afraid of the truth coming out. Was he protecting her? Or himself? Was he worried about the scandal of having a murderer in the family? That wouldn't be good for a judge, who depended upon being elected to his post term after term. Or was he covering up his own guilt? And what about Tillie, who was engaged to Jones at the time of the shooting? If she knew he'd betrayed her with Charmelle, how strange that the two women had remained such fast friends all these years following the murder.

I was bothered by the fact that Roland Richardson hadn't told me that he was present the night of Wanamaker Jones's murder. It seemed to me that he could have offered that at the outset. I made a mental note to query him about that lapse.

I went to the edge of the park and waited until a vacant taxi came along. As we drove back to Tillie's house, I thought of my meeting with Captain Mead Parker. Obviously, things had changed dramatically in the Savannah police department since Sheridan Buchwalter's days on the force. For one thing, it was now the Savannah-Chatham Metropolitan Police Department, a merging of the Chatham County and Savannah city police that had taken place in 2003. Detective Buchwalter had described a racially tense and divided department, a state of affairs that thankfully no longer existed. Captain Parker was a black woman, as were the two officers at the desk when I arrived. It was good to see that sort of racial progress taking place, made more significant in a distinctly Southern city like Savannah. That reality was the only uplifting thought I had during my brief trip to the house.

Chapter Nineteen

I'd no sooner walked into the house than the phone rang. Mrs. Goodall answered and said it was for me.

"Hello?"

"Mrs. Fletcher, it's Captain Parker. I was wondering whether you'd like to witness the testing of the revolver you delivered to me."

"Yes, of course I would," I said. "When will you be doing the test?"

"This afternoon at five, at our regional crime lab."

"I appreciate being invited," I said, surprised that I had been. I'd left Captain Parker's office concerned that the police wouldn't be especially cooperative. Obviously, I'd misread her. "Just tell me how to get there."

"I'll have you picked up at four. You'll be at Mortelaine House?"

"Yes. Thank you."

I was standing in front of the house that afternoon when a marked squad car pulled up, driven by a uniformed female officer. I'm sure the sight of the official white car with SAVANNAH-CHATHAM POLICE emblazoned on its sides caused a few curtains to be parted in neighboring homes, and generated speculation about whether something nefarious had occurred at Miss Tillie's mansion—again. I looked back and saw that the Grogans were witnessing the scene through one of the front windows of the guesthouse.

"Mrs. Fletcher?" the officer asked as I opened the rear door of her vehicle.

"Yes."

"I'm Patrol Officer Lee. Captain Parker sent me to bring you to the crime lab."

"I appreciate being picked up," I said, climbing into the backseat and closing the door behind me.

She navigated traffic, including the many slow-moving sightseeing trolleys that seemed to be everywhere, and proceeded around Calhoun Square past "The Book" Gift Shop, headquarters for everything related to *Midnight in the Garden of Good and Evil* by John Berendt, whose wildly popular book, helped along by Clint Eastwood's film version, put the city on the tourist map. We followed Abercorn Street out of the downtown area until it became a highway running south, passing all the vestiges of the inevitable suburban sprawl, including restaurant and clothing chains, numerous large signs promising instant cash for a variety of reasons, and the Oglethorpe shopping mall, one of Melanie Goodall's favorite spots.

We turned off onto a road whose sign read MOHAWK STREET and continued on it until reaching a series of low buildings on the left. Signs indicated that they housed the Georgia Bureau of Investigation and one of its divisions, the Coastal Regional Crime Lab.

Officer Lee pulled into a parking lot and turned off the engine. I followed her through a door into the lab, where she was greeted by a large man with a pleasant smile who introduced himself to me as Charlie Elison, the laboratory manager.

"The others are already here," he said. Officer Lee and I fell in step behind him through a series of doors to a room where every flat surface was covered by thick black foam shaped like the bottom of an egg crate. Captain Parker was there with two other people, a uniformed forensics officer and a casually dressed young man who was in charge of tool-mark testing. His name was Richie Gollub.

I sensed that my unexpected presence caused a modicum of unease in the room, which Captain Parker put to rest. "Mrs. Fletcher is here in Savannah to . . ." She glanced at me, and I detected a small smile on her lips. "She's here to look into the murder of Wanamaker Jones forty years ago."

"I read about you in the paper," Gollub, the tool-mark expert, said eagerly. "You were mentioned in somebody's will."

"The victim's fiancée," I said.

"Right," he said. "There's a million bucks riding on it for you?"

"I'm afraid so," I said.

I glanced at a table dominated by a sophisticated microscope connected to a computer screen. Lying next to it was the revolver that had been discovered behind the wall in Tillie's house.

"I've never witnessed a ballistics test before," I admitted, "although I've visited other labs where tool-mark testing takes place. I've seen them match a screwdriver used to pry open a window with the marks on the window itself, and there was also the mark left by a pair of clippers on the hasp of a padlock that had been cut through."

"I'm sure it's no different than this lab," Gollub said as he picked up the revolver and walked to a corner of the room where a huge barrel, at least ten feet deep, stood. "Ballistics testing is just a glorified form of tool-mark testing," he explained as the forensics officer handed each person in the room a set of sound isolation earphones, the kind used at airports to muffle the roar of jet engines for those working on the ground. "The water in the tank is eight feet deep, enough to stop a bullet fired into it." He laughed. "When I test a rifle or other long gun, I have to stand up on that platform to fire down into the tank. So far, I haven't fallen in."

"Even with your earphones on," Mr. Elison said, "it'll still be pretty loud. Whenever he tests a weapon in here, the whole building shakes. You can stand outside the door if you prefer."

"This thirty-eight special is at least sixty years old," the tool-mark specialist said, turning the weapon over in his hands. "Small, too. You don't see too many of them."

We all donned our earphones and stood back as he aimed the revolver into the tank. He pulled the trigger. The lab manager had been right. The report was painfully loud despite the protection for our ears and the sound-muffling thick foam on the walls. It seemed to linger in the room for a very long time, along with the acrid odor of gunpowder.

Gollub retrieved the bullet from the tank, dried it, and placed it under the microscope. "The bullet I'm comparing this one to is the one that killed Mr. Jones forty years ago," he said. "I'm looking to see if the grooves on the one I just fired match up with the grooves on the original." I watched with fascination as the twin images of each bullet appeared on the screen, side by side. The grooves made on the bullets as they spiraled through the gun barrel came into focus, and he rotated one bullet, seeking to find similarities in the markings. A minute later, it was obvious even to my untrained eye that the marks matched perfectly.

"Both bullets came from that same gun," the specialist announced. "They're identical."

"Now, the question is who fired that weapon and killed Wanamaker Jones," I said, more to myself than to others in the room.

"We couldn't get any prints off the weapon, except those that probably belong to the plumber," the forensics officer said.

"That's a shame," I said.

Captain Parker thanked Elison and Gollub, and we walked together from the building. "It seldom goes easily," she said once we were outside. "At least we have the weapon that was used."

"One step at a time," I said. "I want you to know, Captain, how much I appreciate being included like this."

A sound that passed for a laugh came from her. "To be honest, Mrs. Fletcher, I'd love to see you solve this murder. It would be nice to close the books on it. Besides, I'm getting a kick out of it. Miss Mortelaine was a true Southern eccentric to have done what she did in her will." Her laugh was more full-fledged this time. "I wish you all the best," she said. "Give a call anytime you think you've come up with something."

I watched her walk away and join the forensics officer at the car in which they'd arrived. Officer Lee and I got into our car and she drove me back to the house. As I was about to get out, she said, "So you're the lady I read about in the paper."

"Unfortunately, yes," I answered.

"Everyone was talking about you at headquarters," she said. "We even have a couple of side bets on your success—no money, just bragging rights."

"Which side did you bet on?"

"I bet against you, but now that you found the murder weapon, I'm thinking I'll go change my bet."

"I appreciate your confidence in me," I said, wishing I felt the same way.

She started to laugh and shook her head. "You have a nice day, Mrs. Fletcher," she said as she put the car in gear and pulled away, still shaking her head.

I certainly understood her amusement, and found myself also shaking my head as I went up the steps and entered the house.

What's my next step? I asked myself as I went up to my room, slid off my shoes, and sat by the window. The answer came to me. I found my cell phone in my handbag and dialed Seth Hazlitt's number. I felt very far from home at that moment, and needed to hear a familiar voice, even via long distance.

Seth, as always, was generous with his time, and our talk reassured me. I'd needed an objective ear, someone unacquainted with the people in Savannah, who presented a bewildering picture of their relationships to each other and to the victim. Wanamaker Jones had been as thoroughly rejected in death as he'd been welcomed into their homes and their hearts in life. Without doubt, he had considerable personal charm, which allowed him entry to areas that would have been denied to others who were less talented. Yet, the completeness with which they had locked arms and refused to permit the authorities a glimpse into the circumstances leading to his demise was, to me, baffling. It was almost as if they were embarrassed to have been taken in by a charlatan and were not about to let that weakness be made public.

I used Seth as a sounding board for my theories and laid out for him the little I thought I knew.

"I can't help you, Jessica," he said, "but seems to me you have a pretty good handle on the situation. Ought to be able to wrap it up in a week or two."

"I hope you're right. I keep thinking that somehow I'm missing something."

"You'll find it. You always do. And make it quick, please. My cookie jar is almost empty."

Chapter Twenty

Mr. Basker, the plumber, was scheduled to come back in two days to close up the opening that had exposed the cause of the leak. The extra time was allotted to enable the police to inspect the site where the murder weapon in the Wanamaker Jones case had been found. The Grogans were ecstatic, sure that Jones had turned on the water to make his presence known. And for all I knew, they might have been right. No one had come up with a reason for why a shower, buried in the wall for forty years, would come to life. What unseen hand could have twisted a rusted tap, allowing long-dry pipes to flood with water, spurt out the showerhead, and fill the basin until it spilled onto the dusty boards and flowed down to the ceiling of the study?

The plumber, who was the most qualified to hazard a guess, remained mystified.

Mrs. Goodall clucked over the mess in the hall and muttered to herself about people coming back when they should have stayed dead.

I was inclined to be philosophical. While I couldn't quite convince myself to credit the ghost of a dead man with helping me find the weapon used to murder him, I had no other explanation. I was willing simply to accept my good fortune in discovering what Detective Buchwalter had called "the smoking gun."

The Grogans, aglow with their success, took the open wall as an invitation to focus all their electronic detection devices on what they bragged was solid evidence of paranormal activity. As a consequence, my sleep was accompanied by clicks and whirs outside my closed bedroom door as Artie and Samantha attempted once more to commune with the spirit complement of Mortelaine House through a hole in the wall. To be perfectly honest, I found the noise and the knowledge of their presence less unsettling than the eerie sounds in the house when it was supposedly empty, and more palatable than the Grogans' previously unannounced investigations in the middle of the night.

The dining room was vacant when I went down to breakfast late the next morning. The Grogans had returned to the guesthouse to sleep off their all-night research, and General Pettigrew was nowhere in sight. I took a muffin from the buffet Mrs. Goodall had set up, picked up the local newspaper, and wandered down to the kitchen, where I found the housekeeper preparing crab cakes for supper. Melanie was sitting at the little wooden table, typing on her laptop computer. In typically chic fashion, she wore dark blue jeans and a black pullover with a squared collar, which framed the multiple strands of beads around her neck. At least six thin gold bangle bracelets adorned her wrist and I wondered how she typed with them. When I wear a bracelet, I usually have to remove it if I sit down at the computer.

"Mama, did you know that when Miss Tillie put in the new bathrooms, she covered up the old ones?"

Mrs. Goodall caught sight of me coming into the kitchen and nodded. "I really don't remember, child. That was a long time ago."

"Good morning," I said. "May I join you?"

"Hi, Mrs. Fletcher," Melanie said. "You can sit next to me. I was just asking my mama about the bathrooms." She scooted her chair over to make room for me at the table.

I put down the newspaper and the plate with my muffin and took the seat next to hers. "Are you still working on the report?" I asked.

"Sure. There's lot more to add now. Mama was here when the renovations took place. Mama? Wasn't Daddy one of the carpenters working upstairs?"

"I got too much to do today to worry about what happened all those years ago."

"But I need to know for my report."

"I best not hear that tone from you, girl. When you finish mashing on that machine, I got an errand you can run for me."

"Okay," she said, drawing out the word with a dramatic pout.

"I'm going to clear the sideboard. Be back directly."

"She hates talking to me about when she started here," Melanie said after her mother had left the room. "And I was counting on her for the report, especially now with the gun found and all. I talked with my professor about the murder, and he said what you said, that it's an important part of the history of the house. So now I need to know everything, and she won't help." Melanie frowned as she closed her computer, then brightened. "But Mama said there's stuff in the newspaper today. An interview with the Kendalls. Did you see it?"

"I haven't read the paper yet," I said, "but I'll be sure to look for the article. I'll save it for you."

Melanie took a faux fur jacket from the back of the chair and pushed one arm through a sleeve.

"I wonder if could ask a favor of you, Melanie?" I said.

"Yes, ma'am."

"While you're out, may I use your computer for a few minutes?"

"Sure," she said slowly. "Do you know how it works?" She looked at me skeptically.

"I have one of my own at home, so I'm pretty confident I can find my way around yours. Are you able to access the Internet from here?"

"Not from here," she said, "but you can go next door

to the hotel. They have wireless everywhere. It's a hot spot."

"You wouldn't mind if I took your computer over there?"

"No, ma'am. You're welcome to take it with you. I figure you'll make sure to get it back to me."

"I certainly will."

Melanie showed me a few features on her computer and left, carrying her mother's grocery list.

I checked at the front desk of the hotel and the clerk told me I could access the Internet from anywhere in the building. I took Melanie's laptop into the dining room, checking first to see if General Pettigrew was present. The breakfast crowd had dispersed and the restaurant staff was setting up for lunch. Only a few tables were occupied. A waiter guided me to one away from the windows where I wouldn't get a reflection on the computer's screen. I ordered a cup of tea and opened the newspaper, scanning the pages for the interview with Rocky and Rose Kendall. I knew I'd found it when on page two, I saw the headline SOLVE A MURDER OR STEAL A MILLION? beneath which was a photograph of the siblings standing in front of Mortelaine House.

What's the real motive behind mystery writer Jessica Fletcher's trip to Savannah? That's what Savannah residents Roy Richard Kendall and his sister, Rose Margaret Kendall, heirs to the estate of the late Ms. Tillie Mortelaine, are asking. Miss

Mortelaine, one of Savannah's grande dames, who passed on last month at age ninety-one, left a million dollars to the Yankee author with the proviso that she donate it to Savannah's literacy program, one of the departed's favorite charities. But first Mrs. Fletcher must solve a murder that took place at Mortelaine House forty years ago.

"If she gets the million dollars, there's no guarantee she'll turn it over to the literacy foundation," said Mr. Kendall, who goes by the nickname Rocky.

Ms. Kendall agreed with her brother's assessment, and added, "Aunt Tillie always wanted us to inherit her house. After all, we're her only living relatives. And the will is being held up while we all sit around waiting for Mrs. Fletcher to play detective."

Meanwhile, the writer seems to be making headway in that direction. Sources at the Savannah-Chatham Metropolitan Police have told this reporter that the suspected murder weapon was discovered by Mrs. Fletcher and turned over to the police.

Nevertheless, that doesn't seem to soothe some concerns. Missy Anderson, executive director of the Savannah Literacy Foundation, expressed her fears about the bequest. "Ms. Mortelaine promised she would take care of us in her will. I'm not sure why she put conditions on the donation. After all, she and Miss Charmelle O'Neill were the original founders of this program. I only hope Mrs. Fletcher will live up to the provisions in the will and not take away our funding."

But Ms. Mortelaine's niece is not so confident the author will come through. "Personally, I think she's trying to raid the estate, and deprive us of our rightful inheritance."

As children, the Kendalls were the ones who discovered the body of Wanamaker Jones in the second-floor hall of Mortelaine House on New Year's Eve 1967. The case was never solved and the brother and sister say that's all right with them. They would just like the will of their aunt to be settled and for them to "get shed" of the visiting author.

I sighed and put the paper down. The Kendalls were trying to cement their right to an inheritance in the public's eye. That they trod on the truth in those efforts ultimately wouldn't affect me, although I certainly didn't care to see myself portrayed as a gate crasher after Tillie's money when it was she herself who had arranged for me to get involved. It wouldn't surprise me if the Kendalls were preparing to sue the estate if the inheritance didn't live up to their expectations. I doubted they had legal grounds, but greed rarely recognizes itself.

The waiter delivered a pot of tea and a slice of Lady Baltimore cake, "compliments of the baker." "He's experimenting with a new recipe," he said, placing the white cake with fluffy icing on the table.

"Please send my thanks to the baker," I said, smiling but inwardly groaning. I had been hoping for a lower-calorie day. I pushed the cake aside, poured a cup of tea, lifted the top of Melanie's computer, and connected to my e-mail account.

The messages had been piling up since last week. I answered the most urgent ones, then turned to Google, which had been my original intent. I typed in "James J. Pettigrew" and clicked on SEARCH. The only general that the search engine found was one with the same name dating from the Civil War. Pettigrew was older than I, but he wasn't a hundred and fifty. There were a few articles about a James Pettigrew who was a real estate developer in the Bahamas, and who'd been charged with fraud in connection with a hotel deal. A brief profile included that he was a native of Virginia, but didn't mention military service, which would seem to me to be an important part of the man's background, especially if he'd achieved the rank of general.

I checked the Web site for the local Savannah paper. When Detective Buchwalter had pointed out the story about me in a previous edition, there had been a photo above it. I hadn't paid attention to it then, but I wanted to see it now. It was about real estate developers and expansion plans for the hotel in which I sat. Using the paper's search feature together with the date it appeared, I found the photo, and looked up similar articles about the hotel and its expansion plans.

A shadow fell over the table as someone blocked the light. I looked up to see General Pettigrew, or perhaps "Mr. Pettigrew" was a more appropriate form of address.

"See anything interesting in there?" he said, joining me at the table without waiting for an invitation.

"What I see is that you have been misrepresenting yourself on several levels," I replied calmly, hoping to flush him out.

"Do say? People are so gullible these days," he said easily. "What did you find?"

"You have no military experience despite your claims to the title of general."

"Military men are always impressive. You find people more willing to hang on your every word if they think you've led men into battle. It's a small deception, but useful. Not unlike a writer of pulp fiction leading a murder investigation. Not exactly her official job, is it? Anything else?"

"You presented yourself to this hotel as an expert in real estate negotiations when you're no such thing. In fact, you were charged with fraud in a similar scheme in the Bahamas."

"Charged, but never convicted, Mrs. Fletcher. There is a very big difference, which you of all people should know, being a pretend detective, so to speak." He pinched off a bite of the cake the waiter had brought and popped it in his mouth. "And actually, the incident in the Bahamas gave me quite a bit of real estate experience, which I've managed to apply in my work for the owners of this hotel. So you don't really have much on me, do you?"

"You courted an elderly woman, proposing to her in an attempt to gain access to her estate, specifically her house. Did you have any feelings for Tillie at all? Or was she just a means to your end?"

"Feelings?" he said, chuckling. "I loved her from the tip of her arrogant nose to the bottom of her little blue slippers. Don't waste any tears for the innocent old lady hoodwinked by the big bad general. She was every bit the con artist I am. It was a challenge to match wits with her. Oh, yes, I had a lot of feelings for Tillie Mortelaine. And she kept a very fine Armagnac on hand for me." He mimed holding up a glass to make a toast.

"Do you really expect to gain the title to her house when the rest of her will is revealed?"

"Me? No. She was too shrewd by half. But I've been working on the niece and nephew, not that they know I'm the one they're negotiating with. I think we're close to a deal."

"And what if the house isn't left to them?"

"Sorry to disappoint, Mrs. Fletcher, but the house is definitely going to the Kendalls."

"How can you be so sure?"

"I have the inside track on that."

He took another swipe at the cake, licking the icing off his index finger, grinned at me, and left the table.

I took a deep breath and tried to relax the tension that had crept into my shoulders. I closed the top of the computer and smiled to myself. The so-called general had intended to provoke me by digging his fingers into the cake. Little did he know I was actually grateful that he'd saved me from eating it. And there were a few other valuable nuggets that had emerged in our conversation.

Artie and Samantha Grogan were in the kitchen of the guesthouse when I knocked on the door. "Hello, Jessica. Are you having computer problems?" Artie asked, noticing Melanie's laptop. "We know all about computers."

"This isn't mine," I said. "I'm on my way to return it. I just stopped by to ask how last night's research went."

"Not as productive as we'd hoped," he said. "But we've got hours of material to review, so there may be more there than we realize at the moment."

Samantha looked at me skeptically. "I didn't think you were interested in our research, Jessica. I thought you shared the general's view that what we do is what he likes to call 'fake science.'"

"To the contrary," I said. "I'm very interested in your work, and I'm hoping you'll show some of it to me."

"See, Sammy? I told you we'd convert them all. Didn't I say from the very beginning that the readings were strongest around the bathrooms? That's where all the paranormal activity was concentrated. And look what happened. You're a believer now, right, Mrs. Fletcher?"

"Let's just say I'm not a nonbeliever," I said. "But I'm going to let you convince me. Do you have a little time to show me your pictures?"

I spent two hours with the Grogans. When I returned to the house, I left Melanie's computer with Mrs. Goodall and went to Tillie's study, where I picked up the phone. It was time I called Roland Richardson III.

Chapter Twenty-one

"Good afternoon, Mrs. Fletcher."

"Good afternoon, Mr. Richardson."

"And what may I do for you this fine day?"

"Your name has come up several times since I started investigating the murder of Wanamaker Jones."

"It has?"

"Yes. I had intended to stop by your office to ask you a few questions, but I've been so busy I haven't had the time to come see you. Everything has happened so quickly."

"Well, no time like the present, I always say. The sooner the better, isn't that right? Fire away."

"I'd hoped to do this in person, but if you don't mind . . . All right. This is what I wanted to ask—"

"Yes?"

"You were here in Mortelaine House on the night that Wanamaker Jones was killed. Why didn't you tell me?"

"Yes, well, give me a moment." He coughed and I could visualize him pulling off his glasses and polishing the lenses while he composed his thoughts. "There, that's better," he said. "You see, Mrs. Fletcher, half of Savannah was at Tillie Mortelaine's New Year's Eve party that year."

"True, but only a select few stayed after the other guests left, and you were one of that group."

"Ah was. That's right. We were drinking a fine bottle of bourbon she had put away for us. She knew how much Ah like my bourbon. 'No use wastin' it on folks that don't appreciate it,' she said to me. That was, I think, one of the first single-barrel bourbons, not a blend as they usually are."

"You were also among those who rushed upstairs when the children discovered the body."

"Ah was?"

"You were. Dr. Payne mentioned it, as did Judge O'Neill."

"They must be right. I don't recall that evening that well," he said. "Age must be catching up with me."

I marveled that the man could remember the bourbon he drank but not the discovery of a murder victim, but I let it go. I had a favor to ask and I wanted his cooperation.

"Mr. Richardson, I think it might be time for us to get together."

"Ah look forward to that, of course, Mrs. Fletcher. My office is open to you at any time. But did I not answer all your questions right now?"

"Most of them," I said.

"Is there something more I might do for you?"

"Yes, there is, Mr. Richardson. I believe I'm ready to fulfill the challenge Miss Tillie posed for me in her will."

Silence on the other end of the line spoke loudly of his surprise.

"Mr. Richardson?"

"Yes. Oh, yes, Mrs. Fletcher. Are you saying that you've solved the murder of Wanamaker Jones?"

"I believe so," I said.

"Well, now, that is news. Yes, indeed, that is very big news. I admit that I did not expect this so soon. After all, you were given a month. It's been less than two weeks since you arrived."

"The sooner the better, wouldn't you say?"

"I suppose you are right about that, Mrs. Fletcher."

"What I'd like, Mr. Richardson, is for you to—"

"At whom are you pointing one of your lovely fingers, Mrs. Fletcher?"

"I prefer to make that announcement under different circumstances, not on the telephone."

"Different circumstances?"

"Yes, and I need your help."

"Well, Ah'm certainly at your disposal."

"I appreciate that. Since you're the guardian of Tillie's estate, I would like your permission to host a gathering here at her house."

"Yes. Of course. I'll let Mrs. Goodall know she is to spare no expense. What date are you suggesting?"

"Tomorrow night?"

"That is short notice."

"I know," I said, "but considering the importance of what I have to say, I assume everyone will be willing, if not anxious, to attend."

"No doubt. Anything else I can do?"

"I'm hoping you will extend the invitations for me."

He coughed a bit, then apologized. "I don't know about this, Mrs. Fletcher."

"You represent Tillie and hold the answers to all the questions about the final disposition of her estate in that sealed envelope. I believe if the request came from you, those asked to attend would be less likely to decline to come. Will you do it, please? Arrange for the people I name to come here to the Mortelaine House tomorrow for dinner at, say, seven o'clock?"

"Let me think about this for a moment," he said.

I waited.

"Who would be on your list of invited guests?" he asked.

I hadn't considered that those assembled for the purpose of identifying a murderer would be considered "guests," but I didn't correct him. I consulted a list I'd jotted down and read him the names. "I'll make sure that the Grogans are there," I added, "as well as Mr. Pettigrew."

"Might I ask why you would want Pettigrew and the Grogans present, Mrs. Fletcher? After all, they certainly weren't there forty years ago when Mr. Jones was murdered."

"I know that," I said, "but they'd gotten to know Tillie recently. I think they might have some insight to offer."

His sigh was deep and prolonged. "Ah shall do my best."

"That's all I can ask. Will you be good enough to call me after you've contacted everyone?"

"If you wish."

"I'd prefer that you call my cell phone rather than the house," I said. I gave him the number.

"I trust it will not turn out to be a wasted evening," he said. His voice was less pleasant now; there was even a hint of a warning in it.

"I'll try not to let it be," I said. "I look forward to hearing from you."

I had considered asking Richardson not to reveal the purpose of the dinner, but had changed my mind before I'd called him. I had my reasons for wanting everyone to know why they'd been summoned.

We rang off and I went to the kitchen, where Mrs. Goodall was busily preparing for dinner that night. "Have a few minutes?" I asked.

She stopped what she was doing, wiped her hands on her apron, and leaned back against the counter.

"I know this is very last-minute," I said, "and a real imposition on you, but I'm hoping you'll be able to accommodate some extra guests at dinner tomorrow evening."

"You're having a dinner party?"

I laughed. "I don't know how much of a *party* it will be," I said, "but I can't do it without you. Can you do it? *Will* you do it?"

She pondered my request for a moment before asking, "How many people you be talking about?"

"Approximately ten," I said.

"And who might they be?"

"You know everyone, Mrs. Goodall." I rattled off the names.

She looked at me quizzically. "I have this feeling, Mrs. Fletcher, that this won't be a happy occasion."

"It may depend upon your point of view," I said. "I really can't say more at this time, Mrs. Goodall, except thank you."

"Ten people for dinner," she mumbled. "Ten people. Well, I'd better get back to what I was doing. Ten people for dinner."

I left the kitchen and went to my room to await Richardson's call. My cell phone rang an hour later.

"You'll be pleased to know that everyone you mentioned has agreed to be at the house tomorrow at seven," he said, not sounding too happy about it.

"Including you, Mr. Richardson," I said.

He paused. "Ah had made other plans for the evening," he said.

"I realize this is a spur-of-the-moment request," I said, "but it's vitally important that you be here, *with* the sealed envelope given you by Miss Tillie."

"Are you suggesting that the envelope be opened at tomorrow's dinner?"

"Yes, I am. After all, her instructions were to open it in the event I solved the murder—or if a month passed and I'd failed. I believe I've succeeded."

"I am afraid this is all happening too fast for this humble country lawyer to digest," he said.

"You'll be here?"

"Yes, I shall be there, and I shall carry the envelope with me."

"Wonderful!" I said, trying to keep the relief from my voice. "I look forward to seeing you then."

The following morning, I awoke early and vowed to spend the bulk of the day relaxing. An invigorating run was out of the question, although my muscles cried out for some exercise. My knee was feeling considerably better, but certainly not up to the pounding it would take if I jogged on the city streets. Still, I was itching to get out of Mortelaine House and into the fresh air. Although I had confidence about what would take place that evening, I didn't want to spend the hours leading up to the dinner thinking about what I would say. Plus, it promised to be a lovely day in Savannah, the sky a clear blue, the air crisp and with a refreshing nip to it.

Artie Grogan stopped me as I was about to leave the house. "I just want you to know," he said, "that Sammy and I are all set for tonight."

"That's good to hear," I said. "Thank you. I'll see you later."

Concerned that a prolonged walk might set me back, I opted instead to find one of the stops of the Old Town tourist trolleys. I bought a ticket and sat back as the driver gave a running commentary about the historic sights and scenes we slowly passed. More than six million tourists visit

Savannah each year, and I was content to be among some
of them. Because riders are able to get off and reboard at
various designated spots throughout the city, I took advantage of the tour and spent some time back at the City
Market, browsing shops and galleries I hadn't been able to
visit on Saint Patrick's Day when I met with the Joneses.

I also strolled to the nearby First African Baptist Church
that overlooks Franklin Square. It was Mrs. Goodall's church
and although I'd visited it on a previous trip to Savannah,
I enjoyed seeing it again. Built brick by brick at night by
slaves after putting in their backbreaking days on surrounding plantations, the church is descended from the oldest
African American congregation in the United States. I was
already familiar with the story of the original floors and
the famous diamond pattern drilled into the boards. In the
nineteenth century, those who entered the church in search
of runaway slaves were told that the pattern of holes represented an African symbol. In reality, they provided breath-
ing air for slaves hidden beneath the floor, the boots of those
hunting for them only inches from their faces. Just thinking
of the terror those freedom-seeking men and women must
have felt caused me to shudder on that first visit, and I had
the same reaction during this second stop.

I hopped on the trolley again, taking in such sights as
the Mercer Williams House, the centerpiece of *Midnight
in the Garden of Good and Evil.* Famed songwriter Johnny
Mercer was a Savannah resident but never lived in that
magnificent building. We also passed the Juliette Gordon
Low Center, the family home of the founder of the Girl

Scouts, and the Flannery O'Connor House, now a shrine to the noted Southern author, and other examples of the rich history and outstanding architecture of this unique Southern city.

I made one stop that wasn't part of any sightseeing tour. I walked to the park where I'd met with Charmelle, hoping to see her—and she was there. Keeping an eye out for Beverly, who wouldn't be pleased to see me talking with her patient again, I told Charmelle of the planned gathering at Tillie's house that night and the time that everyone was expected to arrive. "Could you be there?" I asked.

Abject fright crossed her face. "No, no," she said. "Frank would be furious if I asked. And he won't let me do that. I know he won't."

"But you don't have to ask your brother's permission," I said. "You're an adult. You can make up your own mind."

She shook her head back and forth as though I'd suggested something horrible. "I couldn't," she moaned. "I just couldn't."

There was nothing more to do. Charmelle had never overcome her timidity when it came to opposing her brother's wishes. Tillie would have been disappointed, as was I. I tried one more time. "I know that Tillie would want you there, Charmelle. You were her best friend." But she continued to shake her head, sniffling into a handkerchief.

I walked away burdened with sadness, sorry for Charmelle, whose life had been limited by her brother's firm grip, a restraint from which she seemed incapable of breaking free.

By the time I arrived back at Mortelaine House, my need to touch history had been sated. More important, for much of the day the tour had allowed me to get my mind off the impending dinner. I envisioned how I wanted the evening to proceed, but was realistic enough to know that it would be naïve to assume it would go according to my wishes. I was about to accuse someone of a murder. Granted, it took place forty years ago, but it was hardly the sort of topic destined to promote sanguine dinnertime conversation.

After making a few phone calls from my room, I showered and dressed well in advance of dinner, and checked in with Mrs. Goodall in the kitchen.

"Anything I can do to help?" I asked.

"No, ma'am," she replied. "I've got everything just about ready. Since you've got all these people coming, I figured it would be best to serve the dinner, instead of using the sideboard. I told Melanie to come help me out."

Having such a young person present might not be wise given the subject at hand, I thought, but didn't raise an objection, not wanting to step on the housekeeper's toes.

The dining room looked lovely. Mrs. Goodall had put out the best china, crystal, silverware, and candles. All the elegant tapestry chairs were drawn up to the table. *What a shame*, I thought, *to cast the shadow of murder over such a festive atmosphere.*

The first person to arrive was Dr. Warner Payne. He seemed in good spirits, his greeting expansive and accompanied by a wide smile. Before leaving the foyer, he leaned close and said, "So, you've risen to the occasion, have you?"

"You know," I said.

He winked at me. "Yes, Rollie told me why we're here. I have the feeling that you wouldn't have arranged for this unless you were rock-solid sure."

"I hope you're right," I said.

"Should be a lively evening," he said, his statement accompanied by a knowing laugh.

A knock at the front door announced the arrival of the second guest for the evening, Roland Richardson III. He'd no sooner stepped inside when I looked past him and saw the specially equipped van used by Judge O'Neill pull up at the curb. His nurse got out, came around, and operated a hydraulic lift that lowered him in his wheelchair from the van to the ground. She pushed him up the walk and alongside the house toward the rear door, where Tillie had installed a ramp.

I greeted him there. "Go on now," he said to Beverly, ignoring me for the moment. "I'll call when I need you." I was tempted to suggest that if he could walk in his front rooms at home as I'd seen him do, he could walk here as well, but I held my tongue and simply repeated, "Good evening, Judge."

"I'm here against my better judgment," he fairly growled at me. "Tonight's my poker night. This had better be worth it."

He brusquely wheeled past me. I followed to the parlor where predinner drinks were being served. A silver bucket filled with ice sat on the glass-topped cart Tillie had used when she'd entertained. Mrs. Goodall had also set out a selection of bottles, glasses, and mixers for the guests, whose choices in beverages she knew well.

"I'll do the honors," Payne announced, going to the makeshift bar and surveying everyone in search of their drink orders.

"Two fingers of bourbon, if you please," Richardson said to Payne. "Neat."

"You, Judge?" Payne asked as O'Neill entered the room.

"I'll have the same."

Payne handed the gentlemen their drinks and mixed one for himself. I joined Richardson, who'd moved to a corner of the room. "Did you bring the envelope?" I asked in a whisper.

He answered by patting the breast pocket of his tan linen suit jacket.

I turned at the arrival of someone else, James J. Pettigrew. "Quite a gathering," he said as he went directly to the bar and perused the bottles on it. "Ah, good, my favorite, Armagnac. Mrs. Goodall never lets me down." He looked at me. "I understand you're about to make some monumental announcement tonight."

A knock on the front door drew me to the foyer, where Melanie, who'd been in the kitchen with her mother, now opened the door for Rocky and Rose Kendall. "Good evening," she said, like a professional greeter. I had to smile. She was obviously enjoying her quasi-hostess role that evening and intended to make the most of it.

The Kendalls walked by her without a word, bypassed the parlor, and went directly to the dining room, where they whispered to each other. "Probably counting the silver," Melanie murmured to herself. She made a sour face behind their backs, which caused me to smile. She saw that I'd noticed and gave me a pleading look for understanding. "Ooh, don't tell my mother I said that." She rushed back to the kitchen.

I chuckled and was turning toward the parlor when another knock sounded at the front door. As far as I knew, everyone who'd been invited had arrived.

Mrs. Goodall bustled out of the parlor and reached for the knob before I could open the door. Standing there was Charmelle O'Neill.

Chapter Twenty-two

Charmelle was wrapped in a heavy red-and-black-plaid shawl and wore a matching plaid tam on her head. She looked particularly old and frail, her bony face ghostly pale, wisps of white hair protruding from beneath her small cap.

Mrs. Goodall keened at the sight of Charmelle, and the two women squeezed each other's hands, tears dampening their cheeks. I was sure they wanted to reach out and hug, but years of formal behavior between them were too hard to overcome.

"Come in. Quick. It's too cold for you outside," Mrs. Goodall said. "It does my heart good to see you doin' okay. I was so worried."

"I'm all right, but it's hard without her, isn't it?" Charmelle said, her voice almost a croak.

Mrs. Goodall nodded, dashing away her tears. She saw me waiting to greet Charmelle. "Here's Mrs. Fletcher for you," she said.

I wrapped my arm about Charmelle's shoulder and said, "I didn't expect you to be here."

She responded in a thin, feeble voice. "I wanted to."

"And I am very glad you did, Charmelle. Come inside."

"Is Frank—?"

"Yes, Frank is here, but don't worry about that. I'll take care of him."

Mrs. Goodall helped her out of the shawl and took her hat. I stayed close in the event she might fall. "Ready?" I asked.

"Yes," she said, but not without first checking her appearance in a mirror. I noticed that she'd applied lipstick, not particularly evenly, but that didn't matter. The fact that she'd cared about how she looked was heartening.

I put my arm around her and we slowly left the foyer and stood in the doorway to the parlor. All conversation ceased. Richardson broke the silence: "Mah, mah, Miss Charmelle," he said.

Judge O'Neill's back had been to the door. Upon hearing his sister's name, he swung around in his wheelchair. "What are *you* doing here?" he demanded.

"I invited her," I answered, "and I am delighted that she's accepted my invitation."

"I suggest that—" the judge started to say.

"And *I* suggest that we enjoy our drinks and look forward to dinner," I said.

"I second the motion," said Dr. Payne from where he stood at the bar.

I got Charmelle settled in a chair, and asked if she wished something to drink.

"I believe some sherry would go nicely," she said in a weak, but hardly inaudible voice.

The O'Neill siblings kept their distance from each other until Mrs. Goodall poked her head into the parlor and announced that dinner was about to be served.

I went to her and asked, "Where are the Kendalls?"

"In the dining room," she said, "studying all Miss Tillie's things. An unpleasant pair, those two."

I didn't debate her evaluation.

As we headed for the dining room, Artie and Samantha Grogan appeared on the stairs leading down from the bedroom level. Artie grabbed my elbow and pulled me aside. "We've just seen him again," he said in a hoarse whisper.

"Who?"

"Wanamaker Jones." His grin was smug. "He must know why everyone is here tonight."

"Perhaps," I said. "But let's deal with your sighting later."

He looked disappointed but didn't press the issue.

Rocky and Rose Kendall were already seated when we entered the dining room, their faces glum. "I hope someone has done an inventory of my aunt's possessions," Rocky said. "We would be very upset if some of her things went missing. It's enough that you're all eating her food and drinking her liquor."

Richardson ignored Rocky's comment and went to his customary seat at the head of the table. "Since Mrs. Fletcher is our hostess for the evening," he said, "Ah suggest she be given the place of honor."

"I'd like Charmelle to sit next to me," I said, and pulled out her chair. Judge O'Neill positioned himself as far away from his sister as possible and glared at her. I was pleased to see that she effectively ignored his stern, pointed looks.

Our first course, bowls of gazpacho, waited at our places. Mrs. Goodall arrived carrying two wine bottles, one red, the other white, and filled glasses according to each guest's preference. There was little conversation as everyone enjoyed, or pretended to enjoy, their soup. As the bowls were cleared and Melanie delivered salads, conversation opened up a bit. I kept my eye on Charmelle, who glanced around the room, most likely remembering other dinners with Tillie presiding over the table. She sighed but appeared to be in control. Judge O'Neill and Rollie Richardson pressed me to make whatever announcement I'd planned, but I deflected their requests and tried to keep the dialogue flowing in other directions.

Mrs. Goodall had outdone herself with the meal. A crusted rack of lamb was superb, expertly broiled and seasoned, the vegetables perfectly cooked, the biscuits hot and tasty. I knew that I couldn't stall much longer, and decided I would raise the issue of Wanamaker Jones's murder over dessert. Melanie distributed parfaits of strawberries soaked in Amaretto and covered with whipped cream, while her mother poured coffee for everyone except Charmelle and me, to whom she served tea.

I cleared my throat. "Tillie Mortelaine was renowned as a great hostess, so it's appropriate that we remember her this way," I said while rising from my seat. "None of us knows if this dining room will be the scene of more great dinners after tonight." I didn't let my eyes fall on the Kendalls.

"To Miss Tillie," Dr. Payne said, raising his glass.

We all took a sip of wine. "I know you're anxious to get to the reason I asked you here this evening," I said and put my glass down. "I believe Mr. Richardson has informed you that I intend to make an announcement about the murder of Wanamaker Jones. You're all aware that Tillie's last will and testament included a challenge to me to solve that homicide. I must admit that I was not eager to accept that assignment, but the stakes are high. If I'm successful, the literacy program that Tillie, Charmelle, and I launched here in Savannah will have the funding it needs to move forward and to help that many more deserving people." I allowed what I'd said to sink in, taking in everyone's face. Judge O'Neill's and Roland Richardson's expressions were a melding of impatience and annoyance. Pettigrew looked bored. Dr. Payne's bemused smile told me that he was finding the evening entertaining. Rose and Rocky Kendall sat rigid in their chairs and looked straight ahead. Artie Grogan demonstrated the most animation, like a boy having trouble waiting for his chance at a favorite game. His wife gripped his hand on the table. Charmelle sat very still, staring down at the napkin in her lap.

"I won't waste any more time getting to the point," I said. "If you read the local paper, you already know that the weapon used to kill Wanamaker Jones was found right here in the house, behind a wall that was erected shortly after the murder. Someone in the Savannah police leaked the information to the press that I'd delivered the gun to police headquarters. Unfortunately, the only fingerprints the forensics lab were able to recover were those of the plumber, who was the one to retrieve the weapon from behind the wall—no others were found. But that shouldn't pose a problem. I don't need fingerprints to identify the murderer."

"Good enough," the judge snapped, "but we don't need to know what you *don't* need. You think you've solved the murder? Then get to it, although don't be surprised if what you've come up with is summarily dismissed. I find it the height of arrogance that you come down here to Savannah and claim you can get done what our police failed to accomplish. Frankly, it's laughable."

I dismissed his barb and continued. "I wondered," I said, "whether one of you would fail to show up here tonight once you knew the reason for this dinner because— well, because that person would know that he or she was the killer. But since you're all here, I can only surmise that even if one of you shot Wanamaker Jones, you aren't concerned that you might be indicted. After all, it happened so long ago, and the victim wasn't exactly what you would term a model citizen, at least from what some of you have told me."

Pettigrew had said little during dinner aside from an occasional brief response to a banal question. "I sure as hell know that I didn't shoot this Jones character," he said. "I never even met Miss Tillie until just recently, although I'm delighted to be included at this dinner." He looked around the table. "So, which one of you did the deed? Come on, fess up and save Mrs. Fletcher the trouble of having to name you."

"Honestly," Samantha Grogan said, "don't you ever know when to shut up?"

"Just because you never have anything interesting to say—"

"Don't you dare speak disrespectfully to my wife, you phony blowhard," Artie said.

"Please," I said, holding out my hands in a peace gesture. "Let's avoid such distractions. Yes, neither Mr. Pettigrew nor the Grogans could possibly have killed Wanamaker Jones." I paused. "But someone did, and that person is very much with us tonight. You three gentlemen certainly had a motive to kill Jones." I looked from Payne to Richardson to O'Neill. "Each of you discovered Jones was not who he made himself out to be. Furthermore, each of you was smitten with Tillie. No, I think it was more than that. I believe that each of you had wanted to marry her, but she wouldn't let herself be pinned down. Until Wanamaker Jones came along."

I took in their reactions. Richardson seemed confused, as though he either had to process what I'd said or was trying to remember back forty years. Judge O'Neill, as expected, muttered obscenities under his breath and guffawed. Payne laughed, not scornfully but with what appeared to be glee. "Go on," he said. "I feel like I'm in one of your novels."

"So?" Pettigrew said to me. "Which one of these guys did it?"

"Shouldn't the police be here to arrest the murderer?" Rocky asked.

"That's right," Rose agreed. "Whoever did it is liable to kill again." She stood. "I'm getting out of here."

"Sit down," Richardson said in a firmer voice than I'd ever heard come from him.

"Yeah, c'mon," Rocky said, grabbing her arm and pulling her back into her chair. "I'm not leaving till I know what we get."

"The three suitors for Tillie's affections at this table," I said after things had settled down, "are all professional men with reputations to uphold. I think you were jealous of Wanamaker Jones for having captured Tillie's heart, but out of respect for her I doubt you would have killed him."

Judge O'Neill said to his sister, who sat stoically throughout the exchanges, "I don't see anything new here. Get your things. We're leaving!"

She didn't move.

"You heard me, Sister," he said, louder this time. "We're leaving. I'll call for the car and—"

"Be quiet, Frank," she said. Her voice, like Richardson's, was stronger than I'd ever heard it.

"Charmelle!"

"I am staying!" she said.

Her brother, who'd used his arms to push himself to his feet, slumped back as though she had poked a hole in him and all his energy had seeped out. "You're going to be sorry," he growled.

I hid my satisfaction at Charmelle's stiffened backbone. "I don't believe any of you shot Wanamaker Jones. But that doesn't mean that you weren't pleased at his demise. Far from it. Finding his body must have been a source of satisfaction for each of you. And you waited a long time before calling in the authorities. Enough time for the judge to calm his sister, who had been hysterical. Enough time for Tillie to make her plans with Dr. Payne. Enough time for Mr. Richardson to hustle the Kendall children and their parents away from the crime scene. Enough time so that everyone could be found sitting serenely in the parlor when the police arrived. Wanamaker Jones must have lain dead for at least two hours before the judge made the call."

None of them uttered a dissent.

"I said earlier that Jones's murderer was with us tonight. That's true. But that person is with us in spirit only."

"Huh?" Rocky Kendall said.

"Tillie Mortelaine killed Wanamaker Jones," I announced.

There was a moment of stunned silence until Dr. Payne began applauding. "Well done, Jessica," he said, his words filtering through a hearty laugh. "Congratulations! You've just won a million dollars for your literacy project."

Judge O'Neill turned to him. "How the hell do you know she's right, Warner?"

"Because Tillie told me she'd done it," Payne said.

"What?" exclaimed Richardson.

Payne stood and joined me at the head of the table. "Oh, yes," he said. "Our Miss Tillie pulled the trigger, all right. Didn't any of you notice how scarce she made herself later that evening—or early morning, to be precise? Once these two discovered the body and started wailing—" He pointed to Rose and Rocky. "Once the body was discovered, Tillie was a wreck, as you can imagine. I took her aside, closed the door behind us, and talked sense into her. That's when she told me what happened."

The judge fixed Charmelle with a fierce look. "And all this time, you let me think—" He turned to the doctor. "And you didn't do anything, didn't tell anyone?" he demanded.

"No, I did not, Frank. As far as I was concerned, that sleazy con man got what he deserved. No way was I about to give Tillie up to the authorities. I told her everything would be all right as long as she listened to me and did what I told her to do."

"You've known all along," I said, unable to keep the pique from my voice.

"Afraid so," he said. "I could have said something to you, but that would have been cheating."

"Did you tell Tillie where to hide the weapon?" I asked. "The police never found it."

"Didn't have to," he replied. "She'd already done that,

in the dumbwaiter." He chuckled. "That's how she came down from the scene of the crime without anyone seeing her. She climbed into that dumbwaiter, rode it to the ground floor, and left the gun in it. Then she told Mrs. Goodall that the dumbwaiter was broken. Didn't want her discovering anything compromising. Tillie was a good liar, but the truth is always written on Mrs. Goodall's face."

"Didn't the cops examine the dumbwaiter?" Pettigrew asked. "It's the first place I would have looked if I were searching the house."

"It's so well camouflaged, the cops never found it," the doctor said. "You have to know where it is. Once they were through searching the house, Tillie retrieved it from the dumbwaiter and tossed it through the open wall that was due to be boarded up that day."

"You're guilty of obstruction of justice, Warner," the judge intoned.

"I'm not really worried about that," Payne countered. "You're retired, Your Honor. What are you going to do, tell the DA to bring charges against me? Don't be silly. I just think it's wonderful that Mrs. Fletcher has solved the crime. Brava, Jessica."

"The police will never close the case unless you testify, Warner," Richardson suggested.

"They don't need *me*, Rollie," Payne said. "I think you'll find in that sealed envelope a neatly typed-out confession from Tillie, along with a few other things. By the way, she states in her confession that I urged her to go to the police but that she refused. Gets me off the hook, I'd say."

I glanced at the doorway to the butler's pantry and saw Melanie hiding there, her eyes wide at what she'd been hearing.

"How do you know what's in that envelope?" Pettigrew asked.

"Because I helped her draft what's in it, that's why," Payne said. "She didn't want her confession to come out until she was dead. She asked me to help her find a lawyer out of Savannah who would handle her papers confidentially."

"She was mah client," Richardson said.

"Yes, she was, Rollie," Payne said, taking his seat again, "but she didn't want you to know what was in the envelope. So she told you one thing and put another in there. I took her to Atlanta over a year ago. A lawyer there drew up the other papers she wanted. He didn't know about the confession. I kept that with me until it was time to seal the envelope."

"Miss Tillie said she didn't keep a handgun on the premises," Richardson said. "I asked her the night of the murder. Did she lie?"

"She didn't," I said.

"Then—?"

I turned to Charmelle. "It was your gun that killed Wanamaker Jones, wasn't it, Charmelle?"

She looked up at me and sighed. "Yes, it was mine."

"Wanamaker Jones had lured you into an affair, but he wasn't faithful. You had betrayed your best friend for him, but he wasn't willing to stand by you. You brought the gun to the New Year's Eve party to kill Jones. But when you were face-to-face, you couldn't pull the trigger. You lost your nerve."

"Now, wait a minute," O'Neill shouted. "Charmelle! Don't answer that."

"I suggest you settle down, Judge," I said. "You knew your sister had a gun. You'd bought it for her for protection. And that night, when you took her home after the police had left, she wouldn't tell you where it was, would she?"

He made a false start but fell silent.

"Did you think for all these years that it was Charmelle who'd killed Jones?"

"I warned her about him. He was playing both of them. Making love to Sister, while all the time planning to marry Miss Tillie."

While the judge was speaking, I nodded at Artie, prompting him and his wife to get up from their seats and quietly leave the room.

I faced Judge O'Neill again. "Charmelle didn't want to admit to you or to anyone else that her dear friend, Tillie, had killed the lover who had two-timed them both. She's kept that secret for all these years, allowing you to believe that she was the murderer. I'd say that your belief in her guilt might constitute obstruction of justice, too."

"How did you figure that out?" Payne asked me. "About it being Charmelle's revolver that Tillie used? I knew it, of course, but what brought you to that conclusion?"

"A few things," I said. "In her will, Tillie called for

Charmelle to show some gumption. I wondered what had prompted that. The police said Charmelle didn't have a gun, but they were wrong. She did. And they never found out that she'd had a disappointing affair with Jones, because you all closed ranks and wouldn't talk to them. Charmelle felt a lot of guilt for having been disloyal to her best friend, but she was also afraid Tillie would blame the murder on her. I connected those dots, as they say. I didn't know for sure, but that scenario made sense to me."

I reached over and patted Charmelle's hand. She smiled at me, and a satisfied smile crossed her lips. Her subtle nod confirmed what I'd said.

"Tillie had always been protective of Charmelle," I said, "but at the same time she urged her to stand up for herself. When Charmelle finally took that advice and faced down Wanamaker, she found she couldn't kill him."

Charmelle gave a small snort. "She came upstairs just when I had the gun pointed at him. But I was shaking so hard, I couldn't aim. He was trying to talk me out of it, and his face just lit up with happiness when he saw Miss Tillie come to stand next to me. She grabbed the gun away and said, 'This is how you do it, Charmelle.' And she shot him. Then she told me to go downstairs and pretend nothing had ever happened." She looked at her brother. "Frank knew something was wrong and he kept after me. But I wouldn't tell him. When the body was found, I couldn't hold it in anymore. I started to cry and I couldn't stop. He just assumed—and I let him."

They'd all fallen silent when Charmelle had spoken.

"Well, well," Richardson said at last, patting his mouth with his napkin and rising. "Ah think it's time for me to open this mysterious sealed envelope left behind by Miss Tillie. It appears that Mrs. Fletcher has fulfilled the terms of Miss Tillie's will."

"May I suggest," I said, "that we hold off on that for a little longer?"

"Why?" Rocky Kendall asked. "Let's open the envelope and settle once and for all who gets the house."

"You know, Mr. Kendall," I said, "I didn't appreciate the comments you made to the local newspaper about me. I did not come to Savannah seeking personal gain."

"That remains to be seen," Rose Kendall said.

"Yes, I suppose it does," I said. "The Grogans have volunteered to serve after-dinner drinks in the parlor. Let's join them. They have something to show us."

"I'm leaving," the judge said. "As far as I'm concerned, this evening is over."

He stood and took a few steps toward the door.

"Your wheelchair, Judge," I said.

Red-faced, he returned to the chair, sat heavily in it, and wheeled himself from the room.

"He can walk," Pettigrew said.

"Yes, he can," Charmelle said. "When he wants to."

I asked Mrs. Goodall to join us and we went to the parlor, where we found Artie Grogan at the bar waiting to serve traditional postprandial drinks. The judge had preceded us into the room and was using the phone to call Beverly to come and get him.

Roland Richardson asked me when I wanted the envelope to be opened.

"As soon as we've had a chance to view the show-and-tell." I said it loud enough for everyone to hear.

"What is this show-and-tell business?" Pettigrew asked.

"I think it's time to show and to tell how Tillie Mortelaine died."

No one said a word as they stared at me.

"Artie?" I said. "Ready?"

He motioned to his wife, who dimmed the lights.

"The Grogans have spent considerable time here at the house looking for otherworldly spirits."

"A couple of charlatans," Pettigrew pronounced.

Artie Grogan went to a projector in a corner that hadn't been there during the cocktail hour. No one seemed to have noticed it until he turned it on. The lens was directed at a section of bare white wall.

"What is this?" O'Neill barked. "More nonsense?"

"Go ahead, Artie," I said.

As he began projecting a series of images contained on a memory card from one of his many infrared cameras that had been positioned throughout the house, I explained. "The cameras used by the Grogans have taken hundreds of photos of various parts of the house. They operate when they detect motion. I was surprised at how sensitive they are. Even a fleeting shaft of light, or a shadow, activates them. Because of the large number of images captured, the Grogans fell a bit behind in viewing and analyzing the pictures, and they graciously allowed me to go through their unviewed shots with them." I looked at the wall, where a new image came to life. "Like this one," I said.

It showed Tillie leaving her bedroom and heading for the top of the stairs.

"And this one," I said.

Now, the images came faster on the wall. Everyone was transfixed as one picture followed another, creating a montage of still images that had the effect of projecting a continuous story. *Tillie reaching the top of the stairs . . . Tillie looking down at the rug beneath her blue slippers . . . Tillie tentatively reaching for the banister . . . Tillie about to take her first step on her way down the stairs . . . Tillie stopping and turning . . . Tillie's face reflecting surprise, and fear . . . and then . . .*

James Pettigrew coming up behind her and sending her tumbling down the long staircase.

Mrs. Goodall and Charmelle began to cry. Warner Payne slapped his hand on his knee, and exclaimed, "I knew it!"

All eyes turned to Pettigrew. He stood in the middle of the room, motionless, unsure of what to do or where to go. He suddenly took long strides to the door. We followed. He reached the foyer, glanced back once, opened the front door, and stepped through it—into the arms of two Chatham-Savannah uniformed officers.

We watched the policemen cuff him and lead him away before we returned to the parlor, where Artie, with a large grin on his round face, eagerly poured drinks for everyone.

"Remarkable," Dr. Payne said, taking my hand and patting it. "I am truly impressed."

Richardson asked for everyone's attention. "With Mrs. Fletcher's permission," he said, "I shall now open the sealed envelope left behind by Miss Tillie Mortelaine."

"About time," Rocky Kendall said. His sister kept mum.

I went to the bar, poured three glasses of sherry, then handed one to Mrs. Goodall and one to Charmelle. I touched the rim of my glass to each of theirs.

The moment had come for Tillie's *final* final wishes to be revealed.

Chapter Twenty-three

I t was good to be back in Cabot Cove.

Sheriff Mort Metzger and his wife, Maureen, hosted a potluck dinner party to mark my return, and to celebrate my having secured the million dollars for the Savannah literacy project. Seth Hazlitt was at the dinner. So were our leading veterinarian, Jack Wilson, and his wife, Tobé; Richard and Mary-Jane Koser; Tim and Ellen Purdy; Mayor Jim Shevlin and his wife, Susan; and a few other friends from town. Maureen had instructed everyone to bring a dish based on recipes she'd seen on Paula Dean's TV cooking show. I hadn't had an opportunity to eat at the Lady and Sons restaurant while I was in Savannah, so it was fun to try the very Southern, very rich dishes, all created with a bit of Maine tweaking. But the food wasn't the centerpiece of the evening. Everyone wanted a detailed report from me on what I'd done on the trip, and especially how I'd solved the forty-year-old murder of Wanamaker Jones.

I recounted for them what had led me to the conclusion that Tillie Mortelaine had shot her fiancé to death and that she'd used a gun brought to the party for that purpose by Charmelle O'Neill, who'd intended to do the deed herself.

"So the old lady wanted to wait until she died before admitting she murdered Jones," Mort said.

"Right," I said.

"I still find it inexcusable, Jessica, that Miss Tillie suckered you into solving the crime," said Seth. "And she put you in further danger: You were living next door to a man who turned out to be a murderer."

"Pettigrew?" I said.

"Who else would I be talking about?" my physician friend said.

"Did you know he'd pushed your friend down the stairs from the beginning?" Tobé asked.

"No," I replied. "I considered him to be a harmless, if annoying, eccentric. Of course, I never did believe that Tillie had accepted his proposal of marriage. It was when I learned of his connection with the hotel next door and its plans to expand onto Tillie's property that I began to suspect his motives for courting her. When he mentioned the color of the slippers she'd worn the night she died, that was when I knew he'd been responsible for her death."

"How did the slippers figure in?" Mayor Shevlin asked.

"Mrs. Goodall had said they were a gift from Charmelle,

and that Tillie had taken the box upstairs to open it. So Pettigrew could not have seen those slippers unless he'd been there when Tillie fell down the stairs. Of course, that wouldn't have been easy to prove. But when it occurred to me that the cameras the Grogans had placed around the house might have caught something the night she died, I had my proof of the murder. Fortunately, I was right. His guilt was beyond question, right there in black and white."

"The pictures weren't in color, Jessica?" Maureen asked.

"Yes, they were in color," I said. "I was just using an expression."

"What I'm wondering," Tim Purdy said, "is how the police happened to be there when this Pettigrew character tried to escape."

"I'd called them before the dinner. Once I knew Pettigrew had killed Tillie, I alerted the police captain and suggested she have some officers watching the doors."

"*She?*" Mort said.

"Yes, Mort. Captain Mead Parker, a lovely and very capable law enforcement officer."

"Good to see a woman get that far," Mort said.

"So who got the house?" Mary-Jane asked.

"It wasn't the niece and nephew," I said.

Seth drove me home after dinner.

"Tell me about this Dr. Payne," he said as we sat in his car in front of my house.

"A charmer, but not a straight shooter," I said. "He knew everything about Wanamaker Jones's murder from the very beginning."

"Why didn't he share what he knew with you?"

"Good question. It would have been helpful, but he seemed to enjoy watching from the sidelines while I tried to solve the murder. He and Tillie had a lot in common; both of them were fond of playing games. I like to think he would have solved Jones's murder for me if it had gotten down to the wire, but I can't be certain."

"Sounds as if you took a liking to him."

"Romantic interest, you mean?"

"*Ayuh.*"

"There wasn't any such thing, Seth. He's just an interesting man. Although he did ask me for a kiss good night."

"See?"

"I said no."

"Uh-huh. That's good."

"Good night, my friend."

I'd shared just about everything from my Savannah trip with my friends that evening. The legal papers Tillie had placed in the sealed envelope revealed more than her murder confession. She'd left her historic house to Melanie's school, the Savannah College of Art and Design, with the condition (of course) that they use it to further the study of Savannah architecture and keep it on the rolls of historic buildings to be maintained but never changed. Melanie was ecstatic when she heard the news, as was her mother. Tillie had declared in one of the legal papers that Mrs. Goodall was to have the option of staying on as "manager" in charge of the house, and provided a sum of money to SCAD sufficient to pay her for that service. Fine people, the Goodalls. I would miss them, although I had a standing invitation to stay at the house anytime I wished to visit again.

The big surprise had been a bequest for the Grogans. Tillie had left funds for them to continue their paranormal research at Mortelaine House. It wasn't much, but they were thrilled to have any money with which to finance their research. Tillie stipulated that they were to remain in the guesthouse for a period of up to six months, and to have the run of the main house in order to continue their quest for proof that Mortelaine House was haunted, at which time they should be able to establish more permanent quarters. They were a strange couple, but I'd grown to like them, and I wished them well upon my departure.

Tillie did have a token bequest for Pettigrew. She left him a single bottle of Armagnac, but it wasn't the brand that he liked.

What I had not shared with my friends at dinner that night was the ghostly aspect of my visit, although I did recount the story of the haunted shower turning on suddenly, and how it led to the discovery of the murder weapon.

Try as I might, I couldn't come up with a rational reason for how the shower was turned on, nor could I explain the old lamp in the foyer coming to life in the midst of a power outage, nor did I know how the door to the tunnel, which ran between the house and the guest quarters, managed to unlock itself.

But it was the apparition I'd seen on my final day that gave me the shivers. It occurred as I came downstairs with my small suitcase. Melanie and her mother stood in the foyer waiting for me; Melanie would drive me to the airport for my flight to Boston and then to Bangor, Maine. I'd started down the staircase when I felt a sudden chill, a swirl of freezing air, raising goose bumps on my arms. It stopped me cold. I sensed something to my right, turned and caught a reflection in one of the series of small mirrors that lined the wall. I blinked rapidly to ensure that my eyes were working properly. A faint outline of a face peered back at me from the mirror, a man's face—Wanamaker Jones. He winked and was gone as quickly as he'd appeared. *It can't be*, I told myself.

"Is something wrong, Mrs. Fletcher?" Mrs. Goodall asked.

"What? No, nothing is wrong. Did you see anything?"

"Where?"

"In the mirror."

"Only your reflection, Mrs. Fletcher."

"I didn't see anything at all," Melanie said.

"It must have been my imagination," I said.

I would never know for sure.

A month after my return from Savannah, I received a call from Dr. Warner Payne. After some pleasant conversation, he informed me of two things. The first was that Roland

Richardson, Tillie's attorney, was under investigation for conflict of interest. It seems he was in league with James Pettigrew—"in cahoots" was how Dr. Payne actually put it—to get hold of the rights to Tillie's house and arrange for the hotel next door to take it over. According to Payne, the "general" had wormed his way into Tillie's life in order to influence her. When that didn't work, he'd taken it upon himself to kill her to hasten things along. The hotel's owners disavowed any complicity. Pettigrew had implicated Richardson, spilling everything to the authorities in the hope it would lessen his sentence in the murder of Tillie Mortelaine. I hoped it wouldn't.

Warner's second message was a sad one. Charmelle O'Neill had passed away. I was grateful I'd had an opportunity to spend some time with her before leaving Savannah, and was glad that she'd been able to free herself of the heavy burden of guilt she'd carried for so many years. Payne promised to stay in touch and keep me informed about the Richardson-Pettigrew investigation.

Two other things occurred having to do with my Savannah adventure.

I received the check for a million dollars, which I promptly arranged to have transferred to the literacy group in Savannah.

The second was a delivery, a very large, heavily fortified package. I tore open the brown paper and had to use a crowbar to dismantle the wooden crate. It was just as I feared. Tillie had left me the oil painting *Judith Holding the Head of Holofernes.* A slip of paper fell out when I pulled